BOOK INFO

A Taste for Death
A Finger Lakes Wine Mystery
Copyright ©2015 by Don Stevens
http://donstevensauthor.com

Merge Publishing
Finger Lakes, New York
http://www.mergepublishing.com

Publisher's Note: This is a work of fiction characters, places and incidents are a prod author's imagination. Locales and public n sometimes used for atmospheric purpo resemblance to actual people, living or de businesses, companies, events, institutions or

completely coincidental.

Book design ©2014 Ros Welpy
http://bookdesignfactory.com

ISBN: 978-0-9904432-2-3 Print
ISBN: 978-0-9904432-3-0 Digital

ACKNOWLEDGEMENTS

Special thanks go into writing any piece of work, fiction or not. Here are my kudos.

Thanks to some Finger Lakes wineries, especially Kim Gardner Aliperti from Billsboro Winery, who answered questions, was the first wine expert to read this, and brought superb dry wines to the area. Also thanks to the Miles family from Miles Wine Cellars for countless hours of being in the field with them and being able to help them produce their wonderful elixirs.

The Finger Lakes wineries are a precious commodity to the area. More and more people need to explore and support this growing industry regardless of how many murders will be committed there in my imagination.

Thank you to my already dedicated readers, including beta readers, especially Jodi and Rick, who helped me polish this one out.

Also thanks to my family, friends and those who I will always love who I call my family.

PROLOGUE

Sydney Keller arrived at Allenwood Winery in a hurried state. As usual, she was running late. You'd think after opening the winery for a few weeks she'd have the routine down. But the Finger Lakes didn't have the rushed pace of New York City, where everybody was busy bumping into the next person, too busy getting into everyone's business. The laid-back lifestyle of upstate left her with more time on her hands. In the big city, she was busy trying to survive and had a lot on her plate—her job, her boyfriend, her friends—all of which were insecure. It's funny how it can all be taken away and you're left with your conscience. She could clearly hear what the spirits were saying or maybe, she had more time to read the signs of destiny.

Destiny told her to come to the Finger Lakes and work at her aunt and uncle's winery. When her aunt had asked her to move here and help out, Sydney had just ended a relationship and her catering job wasn't producing enough income. Now she was learning more about wine than she ever thought possible. Memorizing all the wine in this region wasn't necessary, since their winery produced only a few varietals, but she believed she should possess as much knowledge as she could.

Allenwood Winery was located on Route 14 on the west side of Seneca Lake. Working here could lead to better things. This new life will have to be better than her old one, serving ungrateful customers food that she slaved over. She worked all hours, every weekend, for a wonderful moment when a spoiled debutante or clueless hostess gave a smirk of approval. After discovering catering didn't satisfy her passion for food, she tried other jobs, and after the break-up, her aunt told her she was opening a winery. Aunt Marianne, along with Uncle Frank, had been successful real estate agents, took a risk and asked Sydney her thoughts. Sydney, who dabbled with astrology and Tarot told them to go for it. This would bring them many fortunes and much happiness. The cards didn't exactly say this. The planets were not in the right houses, predicting confusion and turmoil. That damn Tower card always turned up. Never a good sign but Sydney reasoned that starting any new business was risky. Persuading her aunt that the cards recommended she should hire her was bending the truth; but being two months late on your rent allowed her to stretch the truth.

When she remembered this it upset her. She didn't want to take advantage of her relatives, or anyone, but her desperate situation caused her to take risky actions. After parking her car at Allenwood, she spotted one corner of the "NOW OPEN" banner on the front of the building flapping in the breeze. Last night's grand opening party was her idea. From a marketing perspective, such a party told the world and convinced the owners they were ready to run a business. She secured the banner and went inside. Cleaning up glasses, napkins, food and plates, she prepared for the day ahead. She thought about the night before when guests were all having fun. *Bravo*, she thought to herself. The party was a great success, in spite of what the cards had said. While clearing up the wine bottles she noticed three were lined up on the table where her Uncle Frank had been sitting.

After filling up two trash bags she dragged them to the back of the building. She didn't mind this task. The best view of the winery was in the back. Besides the endless rows of grapes, a hill lay beyond where the sun shone across the vines. In the distance the rented cottage created a picture perfect postcard for her reverie during troubling times.

The birds were out unusually early. They crowded around the vines, congregating in the front area, where the vines began. After placing the trash in the bins, she walked toward the vines, eager to see what all their fuss was about. The sun's rays made her squint so she used her hand for shade and kept walking uphill. It appeared the wind knocked down a scarecrow.

Funny, she didn't recall it being windy last night. Then she remembered Uncle Frank hadn't set up the scarecrow yet. He had planned on doing it for days. When she arrived at the spot where the birds were stirring she would no longer see this as a tranquil postcard. In fact, this image of death and evil so plainly visible jarred her more than any scarecrow could.

CHAPTER ONE

The body lay in the vineyard, fully dressed in a sharp tailored suit, loose tie and polished shoes. Its hands, stiff with rigor, showed fingers digging deep into the earth. Investigator Louis Deville from the Violent Crimes Investigative Team took a moment to view the scene. Not the murder scene but the surrounding view from where he stood. The brisk November morning brought a blanket of mist across Seneca Lake. Crime presents itself everywhere, he thought. Even in the most serene of places.

He looked more closely at the ghostly blue color of the victim's face and the ligature mark circling his neck. Deville studied the scene, took his own photos and notes, careful to record everything. If there's anything he learned from crime textbooks was to record everything. Even with the forensics team by his side, he decided to spend the extra time.

He wondered if the strangulation had lasted long enough for the victim to see his assailant. He couldn't imagine watching your killer squeeze the life out of you. The sheer terror of it could be enough to weaken anyone's heart, especially if you recognized your killer. Did the victim try to scream or escape?

Strands of heavy-duty trellis wire around the body suggested the readily available weapon. Grapevines on either side lay on the ground, detached from the trellis. The crime scene officers practiced caution not to step on them. Not to disrupt evidence is normally the rule but Deville thought perhaps no one wanted to step on the grapes (in the Finger Lakes or any wine country that worshipped grapes).

Senior Investigator Jessica Malone stood beside him, which didn't help their relationship. Or the end of it, he said to himself. Jessica Malone read aloud the identification found in the victim's wallet.

Deville remembered the victim's name when he heard it. Gerard Bellamont. A critic from France, where Deville had lived. Bellamont critiqued books and art—but why was he in the United States?

He recognized Bellamont from photos in newspapers or magazines, showing the victim at lavish parties or sailing on impressive yachts. Harsh words, lofty criticism and an insidious temper had made Bellamont into somewhat of a celebrity. Deville had never met the victim in person but suddenly a womanizer came to mind. Bellamont had an infamous past and the French had a bad name because of people like him.

Jessica Malone stood over the body. Her looming but shapely figure still tempted him, even if she covered herself with a dowdy trench coat. She shook her head. "It's a shame to ruin a perfectly good vine," she said, while inspecting scattered pieces of trellis wire around the body. The wire stretched from post to post, wrapped in vines of leaves and fruit from an unknown grape.

"Was he strangled with the trellis wire?" Deville asked.

"I can't tell," she said. "Looks so." She took a deep breath and began examining the pockets of the deceased. "He's a foreigner. Look familiar?"

He nodded. "A critic from France. He's been in the

news."

"A wine critic?" she asked.

"Yes but he also may have reviewed books and art."

"Imagine that. Our victim is from your native land," she said. "You go in and interview the person who discovered the body and I'll stay." She walked away, spoke with the team, and helped remove all contents from the victim's clothing.

The New York wine industry makes more varieties of wines than almost any wine region in the world. Its cool climate creates an ideal environment to grow grapes. Allenwood Vineyards was one of many on this side of Seneca Lake. The officers told Deville that Allenwood had recently opened and specialized in table wines. As he walked toward the entrance, Deville noticed the vineyard was somewhat of a mess. He discovered broken strands of trellis wire in other areas, not just where the victim lay. Smashed grapes covered portions of the grounds, making him wonder how difficult it would be to retrieve evidence from this crime scene.

The building stood several hundred feet from the trail of vines, where a party had taken place the night before. The one-story building had a wraparound porch, with a party room of tables and chairs. In front of that was a medium-sized parking lot, where a few streamers, lights and a banner hung. One corner of the "NOW OPEN" banner on the front of the building was flapping in the breeze. What a way to celebrate an opening, he thought, as he stepped onto the deck.

Everyone from the state police barracks moved about with respect. Deville did his best to remember names of the officers from the Bureau of Criminal Investigation (BCI). The local police didn't handle violent crimes. His troop was comprised of a few investigators assigned to the Finger Lakes. There were no detectives in the

Violent Crimes Investigative Team (VCIT) nor in the BCI division. All the investigators were state police officers.

Inside the building the familiar layout of a tasting room held shelves of wines, a fridge of cheese, a gift area and a long bar where tastings took place. At the bar, a troubled looking woman sat on a stool. She had found the body. She was dressed in a blue jean jacket over a simple cotton dress, dark hair to her shoulders and when she turned to greet him, she seemed relieved at his presence.

"Miss Keller?" he asked, reading his notes.

She nodded and brought out a small hand with bitten nails. She looked to be in her late twenties. "Sydney. My aunt and uncle own this place and I moved here. From New York. The city, that is." Her thin-lipped mouth tried to say something else but before she could, she buried her head in her arms and cried.

"It's okay. You've had quite a shock," he said. He went around the bar, found a clean wine glass and poured her some water out of the faucet. She took the glass and drank.

"Thanks. Aunt Marianne and Uncle Frank don't need this attention for their winery. This could kill their business." She looked at him. "That awful man. I can't get him out of my head."

"Sorry you had to see it. What do you know about Mr. Gerard Bellamont and why is he so awful?"

"Others called him awful. He attended the party last night, along with other people. The party was my idea. I wanted to celebrate the opening of the winery." Her face showed disgust. "All my idea—to have a party. Open with style."

"You mentioned there were other people?"

She nodded.

He flipped open his pad and gave it to her. "List all

the names of guests you remember from last night. Where are your aunt and uncle?"

"They'll be here any moment now. Oh my, what do I say to them?" She wrote hurriedly. "This place is supposed to be open now. What will my aunt say? What will others think?" The quick act of writing notes seemed to make the scene more real to her as if forcing her into accepting a living nightmare.

"I'm sure your aunt will understand why the winery isn't open." He noticed her script. "Take your time and print please. I need it legible."

She nodded, took another sip and said, "We didn't plan for this to happen. I'm here from New York. Did I say that? I needed to escape the city. Too many bad memories. I also came to help keep things organized at the winery." She watched officers moving about and sighed. "I'm staying until I get back on my feet—but now I'm not sure what will happen." Sydney searched her dress and jacket until she found a tissue. "I destroy everything. It's all my fault. All of it."

Deville cocked his head. "Are you responsible for the death of Mr. Bellamont?"

"Oh, no. I didn't kill him. Bellamont always had an aura of death around him. It was only a matter of time. I mean the circumstances may have been my fault—things happen around me." After he asked her to explain, she told him about her history of bad luck. Her parents dying while on holiday in Africa, her friends getting hurt, her boyfriends losing their jobs, her fiancé getting poisoned. He encouraged her to write this down as well, especially the poison part. She continued talking and Deville listened. Her ex-fiancee apparently lived but they had gone their separate ways.

"After getting sick he said he shouldn't risk being with me anymore. My bad luck makes me a walking time bomb." She saw him looking confused. "It's already been written," she pointed up, "in the stars." She explained that horoscopes and birth charts predicted her destiny to always to flirt with disaster, natural or man-made.

"Are you finished writing down the names?" he asked.

She looked back to the pad as though he'd interrupted her train of thought. After she finished writing she seemed calm. "I never expected anything like this to happen."

"To Mr. Bellamont?"

"Oh, no. It was a matter of time before someone killed him. I meant I never expected anything like this to happen at Allenwood Vineyards."

"Why aren't you surprised that Mr. Bellamont is dead?"

She spoke with ease as if talking to a classroom of students. "Such a bad man. He was a writer; one of those wine critics. He did so much harm to wineries." She paused, remembering. "His reviews proved to be merciless to some of the vineyards in the area. If he liked the wine, people saw an increase in sales—but if he didn't—it could mean the end!"

Deville learned Gerard Bellamont had been assigned to write a huge story for *Wine Sipper*, a national wine magazine, one of the many publications to which he had contributed. Recently the press had been kind to the region, with over twenty vineyards reaching the Wine Spectator's rating of 80 or more. Gerard Bellamont arrived to the Finger Lakes because a handful of wineries appeared in *Food and Wine* and other periodicals.

Sydney continued. "He's here from California for a few months. Before that he lived in France! Why would an international wine critic get killed up here in Western New York? At Allenwood Vineyards?"

Deville believed almost anything. He was waiting for her to say something like the victim deserved to die because he was French. Deville prepared to hear the worst.

Living as a foreigner may be easy in the United States, the melting pot of the world, but the French held a certain stigma, reputed to leave a bad taste with Americans. No one had ever been rude to Deville because of his nationality but some not as friendly. "Miss Keller, what else can you tell me?" he asked, wondering if she noticed that he, too, was a foreigner. "Who would want him dead?"

She said bluntly without any thought, "Anyone from a winery. Since he's been here, he's written other pieces for other magazines. He's a disease."

"A disease?" he repeated. Such a harsh word. What had made the victim such a tyrant to this woman? He tried to get back to the subject of last night. "Are you finished with the list?"

She pushed the notebook back to him. "These are the guests from last night." She looked around and sighed. "I need to get ready to open. Can I even open?"

"I'm afraid—"

Suddenly a woman from across the room shouted. "What is going on! What crime scene? I own this place. Who are you?"

They both turned around and Sydney jumped off her seat to run to the other woman. "It's my fault, Aunt Marianne. I'm sorry. I realize you didn't want the party, none of this would have happened."

"It's okay, Sydney. It's not your fault. There. There," Marianne Keller said to her niece while holding her with her thick arms. She looked around and spotted Deville. Shock was not the only word to describe her face. Deville also saw confusion, disgust and discouragement. To come to work and discover a small army of uniformed police floating around, asking her questions and ordering her around, seemed too much to deal with at this early hour.

Investigator Malone appeared and touched Marianne Keller's shoulder. "Is there anywhere we can talk?"

Moments later they gathered in what appeared to be an office, a room off to the side of the tasting room. They closed the door for privacy and Marianne Keller sat at a desk while Jessica sat on the other end. Deville stood.

Marianne Keller was medium height, had a round face, dark hair and a simple look about her. Dressed in a blue suit, flats, with a touch of makeup. The office was simply furnished, an offset to its decorator perhaps, with scarce furniture, a laptop, file cabinet and wine boxes. Cases of wine ran around the edge of the room, making it appear smaller. Deville scanned the cases of wines, curious how many blends Allenwood produced. He saw Riesling, the Finger Lakes-known grape, Cab Franc and several other blends. The familiar grapes did nothing to trigger any memory of taste for him. He felt that not being able to drink because of his alcoholism was a curse for him. He didn't mind but to live in an area known for splendid wine and not being able to taste it, was an encumbrance.

A single window exposed the vineyard in the back. The sun shone from behind the clouds and he noticed the crime scene techs finishing up. Mrs. Keller looked through the window, following his gaze, as though the window were a television screen. "Now what will happen?" she asked, as a group lifted the body onto a gurney. "I can't look at it." She turned her head back and covered her face with her hands.

"Please don't look," Jessica said. "It will be easier once the evidence is removed."

"Mrs. Keller, do you know what happened?" Deville asked.

She nodded and stared at her computer screen.

"Did you know the victim?"

She nodded again. "Sydney told me about Bellamont." She shook her head. "What a cruel thing to do. He has a wife and child. What will become of them?" She didn't wait for him to speak. "I guess they'll move back to California."

"How long have they been staying here?" Jessica asked.

Marianne shrugged. "A few months. Jan, his wife, said she didn't expect to stay this long. The piece he wrote was more of a guide of his favorite wineries up here. His articles were being published as a book. However, he did a lot of damage with his writing."

"Did he do any good?" Jessica inquired.

"Yes, he did. He helped some small wineries. Put them on the map, so to speak. Nice to us. Never sure what or when he would write. I'm surprised that he gave us a positive review. Quite relieved." She sighed, closed her eyes and said, "He told me I was special. I had a famous name, a symbol of liberty and freedom. Not familiar about the history of France."

Deville cleared his throat. "The name Marianne, just the way you spell it, is also known as a symbol of wisdom. She is usually represented in bronze statues or busts."

"Busts?"

"Yes. You know, like Beethoven?"

Marianne considered this. After a few moments, she peered back to Jessica. "The name seems wasted on me —I'm not wise at all. This business seems a bad move. I should have listened to my husband."

Marianne Keller seemed sensible, in her early fifties and easygoing. She and Frank Keller had been successful real estate agents. A power team, she said, selling the most non-commercial listings in a ten-mile radius. Another agent told her about this property and she gave winemaking a try. "It's a cutthroat business, real estate.

Not that the wine business is any better. I had hoped to bring Sydney to a less stressful environment. She's been through so much. She had a nasty break up and lived all alone. Poor thing. Thinks everything is her fault. I encouraged her to come here to help us. Told her it wasn't like the city, less crime.'"

"And a murder occurs," Deville said, handing her the notebook. "This is the list from last night's party, from what Sydney remembers."

"The party I didn't want," Marianne said. She took hold of the notebook. Her eyes became glassy. "Let's not be too proud, I said. Let's have a quiet opening." She wiped a tear away.

Jessica said, "You didn't know this would happen." She paused. "Look through and check all the names, please."

"Tell me if there's anyone else you should add or anything you remember," Deville uttered.

Marianne shrugged her shoulders. "It looks fine. A few news reporters not on this list left early. Gerard— Mr. Bellamont—was here with his wife, Jan. She's very nice. There's me, Frank, my husband and some friends from other wineries. Roger and Kelly Owen, from Owen Winery, which is the winery next to ours. Ryan and Stephanie Ferris, a young couple also from Owen Winery. He's the winemaker and she's the manager. Then there's Paul Shepard, from Catalina Vineyards, the winery next to ours on the other side." She handed the notebook back. "The party lasted until midnight and everyone left."

Deville said, "Either Mr. Bellamont never left or he came back. And someone met him. But why here?" He walked over to the window where rows of grapevines and officers could be seen.

Marianne appeared next to him. "They've rented the cottage just over the hill, pass our vines. We're their landlords."

Deville left Jessica recording more statements from Marianne Keller and met her husband outside. Frank Keller already looked as if he started mourning, although Deville guessed it wasn't the victim Keller mourned for but something else.

"It's over before we even began," Keller said with a twisted, sad mouth. He wore sunglasses and his bald head shone. A tropical shirt with khakis and sandals comprised his outfit, even on this autumn day. They stood a few yards from where the body was found. "I came as soon as I heard. My wife's hysterical rant on the phone made me hurry. I didn't believe her at first. She is trying to keep cool but she'll lose it before the day is done."

Deville gave him a card. "I'm sorry. Would you mind if we talk now?"

"Now is as good a time as any." He looked at the card. "Deville, like the Cadillac?"

Deville nodded. "Why don't we walk? The fresh air may do us some good?" Deville hoped his attempt at making matters light would make Keller more at ease. Deville hadn't much experience interviewing suspects for homicide but the usual brash way of asking questions, with a robotic tone and pinpoint expressionless guise, didn't seem his cup of tea. The facts worth investigating could be uncovered in almost any way, regardless of whether sweating in an interrogation room or walking along a vineyard in pleasant temperatures. I could get used to this, he said to himself.

"I know all about fresh air," Keller said. "Every morning I pick the grapes and make the wine myself." He walked, and stopped where crime scene tape began. "She's been telling me to fix some of these wires; some have fallen off the trellis." Deville asked about the layout of the vineyard and Frank Keller explained specifics to him. Deville noted each panel had four vines; each row about five hundred feet long with posts aligned about every twenty feet. "It's harvest time," Keller added. "This is a busy time for wineries."

Deville paused a moment before saying, "I'm afraid Gerard Bellamont may have been killed by the steel trellis wire. Strangulation." He noted some of the wires disconnected to the posts. "Are the wires always this loose?"

Frank Keller turned to look at him. "I try to tighten them all the time. Sometimes the wires break. How would I know someone would kill him like this?"

"Mr. Keller, I'm asking questions and giving you information about the crime."

Keller looked exhausted. "Winemaking is more than I bargained for. And now this tragedy."

Deville asked how much further to the cottage. Keller told him a few minutes' walk over the hill.

As they continued walking to the cottage, Deville asked about the party.

"Sydney, my niece, wanted it. My wife didn't. Marianne doesn't like people to see our accomplishments. Why invite jealousy?" He shook his head, "She always makes sure we are thankful, down-to-earth people."

"Mr. Keller, the party—"

"Oh, yes, that's right. Sorry."

Deville learned the grand opening party for Allenwood Vineyards had been a private one. Allenwood was his wife's maiden name. She didn't want to use his name for the same reasons he mentioned earlier—to draw attention. "A few friends were at the party." He scanned the list given to him and agreed to the attendants.

"Did everyone know each other?" Deville asked.

"Pretty much. We've known the Owens for about a year and they have the winery next to us."

"And what about the winery on the other side?"

"Catalina, yes. Paul Shepard has been wonderful. They all support each other, help each other."

"Your wife doesn't seem to agree."

Keller stopped. "What do you mean?"

Deville looked at his notes. "Your wife said the wine business is no better than real estate, which she described as cutthroat."

Keller said, "Maybe the wine business can be but why would she say that? Everyone's been so friendly." He started walking again with Deville following. "What do I know? She's the business woman. I work on the vines and make wine." They reached the top of the hill with the vineyard no longer in view.

Deville spotted the cottage a few hundred yards before them. He imagined it was something out of a postcard from another country. Two stories with one chimney, both quaint and charming. He heard the previous owners of the land used it as their summer quarters. He noticed the lawn ill kept in places, uneven, and bushes untrimmed, and guessed Frank Keller was not an avid gardener.

Keller said, "I'm outside most of the day, working on the vines. Very different than real estate I tell you—never thought I would do this."

"It was your wife's idea to open this vineyard?"

"Yes. She has all the ideas. I just follow and try to keep out of trouble."

"How did everyone seem last night? Everyone in good spirits?"

"Everyone seemed happy, I think. Harvest time makes everyone tired but with the leaves changing this place gets bustling. We've been open for a few weeks now—and I cannot believe how many people tasted our wine."

He stopped to catch his breath. Deville thought Frank Keller rarely went to the gym and possibly avoided exercise completely. His potbelly reinforced this. His face turned a shade of red and his short pauses painted a picture of a lazy winery operator. No wonder the vines had unattached wires and the grounds were in need of help.

"Mr. Keller, I hope you don't mind me asking this, but why on earth would you open a winery?" Keller looked at him, baffled. Deville continued. "You can't walk fifty feet without pausing. The grounds need serious help and your skills as a harvester are less than what I or anyone expects from a winemaker." He looked at him apologetically, "Why would you do this?"

"Because my wife told me."

An unusual response, Deville thought. Although quick, the response seemed honest and somehow expressed Frank Keller's attitude about his position in the business and his role in the marriage. They continued their final march to the cottage.

"I guess he wasn't well-liked?" Keller asked. "Anyone who gets killed, gets it for a reason. Not sayin' he deserved it or anything."

"Bellamont gave wine reviews, didn't he?" Deville asked.

Keller nodded.

"Any bad reviews of your wines?"

"He liked our wine. Gave it a good review—not glowing—but we'll take it. We're known for our table wines. These aren't as difficult to make. I read some of his other reviews but I don't care for reviews myself. If I like something, I like it."

Deville guessed Keller cared little about anything, at least in the wine industry.

As if he read Deville's mind, Keller said, "I don't much care for wine myself. Again, it's the wife. She likes to drink wine occasionally—but it's really for business. Bought this property at a good price; built a winery and plan to sell it when it gets on its feet. She's the smart one. I never claim to be." He stopped again. "I think Bellamont gave a bad review to the Owen Winery. Don't ask me which varietal. He hated their wine. He said something strange last night while sitting with a few of us at the table. It was me, Bellamont, Paul Shepard, Roger Owen and Ryan Ferris. Ferris makes the wine for Owen. Bellamont announced something he didn't like." He paused and scratched his bald head. "Actually he said he didn't like it the first time he saw it either. Strange. Didn't know what he meant but a few moments later I forgot about it."

"What was he referring to? The wine?"

"Everyone thought so. What else could it have been? There were a few bottles of wine on the table. The Owens brought a few, Shepard had some and our wine. What I thought was unusual was that he finished the glass. Later I asked Marianne why did he finish it if he didn't like it. Most critics spit it out. They don't drink or finish up something they hate. I don't even bother. I take a few sips of our wine because Marianne tells me I should sip and when the guests leave I drink my Coors beer."

Deville asked, "Do you remember which wine in particular Mr. Bellamont referred to when he said this and what kind?"

"Why? Was he poisoned? You told me he was strangled."

CHAPTER TWO

Deville learned Frank Keller didn't know which or what kind of wine Bellamont referred to the night before when he gave his mysterious rant. Deville also couldn't tell if this was important to the case yet. When they reached the cottage Deville expected Keller to knock on the door but instead he chose to sit on the swinging chair that hung on the cottage porch. Deville took out his video camera and began shooting. Keller eyed him curiously. After a few moments Keller stood and left, walking down the hill and passing Jessica Malone, who had walked up. Under her trench coat she wore a pantsuit, hair all done as if she'd been expecting a murder. She was older than Deville, a mother of a daughter going to college, and despite their complicated romantic past, he still respected her.

"Making a movie with me in it?" she asked. "I thought you no longer viewed our relationship that way?"

"It's for the investigation, my records. Although I'll keep you in this scene."

"With my hair being this frightful? Gray streak and all?"

He smiled and turned the recorder off. "It looks perfectly fine, gray streak and all."

After an awkward pause she asked, "Time for the grieving widow?"

Deville knocked on the door of the cottage and felt the temperature rising. After a brief absence the sun peered out from the clouds. In just a few weeks snow will fall, changing the hills of the wine region into a different spectacle. At this time residents of the Finger Lakes cherished every last bit of life without snow. At times, the lake effect weather protected them from area storms. It also brought heavy snow in the winter months that seemed more or less unforgiving.

"They planned to stay for at least another month," Deville said.

"Why would a family from California stay any longer than they have to?" she asked.

He knocked on the door again. "Maybe they've never experienced the mercy of cold weather in Upstate New York."

"He died before experiencing the cruel winter months."

The door opened by someone appearing to be in his teens. Dirty blond hair that covered most of his tanned face. Dressed in jeans and a T-shirt, probably in fashion for his age. Skateboarders, freestylers—what were they calling them now? Music from his headphones could be heard from where they stood. The teenager looked them over as if he'd been interrupted from something important. "Mom, it's for you," he said, placing the headphones back in their place and stepping away.

Deville could see the room ahead of them was nicely furnished with a few chairs, a table, wooden floors and some fresh flowers. In front of him, stairs led to the second floor, where a woman came down to meet them. She looked to be in her late forties or early fifties with a look of surprise like she wasn't used to visitors. She wore a robe and she'd been drying her hair with a towel. "You can at least invite our guests in, Wyatt," she said, while ushering them inside. "Hello. Can I help you?" She extended her hand and turned to yell again. "Wyatt, can you make some coffee? Sorry. Kids. You know. No respect for adults."

It starts with the upbringing, Deville thought. "Mrs. Bellamont?" he asked. He gave her his card as they broke the news delicately. Even though he had a way with people, his superior had a way with emotions. Deville let Jessica Malone speak. She had been a criminal psychologist working with the Bureau for several years before joining VCIT. Jessica broke the news with ease while they stood in the hall.

Deville asked if they could sit in the living room. The widow stood there, staring, lost in thought.

Jan Bellamont opened her mouth, gave a short sigh and seemed lost for words. She walked away, leaving them to make themselves at home.

Minutes later, they sat in the comfortable living room. Jan Bellamont seemed to take the news well. There wasn't any screaming, yelling or furniture being thrown around. Her damp brown hair, flowing down to her chest, sprouted over a long oval face that showed no emotion. She shared the same tan as her son and her manicured hands gripped the belt of the robe, as though this simple act kept her from losing it.

Wyatt Bellamont sat beside his mother in silence. His face was flushed with what Deville guessed was anger. He showed vestiges of tears, arms crossed and the music had stopped. The silence became awkward.

"You're French?" Mrs. Bellamont asked suddenly.

Deville nodded. "Yes, I am."

"Do you speak fluently?" she asked in French.

He nodded then brought out his notepad. She eyed it curiously then looked back at him, showing a pinch of fear. "Would it be okay to ask some questions?" he said in French. "If you don't want to right away, I understand."

"Get it over with," she said in a low voice.

Jessica Malone asked about last night, bringing the conversation back to English. "Tell us about the party, Mrs. Bellamont, and the people who attended."

"The Kellers are very nice people, and we wanted to be there for their opening. Few people are nice to us. It comes with the business. My husband can be cruel but emotion sells. The Kellers don't care about their wine, at least that's the way my husband saw it. He liked Frank. They spoke mostly about football. Gerard, my husband, said it was a relief to find people who weren't trying to get something. He told me he found it refreshing to meet 'normal people.' The Kellers weren't looking for a good review."

"How did your husband feel about their wine?" Deville asked.

"Funny thing is, he liked it. His words were 'thoroughly surprised.' This is considered a good thing for Gerard. So many people try very hard for good wine and what they produce is—"

She broke off and Deville accepted her decorous omit. If you have nothing nice to say—

"What about the Owen's wines?" he asked.

Jan Bellamont's stance changed and she appeared to be more guarded. "He didn't get along with the Owens so much," she explained, "because of some reviews he'd given."

Wyatt stood. "I gotta go." He left the room briskly, his mother watching him go while biting her lip.

When he opened the front door to leave she yelled, "Wyatt don't stay late!" She turned back to them and swallowed. "That's what I typically say to him at this time of day. Like it's another ordinary day. He goes off somewhere to spend time alone. He's always been a man of few words."

"Unlike his father?" Deville asked while writing. He looked up and saw her expression.

Jan Bellamont frowned. "Yes, unlike his father, who had a lot of things to say. Finger Lakes wineries produce a lot of sweet wines, something my husband never cared for. Is it wrong for someone to say what he or she feels? What is this world coming to if we have to filter every little thought or action? He hated sweet wine."

Deville asked, "Then why come here. Why do a story on wines he hates?"

"The magazine asked and after some research I—we —came over. Even though this area is known for sweeter wines, such as Catawba or Niagara, there is a lot of great dry wines, too. He had to review the sweet wines, which he did reluctantly, but he did it and was good at it."

"Didn't he review books?" he asked.

Jan nodded. "You remember him from France? And art. He was infamous for being an art critic. I suppose one becomes a critic of many things, depending on the locale." She paused. "He made a lot of enemies." She looked away to a painting on the wall over the fireplace. The painting showed a Finger Lakes landscape in autumn. Deville recognized the piece as one from Judy Soprano, a famed local artist. "Some people can't take criticism well. You have to see something or feel something to critique it. Whether it's a book or a piece of art or even wine. You need to have a taste for it or acquire one. It becomes automatic after a while. You fill in the information and give your best review. If people don't like it there's nothing you can do about it. We've received hate mail, fan mail and I never know what to do with it. It's part of the business." She looked back at the painting. "A taste for death. That's what Sydney called it. She's the girl who works here at Allenwood. She could read his energy. Sydney is a bit of a medium. She's spiritual. I don't believe in everything she says but so far it's been true."

Jessica Malone asked, "Why didn't you report your husband's disappearance last night? Do you have separate rooms?"

Jan Bellamont nodded. "My husband sleeps with his laptop and works till all hours of the night. I am old-fashioned, sleep with eye covers, complete darkness and silence. Didn't know he was gone. I don't go in his room. Our schedules are different, too. Now with the pills I don't have a problem sleeping." She looked away. "But Gerard tosses and turns. Before we had separate rooms I found it was a nightmare to sleep in the same bed."

Deville asked permission to look around the deceased's room. Jan agreed, showing him up the stairs with a brief tour of the cottage. The wallpaper, torn and dark, showed grapevines on an ivory background and ran up to the ceiling. It must have been several decades since the walls were washed. The carpet, thin and stained in certain areas, was a shade of drab beige. A short hallway led to three bedrooms and one bathroom. They entered Gerard's with prudence, as though they didn't want to disrupt any evidence or stir up any ghosts. He was a rude man, Deville thought to himself. He died violently and before he died he may have seen his assailant. If this wasn't the backdrop for a ghost story he didn't know what would be. He made a mental note to speak to Sydney Keller about unrested spirits. "What time did you leave the party last night?" he asked.

Mrs. Bellamont stood by the doorway and crossed her arms. She didn't look like she wanted to come any closer. Her husband is dead and she looked like she was looking for permission to enter his room. "Around midnight I guess, when I left him there speaking to the other men. I was worried about Wyatt. I had expected him to show up at the party and he didn't. When I got back neither were home. I thought Gerard had been looking for Wyatt or out for a walk. Gerard did that sometimes when he couldn't sleep. Although it can get nippy out there in the dark."

"Does Wyatt often leave without telling you where he's going?"

Framed pictures and reviews covered one area of a wall. Gerard Bellamont smiled in many of them, along with famous winemakers across the world. Deville recognized some areas in France and others parts of the globe. He noticed a few photos of the California coast. One thing stood out. They weren't any pictures of his wife or son.

"Lately he's been so unruly," she explained. Deville wondered who was unruly. "Can't say I blame him," she continued. "We took him away from his friends at schools. He and his father weren't close. They argued but not all the time. Wyatt doesn't understand how hard his father works. He tried, though, by helping his father with his writing. But it never lasted long. Wyatt always wanted to do his own thing. And Gerard was trying to teach him the value of money, showing him how hard it is to earn and save it."

"Kids are that way," Jessica said. "I have my own. She thinks money just grows from trees." Her phone rang with a call requesting her outside. She stepped out and left Deville and Mrs. Bellamont alone.

Mrs. Bellamont then said with sudden urgency, "He didn't do it. Wyatt. He would never hurt his father or me." She looked around, warming herself as though she felt a chill. "How did my husband die? You said he'd been killed."

Deville found the laptop on the bed, buried among the sheets, pillows, and blankets. He asked if he could take it. She mentioned he could take anything. He grabbed it, along with a few other things. With Mrs. Bellamont's permission, he took photos and a mini video with his phone.

The bed, small and unmade, stood in the center of the furthest wall. There weren't any windows and the room was dark, even with the lamp. The walls, dark as well, made the ceiling look closer and the room smaller. There were clothes and shoes on the floor. He opened the closet to find several fine suits, shirts and ties. He admired them, touched a few shirts and asked, "How long did you intend to stay in the Finger Lakes? It wouldn't take long for him to write a piece?"

"He was working on something else, too. I'm not sure what. Sometimes he'll contact local newspapers and write for extra money. He does a lot of freelancing but he gets paid well since he's well known. Did you know or recognize him?"

"The name is familiar," Deville replied but didn't want to say anything else. His connection to the victim would bear no hindrance to the case. Having them both come from France was just a peculiar coincidence. The wine, however, may cause a problem.

He sighed, feeling jealous of the victim's wardrobe. A crime to have this clothing unappreciated. There, on the floor of the closet, lay more lifeless shirts and pants. Deville thought the room was in such shambles. Anyone would think this was the son's room if not for the pictures and famed reviews on the walls.

"You still haven't answered me. How did Gerard die?"

He turned around to speak to her. "I'm sorry. He was strangled."

She raised her hands to her throat. "Strangled by someone?" she asked, as she started shaking. "Someone's hands were on Gerard, squeezing the life out of him?"

"Actually, it wasn't by hands. We believe the perpetrator used a trellis wire from the vines of the vineyard."

She looked as if the news was a joke. When she realized it wasn't, she closed her eyes and gave a shrill scream. "Trellis wire" was the last thing she said before fainting forward in a heap of dirty but expensive silk shirts.

CHAPTER THREE

Deville expected Jan Bellamont to wake from her fainting spell but she lay motionless longer than he expected. He lifted her head and placed it gently on a heap of clothing. He left her on the floor, giving her a few minutes while he searched the rest of the second floor.

Mrs. Bellamont had her own private bathroom attached to her bedroom. The medicine cabinet housed a potpourri of prescribed painkillers, mood elevators and sleep aids. No matter what time Gerard or Wyatt Bellamont would have come home last night, or any night, may have been a blur to her. How can anyone get to this level? To need a pill for anything—motivation, reduce stress, keep nightmares at bay—was so common in our society now. Deville wondered if it would ever change. What's next? A pill to fall in love?

Her bedroom displayed postcards from relatives and friends, pictures of her and her son but none of her husband. Deville guessed perhaps they weren't getting along. Her room proved to be just as untidy as his. Poor sods, he thought, as he went back to check on her. Living an itinerant lifestyle made them careless with their material items. He checked Jan's breathing. It flowed erratically from her wide-open mouth. He wondered how often nights ended with her out cold, not unlike her current state.

The third bedroom had a window. He opened it and spotted the other officers and Jessica Malone. "She's out cold," he yelled out. "She seems to have fainted."

Two officers stared back at him. Jessica Malone asked, "Do you need me to come up?"

"You or another female officer to carry her to her own bed."

While waiting for Jessica to come up, Deville closed the window and looked around the room. This third bedroom must be Wyatt's. It was neat and clear of any clutter. Musical groups, recent and older, covered the walls. Soft lighting showed a full size made bed. How odd, Deville thought, as he opened the closet door, eyeing the teen's wardrobe. This room is the neatest one.

Jessica Malone returned and helped him carry Mrs. Bellamont to bed. She placed a cold wet cloth on her head until she came to.

"We've called a doctor to check on you," Jessica told her.

Mrs. Bellamont looked around and noticed Deville standing by the doorway. In a dramatic fashion, she extended her hand. Deville walked toward her and took it. "Catch who killed my husband. Do this for me."

Investigator Malone witnessed this scene but said nothing.

Deville nodded. "I'll do my best." He took his hand away. He collected himself, helped other officers with some evidence and hurried out. After getting into his car, he buckled his seatbelt and took another look at his notes.

Jessica opened the passenger door.

"So she asks you to catch him, as though you were part of the French Embassy or something?"

"Someone's got to represent." He looked at her and smiled.

She smiled back but didn't seem to fall for his light banter. She knew him well enough to know something bothered him. What was going through her mind, he wondered? What did she see in him? He stood over six feet tall, thin, with a wave of dark hair and protruding ears. The man she had bedded several times acted cold, civil. He didn't let emotions rule him. He didn't consider himself the mushy man so many women seek. However, she wasn't the typical woman either. yet none could deny the connection. They shared physical intimacy but he was incapable of giving her anything else. She didn't seem to mind but he felt obligated to give more. For now, they were doing their best to keep it professional.

"Want to interview with me?" he asked, hoping to change the subject.

"Would you like me to?" She didn't wait for an answer. She looked away and bit her lip. "I probably shouldn't."

"I much rather you start all that wonderful paperwork. If we begin now we won't have to spend the night at the station."

"Don't have too much fun without me." She smiled and left the car. As soon as she left she gave orders to the others to wrap up. It was amazing how thorough she could be and how bossy. She seemed to be more human with him. He knew he had a special place in her heart and felt happy at the new level of their relationship. He respected her, now more than ever, and hoped she felt the same. Turning passion into friendship was not an easy thing. It wasn't difficult for him to switch gears because he felt he wasn't vested in the relationship. His brief history with love and women kept him guarded and distant. However, his concern for Jessica continued to inundate him. Her eyes still showed hope and he didn't want to disappoint. She still treated him differently, which wasn't wise. He could lose his post or she, her job.

He turned over a new sheet of paper in his notepad, felt the smooth, flat whiteness and got a bit excited. He enjoyed this part of his job: collecting clues, speaking to witnesses and suspects, brainstorming. The beginning stage of the case moved quickly, sometimes too fast for the investigator. The first 48 hours became a launching pad of gathering evidence, while later the case relied on the careful inquisitive mind of the lead investigator. Even though most cases involved proving your number one suspect is guilty, discovering the motive could be just as challenging.

He started his car and wondered how many officers would be assigned to the case. The fellow investigators in his team were pleasant enough and thorough. Creating a command post was unnecessary because the station was near. Taking other investigative officers to assemble a team was not something he looked forward to but knew it might be necessary. He got along with the other officers but kept his distance. His shyness, indifference and personal problems prevented him from having a strong sense of camaraderie within his own unit. Other than seeing them at the station, there was no other contact. The other officers lived at least twenty miles away. He never ran into them at the store or cinema and when they invited him to a social gathering he always declined. If they dug deep enough, they'd know and understand why.

He watched the crew mill about through his rearview mirror. He glanced at his pale reflection and noticed he looked older than ever before. Sharing a family's anguish after hearing their father or husband has died is something he'd never get used to. He felt like this part of the job aged him and left him uneasy. An uneasiness in the pit of his stomach, like indigestion after a meal.

However, that part was over. Now it was time to piece together the puzzle that had been Gerard Bellamont's life.

He drove his small Honda to the next vineyard south. Catalina Winery could be described as a boutique winery. Its wooden ranch-type building displayed a pleasant sign depicting a sunny coast. He parked in a dusty driveway filled with gravel. Deville heard Catalina didn't grow their own grapes. They got them from growers in the Finger Lakes and California, hence the sunshine coast logo that also appeared on the front door. Upon entering, he noticed a blue bicycle on the porch. Deville picked it up, noticed the kickstand missing, and leaned the bike against the wall. Inside the bright tasting room vivid colors included yellow walls, blue trim and a bar that looked to be custom. On either side of the bar hung floral watercolors of roses, lilacs, hydrangeas and more. The sunflowers were the most prominent. He stood beside a young couple who were purchasing a few bottles. The man behind the bar answered the couple's questions with ease.

"The difference between a winery and a vineyard is a vineyard actually has the grapes. We're a winery. Our vines aren't on the property."

"Aren't the wines made here?" the couple asked. "Yes they are. Some are in the region but not at this location. We are a boutique winery." Next the young couple asked what happened at the winery down the road where they saw several police cars. The man behind the bar said he didn't know and couldn't be of any more help. A moment after the couple left, he turned to Deville. "It's beautiful, isn't it?"

Deville continued feeling the wood of the bar. "Yes. Custom?"

He nodded. Paul Shepard owned the winery. Shepard had a slim build, shorter than average height and looked to be in his late forties. He wore a black polo with the business logo. The short-sleeved shirt showed his long toned arms. Specks of hair sprouted out of his shirt, matching a head of salt and pepper cropped hair over a handsome face. He came around and pointed to a few imperfections. "There are a few cracks here and this part of the wood is bent."

"Do you always spot the imperfections?"

"I speak the truth. Sometimes it is not pleasant though. Take a guess what wood I used."

"Pine?" Deville asked.

"No. Black walnut. I'm a furniture maker, or rather used to be. The wood is from Sonoma." Shepard continued showing off his piece, while giving a brief history of the wood and how he came to own it. His family had owned several companies, one of which was a wood furniture company that he took over. After several unsuccessful years of managing it, he stepped down and discovered woodworking. His true passion was creating the pieces themselves. "My father wasn't too pleased," Shepard explained. "I enjoy woodworking and creating. No starched shirts. No dealing with employees and no dreaded board meetings." His mother and wife both took his side and were happy with any decision he made. "My wife was a painter. This is her work. The winery is in honor of her. She loved wine. Have a glass?"

Shepard brought out a bottle and Deville shook his head. Just then a young man appeared from the back of the building. He wore jeans, headphones and a disheveled look. Deville recognized him as Wyatt Bellamont. Paul Shepard asked, "Wyatt, how long have you been here?"

Wyatt saw Deville then turned away, leaving the room and the two men alone. Shepard shrugged and said, "Kids. Never know what's going on in their heads."

"What is Wyatt Bellamont doing here?"

Shepard's face showed worry. "He's a friend. How do you know him?"

Deville sat on a nearby stool and pulled another close. "You may want to sit and I'll tell you why I'm here."

Shepard followed suit and sighed. "I guess you haven't come to taste." Deville informed him about Bellamont. After hearing the news, Shepard seemed confused and sad. "I can't believe it yet I can." He turned to look where Wyatt had just left. "The poor kid. He probably came because he needed consoling."

"Does he always come here for consoling?" Deville asked.

"Not just here. He goes to Allenwood too. Since the Bellamonts arrived, Wyatt has made these wineries a second home. He rides his bike everywhere and sometimes helps around the building. Hanging art on the walls, moving cases of wines, that sort of thing. Sometimes I think it's more of an escape."

"Who is he escaping from?"

Shepard looked like he chose his words carefully. "Family can sometimes be distant, even though they're near. His mom means well but she seems to be losing him, and his dad, well." He shook his head, as if wondering how the world could be so cruel. "Sydney from Allenwood and I, sort of took him under our wings. He has no other friends here. I should go to him." He stood, looked at Deville and decided not to. "I imagine you'd want to question me about the death?"

"About the murder? Yes."

"Murder, yes," he repeated. "Sounds so inhuman. Was it for money?"

"We are investigating all possibilities."

After a moment Shepard said, "Unfortunately, there are plenty of motives with Bellamont."

Deville flipped his notebook. "Really? Tell me what's on your mind, Mr. Shepard. How well did you know the victim?"

"He wrote about Finger Lakes wines, reviewed them. Heard he was publishing a book. Wasn't a very nice man."

"What did he think about Catalina's wine?"

Shepard shrugged. "My wines escaped his venomous words. Bellamont didn't give us favorable reviews but didn't slam us either."

"Who did he slam?"

The question didn't seem to surprise Shepard. He stepped off the stool, went around the bar and grabbed a cloth. He acted like reviews didn't matter to him. "Come now. I'm sure you've heard about the reviews he gave to Owen Winery. That's the winery on the other side of Allenwood." He wiped the bar with long full strokes.

"So they weren't favorable?"

Shepard sighed. "It's more like he detested that wine. Didn't matter what varietal, year or blend. It's like he had it in for the Owens. Like there's a personal vendetta."

Deville looked through his notes. "You say Bellamont was writing another piece, perhaps a book. What more can you tell me about that?"

"You should ask Stephanie Ferris, Owen Winery's manager. She has something to do with that. Her family is into publishing. They've seen a lot of each other. I don't think it's been all about business either."

"What are you suggesting?"

Shepard leaned closer. "Bellamont and Stephanie Ferris. I saw them last night in an embrace. Right there at Allenwood. I went outside to relieve myself and saw them."

"An affair?" Deville asked.

Shepard nodded. "So risky. Anyone could have seen them—Ryan, her husband, Jan, his wife."

Deville continued writing. "Who else knows about this

alleged affair?"

Shepard shook his head. "I can't stand even thinking about it. I can't believe what people do; how they don't take responsibility for their actions. Thank God my late wife is not around to see such cruelty." He paused. "She died in an accident years ago and it's people like Bellamont who make me relieved she is no longer here. She was quite the opposite of him. So kind, giving, always looking out for people. Artists are nurturing. She helped realize my passion with wood and hopefully now the wine can serve as a vessel for her inspiration."

Deville could almost hear distant chorus bells from the heavens, along with Shepard's disparaging view of life's dark half. The world sometimes seemed as simple as dark and light, good and evil, with people like Shepard ready to arbitrate. He couldn't believe Shepard was as innocuous as he appeared. He also remembered that Shepard had come from West Coast, California, where people viewed life through a shiny lens; a place where people couldn't believe how anyone could be so cruel or unkind.

"Mr. Bellamont's unfaithfulness is just one example of his character," Shepard explained. "I don't understand why people do the things they do."

"Mr. Shepard, it takes two to have an affair. What is your opinion of Stephanie Ferris?"

Shepard continued wiping, this time with quicker movements. "She's obviously unhappy. Like I said, I don't know why people do what they do. They need to stop, observe and be thankful for what they have."

Deville wondered what Shepard thought about what had happened last night. The murder would challenge his morality. "What happened last night?" Deville asked. "Such an evil act doesn't just happen for no reason." When Shepard remained silent with a blank face, Deville added, "Tell me what else went on at this party."

Shepard looked down and shrugged. "The party last night was for Allenwood Vineyards. We all stayed till about eleven then we heard that the kids were missing, Wyatt Bellamont and Chloe Owen. We found them, though, in Bellamont's cottage."

"Who found them?" Deville asked.

"Gerard Bellamont and I. Once we saw them we strolled back to Allenwood."

"Are the kids the same age?"

"Wyatt is older but not as mature as Chloe Owen."

"What happened in the cottage?"

"I can imagine. Two young kids, listening to music, hormones raging."

"Did the kids see you?"

"I don't think so." He threw the rag across the room and it landed in the sink. He smiled. "Basketball. I like to shoot hoops in the back when I'm not busy here." He watched Deville write. "What time did the crime happen?" Shepard asked.

"Between eleven p.m. and one a.m."

"Right there, at the winery? Geez. Who would do that? So risky."

"Risky? The usual response is why would someone do that?"

Shepard tried to explain. "Like I said, there are a lot of motives for Bellamont." After a moment he added, "Owen Winery. There's no hope for them. If you're looking for motives, there are plenty right there. Roger and Kelly Owen, the owners, ignore their wine quality and they're doing nothing about it."

The door opened and people strolled in, looking for tastings. Deville stood, thanked Shepard and left his card. Outside, the bike was no longer there. More people entered Catalina Winery. The bright day promised new adventures. Deville's work was just beginning.

CHAPTER FOUR

Next on Deville's list of places to visit was Owen Winery. He had four names from there: the owners, Roger and Kelly, Ryan Ferris, winemaker, and Stephanie Ferris, manager. He wondered how people staffed their wineries. Did they go by the time of year, staffing heavier during the holidays or summer? Or could it be location of the winery or volume of wine?

As he drove he discovered it was an estate winery. At least 85 percent of the grapes had to be from their vineyard, which began behind a recently painted building. Owen Winery looked like it was growing in size and business. Deville counted at least six employees working and learned the winery produced several thousand cases of wine each year. Several customers were tasting and buying. The vineyard's marketing went beyond wine; shirts, glasses, wine stoppers and much more were for sale, all bearing the Owen name. Deville thought the Owens had a lot to lose if a bad review slowed the business. This winery seemed to more established compared to Allenwood or Catalina.

A young woman ask if he needed any help. He asked for the owners but they weren't available. She mentioned Stephanie Ferris was available and told him to walk to the back of the building to what appeared to be a storage room with a garage door. He noticed stacks of wine cases and another woman lifting a case of wine from a handcart. He thought it might be Stephanie Ferris. She was thin with long, straight blond hair. She wore a tight black dress and looked like she was ready to go dancing at a club. Her balance seemed a little off due to her high heels. Her grasp on the boxes showed long manicured nails.

She was about to fall, case in hand.

Deville caught the case before it fell and she recovered.

"Shit, thanks. Geez. I'm sorry. I never dropped a case before."

Deville offered a friendly smile. "You probably just need a break."

"All these have to go out. They're for orders. I have no time to take a break."

"I think you should," he said as he searched in his pockets.

"But no one else will do it!" she snapped. She took a deep breath and tried to calm herself down. It worked for a few moments until she saw his badge. "Okay, hero. I guess five minutes won't kill me."

Odd choice of words, Deville thought. She admitted she was Stephanie Ferris and suggested they talk outside. She didn't want to go far since the winery was busy. She opened a door that led outside and asked if he minded her smoking. He said no and after lighting up she asked, "So what's this about?" Her voice was sharp.

He decided she was direct so he was also. "Someone killed Gerard Bellamont last night."

She coughed and threw her cigarette. "Oh, excuse me, I didn't expect that."

"Knew him well?" he asked.

"I just saw him last night. He was funny."

"How funny was he?"

"The way he looked at things, full of ideas. We were working on a project, his writing. Something I was helping him with."

Deville asked, "What kind of project?"

She shook her head. "I didn't see it. He didn't show me."

"Why wouldn't he show it to you? Was it a review? Or a book?"

"A book." She opened the door and entered the building. "My family owns a publishing company. Books for travelers, coffee table stuff. He was writing a book about Finger Lakes wineries." She paused and then added, "We met several times about it but I've never read the manuscript. I just sent it off with a referral."

Deville wondered if this was why Gerard Bellamont extended his stay in the Finger Lakes. Could his smaller pieces of work be turned into enough material to write a book? "Mrs. Ferris, can you tell me what Gerard wrote about Owen Winery? I heard he didn't have nice things to say about a lot of wineries."

"He said little nice things period but everyone is entitled to their opinion. Yes, he didn't care for some of Owen's wines but it's not the first time he wrote bad reviews. Owen Winery can handle it. It doesn't seem to affect their dedicated customers."

"That's splendid for Owen's business," he said, realizing how she was distancing herself from the company. Most employees, especially managers, said "we" or "our," but here she was, leaving the owners out to dry. "How long have you worked here?"

She shrugged. "Two years. It's just a stepping stone. I have other plans."

He wondered if her husband, the winemaker, played a role in her future endeavors. "Your husband, Ryan, also works here? He produces wines?"

She rolled her eyes. "Yes, he does. The gifted winemaker. He's the one everyone talks to, the reporters, the magazines." She grabbed a folder from the tower of cases. "You must have read about Ryan?"

Deville nodded. "This winery is always getting press." He guessed it was the number of wines they released, not the quality that grabbed media attention. Owen Winery was not hailed as a serious vineyard. The space and parking lot were large enough to accommodate bus tours and it was a tourist's paradise with all the paraphernalia offered in their gift shop. There was also a small bistro-type dining room for lunch. Please the crowd of masses with everything; food, gifts, entertainment, all while they taste the wine the critics massacre.

"Were you at the party last night?" he asked.

"I'm sure everyone's told you I was." A thin smile appeared. "I guess you need my alibi. I left around eleven. Around the same time the fuss started."

"Fuss?"

"Yes, the kids. They went missing. That Bellamont kid, Wyatt, and Chloe Owen, Roger and Kelly's daughter. They're around the same age. Both missing but I wasn't worried. A few wanted to go find them; Gerard, Jan and Paul. They wanted to start a frantic search party but they were drunk. I didn't even bother. It seems Wyatt is asthmatic and keeps losing his inhaler. You know how kids are."

"How does Chloe fit in?" Deville asked.

"Young lovers, rivaling families. Heard it before? Bellamont writes about Owen Winery, which caused them to argue, then when the kids saw each other, Roger Owen put a stop to it. He forbade his daughter to see Wyatt and that's when the shit hit the fan. Bellamont said that he'd bury the Owens and the vineyard with more bad reviews. He said he wouldn't stop until the vineyard closed." She stopped talking, thrusting her hand in her bosom, where she pulled out a business card. "I hope this helps your investigation," she said with an ingenuous smile, signaling the end of their conversation.

Deville took her card and then added, "A witness saw you and the victim last night. You two were a little more than just business associates. The witness said you were in a liplock with him."

Her jaw dropped. "Me and Gerard? Are you kidding me?" After a moment she said, "Look at me. Does it look like I would have an affair with some old coot? I workout four days a week, do Zumba, aerobics and take Taekwondo." She shuddered and walked away, heels stomping on the concrete floor, not unlike a fashion model on a hapless runway.

Deville took more notes, a short video of Owen Winery and grabbed a coffee in their café. As he sipped, he felt disappointed. Sadly this part of the business had its shortcomings, too. Just as the wines succumbed to the demands of the popularity, the coffee followed suit with lowered expectations. This was more common than one thought. Deville knew perfectly located restaurants with food that could be served in a fast food eatery. Or worse, service so bad they almost expected people never to return. The old philosophy of "getting the tourists in once is good enough" is regrettably not dead, as some businesses with incredible views of the lake seemed to practice just this.

Stephanie Ferris's reaction to his questions about her and Bellamont made Deville wonder if what Shepard saw was true. Maybe Shepard thought he saw the victim, who was hard not to miss in his expensive suit, short stature and receding hairline. Stephanie, for that matter, stood out even more. Long blond hair, thin, heels. There was no confusion. Someone was lying.

Behind the storeroom where Stephanie Ferris left him,

were huge stainless steel containers and wine vats, fermenting the wines. It was here where Deville found Ryan Ferris, the winemaker, and Stephanie's husband. Ryan Ferris was a bright-eyed man in his mid-twenties with a stocky build and dark hair. A handsome boyish face suggested he might have married too young. He looked up and saw Deville with a student's beaming gesture. He stood in front of a vat, glass in hand, studying the color of the wine in his glass. After a moment, he swished the red wine and brought it up to the light. This is when he noticed Deville. "Hello. Are you here to get a tour?"

"No, I'm here for a different matter."

"Well then, I should apologize," Ryan Ferris said slightly disappointed. He placed the glass down delicately and came to greet Deville by putting his hand out to shake. Ferris looked comfortable in white shorts and an Owen Winery colored tee. His grip was tight. Surely he had enough strength to strangle someone. "Glad you're here," he said. "How may I help you, sir?"

So pleasant, Deville thought. Politeness went far with Deville but it didn't exclude one from a murder investigation. He broke the news about murder and after hearing about Gerard Bellamont, Ryan Ferris seemed surprised.

"Someone did the bastard in?" Ferris said, leaning on the counter. "I can't believe anything like this could happen up here. Everyone likes to think they live a neighborhood where murders don't happen." He shook his head. "I guess our winery is suspected. This will mean more press for us."

Deville said, "The winery should be used to getting attention from press."

"Yes but not this kind. We try to maintain a positive image. We sponsor several things throughout the year, golf shows, good causes, etc." Ryan Ferris shook his head. "There are so many wineries that would like to see us go away. But would they resort to this?"

"To what?" Deville asked. "Kill someone to set up Owen Winery?"

Ferris shrugged. "Not just anyone, Gerard Bellamont. I know we've had several bad reviews from him but killing him seems harsh. I hope you don't think we had anything to do with it."

Deville brought out his pad. "What kind of reviews did Bellamont write about your winery?"

"Didn't care for some of our varietals, said we're losing focus. I don't pay attention anymore. It's a bunch of bull. One review was appalling and it seems like he wrote it before the wine was released. Like I said, I think some people would love to see this place close. Bellamont being one. Although there wouldn't be anyone for him to harass anymore."

"Since Bellamont is no longer with us, who else would benefit from your winery closing?"

"Besides the other wineries on this side of the lake?"

"Come now, Mr. Ferris. Doesn't this type of business do better in numbers?" Businesses, such as wineries and antique stores, do well when grouped together. The mall aspect, some would call it. It certainly worked with restaurants, Deville thought.

"Yes but there is such a thing as too many. We all make wine. What do you think sets us apart? The grapes, the barrels, the soil and the year? But what is it really? It's not just a fancy label that brings customers anymore."

"It's the awards?" Deville guessed.

Ferris nodded. He placed his glass on a nearby table and collected his thoughts. Was he disappointed with the wine he had just tasted or the news of the death? Ferris cleared his throat. "I don't pretend to be the best winemaker but I work damn hard. Hard enough to know we aren't the worst winery here in the Finger Lakes."

The frankness Ferris shared was thoughtful and seemed genuine. As if he were defending his honor not just a position. "Would you say you're glad he's dead?" Deville asked.

"Without you locking me up? Yes. I'm glad he's dead but I didn't do it." After being asked his whereabouts the night before, Ferris was almost too eager to shove out his alibi, which seemed weak. He had left the party with his wife a few minutes after eleven. During the party he remembered nothing significant. "Bellamont talked about sports with Frank Keller from Allenwood Winery. Shepard was there and Roger and Kelly Owen, my bosses."

Deville thought he'd ask about Bellamont's scene that Frank Keller had remembered so fondly, just before the victim died. "Do you recall Bellamont saying anything about hating something the first time? Someone had heard him say this."

Ferris shrugged. "He may have said something about hating our wine."

Deville looked at his notes. "I believe Bellamont said he 'hated something the first time?'"

"It couldn't have been our wine. I don't remember him tasting our new Cab Franc, which we just bottled. But that was Bellamont. He liked to get on everyone's nerves. Did you hear about him and Shepard?"

Deville flipped over to a fresh sheet of paper. "No. Please tell me."

"It seems Bellamont is providing some grapes, or juice rather, from California. That's where he's from. Shepard asked for some grapes and Bellamont didn't want to sell him any. Can you believe that? That's flat out business he declined. Stupid."

"Who told you this? Bellamont himself?"

"No. Shepard. Bellamont would never talk about it and I know he already provides California grapes to other wineries here." He provided a short list of wineries. Some were on different lakes in the area. Being a distributor for California grapes and having a possible commission may have provided a reasonable, if not steady, income for Bellamont. The Finger Lakes region had so many wineries. Some weren't estate wineries so grapes or juice could be shipped from other parts of the world. Why would Bellamont refuse to provide grapes and juice to Paul Shepard and Catalina Winery? If what he heard was true about Bellamont's character, he was always looking for more income and any opportunity to make a buck.

"Can you tell me about the missing teenagers?" Deville asked.

Ryan Ferris went back to checking his wine. Whatever experience or expertise he may lack, his patience and work ethic seemed intact. "You know how kids are nowadays, do anything for attention. They found them though. I think they were in Bellamont's cottage. Wyatt is always getting in trouble. He's immature and has a smart mouth. Disrespectful and rude."

The same attributes Deville loathed himself. But those traits were common with teenagers and the way Ryan Ferris reacted when Deville had asked about the teenagers was peculiar. The mood changed and Ferris seemed aloof, wanting to change the subject.

Deville asked, "Are they romantically involved? Chloe and Wyatt?"

Ryan didn't look at Deville when he said, "Don't know. Why not ask them yourself?"

The strong rays of the sun and landscape made Deville think of the past. The life he'd led was an enigma on its own. Pieces of the puzzle came infrequently with images, emotions or smells.

Deville suffered from amnesia for a large part of his past. This past was a battle he shared with almost no one. His mind was eager to unwrap any memories but no methods proved successful. Hypnosis and treatments stopped long ago. He abstained from it due to fear of delirious effects. His body, and in most regards, his mind, functioned well, even when memories surfaced.

Parts of his childhood escaped him, even before the amnesia, before the doctors and hand me downs and the hospitals in both countries. What he remembered, whether it was images, smells or tastes, were sudden and vivid.

From what seemed like another world away, the smell and taste of France were now coming back to him. As a boy, when not studying or in school, he had spent the afternoons in the fields of Bordeaux, a large region off the Atlantic Coast. One such memory erupted now, just by the warmth of the sun.

He could hear the wind blowing, giving off an ocean breeze that made his knees cold. This meant he was in shorts, which were hand-me-downs from cousins whom he didn't recall. He remembered feeling poor but grateful for the little he had. He was running and laughing. His shoes were loose. Deville thought they were also given to him because they were one size too big. He could see the ocean from a distance and it made him happy. How old was he? It must have been summer because it was sunny and he didn't have his schoolbooks with him. While running, he could smell the growing lavender. He thought the tips might be in danger of catching on fire. A child thought of such things; any worries were simple and innocent.

"Don't be silly, Louis. The lavender will be fine," his mother announced. Her voice, strong and sometimes mistaken for a man's, could drown out any noise but did little to muffle his uncle's shouting. The arguments were constant but the details were a blur. The accents were as strong as their voices. He thought maybe the animals outside were afraid of the yelling because when his mother and uncle weren't arguing, stray cats were always running around and he could hear birds chirping. His mother and uncle yelled about finances, education and food. He remembered his mother, a heavy but pleasant dark-haired woman, asking him not to be silly. "If the lavender burns so be it. It is God's will." She winked. "Plus imagine the lovely smell if it burned!"

Where was his father? He could see the lavender fields ahead of him connected to something, a building that looked like a shack. The lavender wasn't burning but the shack was. The fire in the distance didn't change his emotion. He didn't feel at all sad while watching the shack burning. It was a place no family should live in but for some reason he called it home.

CHAPTER FIVE

Deville got the call that the body was ready to be examined. The nearest place equipped to do the job was the medical examiner's office in Rochester. As he drove, Deville's mind kept busy on the facts of the case. Gerard Bellamont didn't have many friends and Deville wondered if the people around the victim could commit such a crime. Bellamont's wife, Jan, was a suspect because Gerard had an affair. His thoughts shifted to Wyatt Bellamont. How was the relationship between father and son? This made him try to remember his father.

No memories, no vestiges or anything his mind wished to share about his father. Just fragments of his mother: gentle, pleasant and working in a lavender field. He also saw images of her and another woman picking grapes and then squashing them. Did he conjure those images? Had he been raised in or around a vineyard? Or a field of lavender? The vineyard would explain a lot of things, he thought, as he touched his forehead. He let his hand caress his face, shoulder, where other hands once probed and imagined a world without doctors, amnesia, missing fathers and God forbid, wine.

An examination of the body showed no surprises. The

medical examiner determined the cause of death to be a ligature from a wire, either the trellis wire found nearby or something similar. The victim, 49, seemed to be healthy, except for high blood pressure that had been regulated with prescribed drugs. He had been medium height and about 20 pounds overweight, an indication that he ate well. The stomach contents were being examined. The body was covered with a thin blue sheet, a dull contrast to the wardrobe Gerard Bellamont once wore. It lay under dull bright lamps, giving off an eerie glow. Deville would never get used to it. Only the head and feet of the victim showed. The well-ventilated room couldn't cover the stench of putrefied flesh, a wafting combination of vomit and rotting grass, along with a layer of disinfectants and steel. The examiner waved Deville over. He gave a wry smile and looked back at the subject.

"French," Dr. Frost, the examiner said. Frost was in his sixties, with a huge head of shocking white hair, a bearded face and fearless eyes. His gaze pierced through small modern eyeglasses, giving him a scholarly air. He looked ready to test anyone he encountered. He wrote on a clipboard. "Never saw a dead one before. French, I mean. Aren't you French as well?"

Deville said nothing. He knew it was impolite not to respond but he also knew Frost didn't care.

Frost kept writing. "Pretty much what you see is what you get. Seems like he tried to fight back but either his hands couldn't reach his assailant or he got too tired." He pulled an arm out from under the sheet to show a hand. "Dug deep in the earth and urinated himself, the usual effects of strangulation."

"Is that blood around his neck and face?"

"No, actually. When blood dries it can be as dark but this is grape juice mixed in with dirt. I imagine there were grapes around the body and when he tried to stop the strangulation he got it around his face, neck and clothes." Frost placed the arm back under the covers and ushered Deville out of the room.

Frost said, "A person with strength did this."

"Is it likely a man?" Deville asked. "Or could a woman with enough strength do this?"

Frost thought for a moment. "I doubt it but it's possible. I've only seen a few strangulations, all done by men. Never like this, with a wire. It doesn't take as much strength as a manual strangulation so I wouldn't rule out a woman. Who's in the running? Or is it too early to tell?"

"The victim had a lot of enemies," Deville replied.

"Don't they all?"

They continued walking the hospital hallway. The humming of the ventilation system was the only noise other than their footsteps.

Frost placed a hand on Deville's back. "This is quite a case for you. I know it's not your first homicide but this one is different. It's not some kid getting shot from a bad drug deal." The older man stopped and gave Deville an earnest look. "Considering what you've been going through, maybe you should consider some help?"

Deville sighed. "Considering nothing. I think I can handle this."

"It's not a question of pride."

"I know it's not. I can do this." Deville forced a smile and tried his best to remain pleasant. "I'll assemble a small team."

"From here? In the city? I can make a few phone calls..."

"No. From our station. Thank you but I know how to do my job."

Frost gave an uneasy, disappointed glare and continued walking. His boys from Rochester were always ready and willing to help and Deville hoped he wouldn't need to seek help outside his station. Frost was well-known in the county and Deville had seen him several times speaking to lieutenants and captains. Frost had influence because of his age, experience and knowledge. Deville, careful of what he said when around Frost, knew that what he disclosed would probably reach others. Frost meant no harm. He just had an old-fashioned way of dealing with officers and remained close with his colleagues. Most investigators from the old boys club were still tight and some like Frost, believed anyone younger didn't have enough experience to handle a homicide. Surely any investigators in farm country, which was anywhere Frost probably thought outside Rochester.

Frost and some of his generational cohorts may think numerous investigators were sufficient for handling a case such as this. This wasn't a serial killing, Deville said to himself. We don't have unlimited officers, a payroll with an overtime staff and people doing legwork computers and software, such as VICAP (the Violet Criminal Apprehension Program). The suggestion of Deville needing help might have been an insult to other officers but Deville let it slide. He gave a slight nod and walked away slowly, leaving Frost like an old scholar who'd just given a speech that fell on deaf ears.

Having enough experience to solve a homicide was imperative. Deville had stood his ground but an uneasy feeling set in while going back to his car. He didn't feel incompetent but now he felt he had to prove himself. For a while, the other investigators on his team seem to be running the show, tackling cases while offering Deville small and meaningless tasks a neophyte could do. At first Deville thought this treatment stemmed from him being so different. Then he realized it was because of his relationship with Jessica Malone. He unconsciously became a teacher's pet. He had taken the role of an investigator who placated their supervisor. Even though he thought no one knew about his relationship with her, he discovered the other officers knew and had treated him differently because of it. He kept her company and busy. They never let him work late and always made sure he spent plenty of time at the station. Eye candy for their supervisor.

The evening became cool when he drove back to the station. The wind blew leaves around the building. The fall weather was in full swing and the crisp air felt pleasant. At the station the crew would be ready for briefing. There was no power trip when one became the lead investigator. They all divided the tasks while making sure everyone put in a full day's work. He entered the station, noticed the grease board ready and counted the officers. There were only three and they stopped talking when he entered the room.

"Where's Smitty?" Deville asked.

A young investigator named Reginald Scudder replied. "They're transferring him, sir. He told me to say he's sorry." Reginald Scudder, the newest investigator of the bunch, could be no more than 26. His short red hair was always groomed. His white shirts were always pressed and he seemed to care about his job. Deville liked that Scudder respected others, especially those who older than him. Scudder sat near the other male and female investigators.

Investigator Malone came out of her office. She walked over to where he stood and looked like she was a proud parent waiting for her child to perform in a school play. Although no one wanted to admit it, a new case was like a bolt of energy to the station. For Deville, and perhaps the other officers, a new case reminded them how important their jobs were.

Deville called Scudder over and handed him a

marker, signaling him to start writing on their dry erase board.

"Gerard Bellamont, 49, strangled with a wire. The victim was a writer who wrote reviews for wines, books and art. From California, he was here to work on projects, possibly a book. Married to Jan Bellamont; father to Wyatt. What else do we know about him?"

The female investigator, Christine Wolanski, stood, holding a notepad. "He moved to the States from France and has been living in this country for almost 20 years." Christine Wolanski, in her late forties, had a raspy voice and kept to herself most of the time. She looked more like a hairdresser, with her curly hair falling on the sides of her face and eyeglasses with frames that curved up toward her ears. She dressed in colorful garbs of mixed fabrics and was well-liked. "The victim was famous for writing bad reviews. If you'd like I can start on all his recent pieces, get together all his harshest reviews. If what they say is true, it will be a big folder."

"Thank you, Christine," Deville said. "More than likely the motive relates to his profession but we can't rule out anything."

"And his career up to this point has been very lucrative," Malone added, crossing her arms. "I've checked his finances and last year he cleared half a million after taxes."

"This is before the book he was publishing," Deville said. "This book could be critical. Did we see any signs of it?"

Scudder, who had been writing frantically, replied, "Computer lab has the laptop now. We'll know in the morning, sir. He has boxes of paper too that we are sorting." He stopped, wondering what everyone was looking at. The grease board showed his erratic small handwriting. Other than the names, it was hard to decipher what had been written. Scudder looked at the board, then back to Deville. "Sorry, sir."

Deville sighed. "It's okay. Write it over please."

Scudder erased the board with nervous hands and started writing again, this time more clearly.

Jessica Malone said, "We've been spoiled with Smitty, who used to be a teacher. We miss his perfect handwriting."

Deville continued, looking at his notes. "Now the suspects. I want to know everything about Frank and Marianne Keller." He gave them all a chance to take notes. "And Sydney Keller, their niece from New York City. Paul Shepard is from Catalina Winery. There's a connection. Paul Shepard and the victim are both from California. Plus, the victim sold grape juice to a number of wineries here in the Finger Lakes but refused to sell to Paul Shepard. We need to know why." He looked over to where the eldest officer sat. "Jerome, can you do some research on the wineries Bellamont dealt with?"

Jerome Miller, near 60, was the most experienced officer they had. He rarely touched a computer, avoiding it at all costs. He did his best work on the phone and on the road. His health wasn't what it used to be. He was clearly more than 40 pounds overweight, had diabetes and took his African American heritage seriously. He had served in Desert Storm, still didn't think of his job as a career and couldn't wait to retire. All of this he happily divulged to any officer passing. "Do you know how many wineries they are in the Finger Lakes?" he asked.

"Oh, about a hundred," Deville answered. "Why?"

Miller didn't look happy. No love lost here, Deville thought. Jerome Miller was argumentative at times and, because of seniority, could win any argument. He had the rest of the officers under his wing. Besides complaining about being tired, Jerome didn't take orders well. However, he had a wealth of knowledge and usually had something sensible to say buried somewhere in all his complaining.

"And Miller," Deville added, "check the ones in California, too."

Miller wrote something down on his pad. Deville guessed it was probably an obscenity. "Miller, since Investigator Wolanski is going over his writings, she can help with the wineries but I need more from you. Look through the victim's past. Start from when he moved here from France, his schooling and such. We need to find out everything about the victim, past and present."

"Anything else you can pile on me?" Miller asked, with a steady gaze.

Deville sighed. "I will be interviewing the suspects, speaking to the coroner, witnesses and collecting more evidence. If you have a problem with any of my orders…" he broke off and stole a glance at Jessica Malone, who shook her head slightly, telling him not to stop. Or was that a signal for him to stop? He wasn't sure and didn't know what to do.

Deville turned around, feeling hot and bad tempered. He saw Scudder stop writing, eyeing him with a proud look on his face. Deville took a deep breath and continued. "Okay. Back to suspects. Ryan Ferris is the winemaker at Owen Winery, which suffered from the victim's most merciless reviews. His wife, Stephanie, is the manager. A witness, Paul Shepard, saw her and the victim kissing the night of the murder. Gerard Bellamont wasn't the best looking man who walked the earth. Stephanie is better than average looking so I don't know what to make of it." He turned around, grabbed a different colored marker and connected the names with a question mark.

"I'm going to speak to the owners of Owen Winery tonight. Any questions?" No one stirred. "Now I know it's important to spend as much time as we can on this. I also realize we are working on other cases but let's do our best. We don't want to have to call on Rochester for help. Please copy everything on the board and let's meet tomorrow morning at 0700 hours. Thank you." Deville exhaled a long breath, glad it was over.

Jessica asked him to join her in her office. A moment later she told him to sit.

Deville refused the seat. "No thanks, I need to go. I want to speak to the Owens tonight."

Jessica nodded. "I'm glad to see you this busy."

"It's certainly about time."

"Louis, come on. Let it go. You've had more than enough to do around here."

"Yes, doing everything that keeps me close to the station, near the phone, near the computers and near you."

She crossed her brows. "Don't do this. Do not come in here thinking I have something to do with your workload. Not completely. The lead investigator is in command. If I think there's a problem then I intervene. You know this." She stretched out her hands. "In case you forgot where you are, there's not a lot of crime here. Since Rochester hasn't called us, our caseload is lighter."

Deville sighed. She might be right. Sometimes he took things too seriously, and maybe personally, but he couldn't stop the way he felt. And he couldn't stop how the other officers felt either. So if they thought he was Jessica Malone's boy toy and he should stay in the station all day with limited work, then that's what they thought. "Why did you bring me in here?"

She gave him a slight smile. "It's been a while since you've been the lead. I wanted to tell you to be more confident. Don't be afraid to give orders. Don't let Miller or anyone else intimidate you. You are all equal here."

Except they haven't slept with you, he thought.

She sat down in her chair and he was reminded why she was senior investigator. She had a way of getting things done in a timely fashion. She seemed to treat each case as a new adventure, trying to make sure everyone acted on their best behavior. "Go on. See you tomorrow."

He gave her a slight nod and left the office. After looking up Roger and Kelly Owen's address, he grabbed his coat and got in his car. While buckling his seatbelt, he thought about the last time he was the lead investigator. The case, a missing woman believed to be dead, took them four days to solve. He hoped this could be done sooner. And he hoped it wouldn't disappoint as the other had.

He yawned as he pulled out of the driveway, turning east. This would be his last interview for the night. The sooner an investigator met all the suspects in a murder investigation, the better. Don't give anyone enough time to collaborate stories or alibis or leave town. Finishing the day knowing you did all you can to jump start an investigation is a good feeling. One didn't want to go home wondering if there was more that could have been done. Besides, what else did he have to do? Go home to his empty house and bring in the night?

CHAPTER SIX

The Owens lived in the better part of Geneva, just five miles away from their vineyard. The house was a large Victorian with exposed trusses that looked like "stick work." It also had brackets and rafters resembling medieval architecture. With all the wood, Deville wondered how fast the home would go up in flames in an event of a fire. Surrounding the exquisite three-story home were a bunch of autumn white ash trees commonly found in this part of the state because they could withstand the cooler temperatures. Not far, just a few blocks, Hobart William Smith Colleges held their own fields of property. This was a worthy college that attracted students from everywhere. Beyond this, the hub of downtown Geneva stood, an impressive small city that looked more intriguing at night than by day. Deville remembered spotting the cities of the Finger Lakes for the first time as a teenager. Although it's been over two decades, the excitement and terror of living a new life still unnerved him.

The tall wooden oak doors were answered by a short white-haired woman in her sixties. She introduced herself as the housekeeper and ushered Deville inside from what she called a chilly night, although it couldn't have been lower than 50 degrees. After he gave her his card, she mentioned she was used to seeing the law often, being so close to the colleges. She could always expect unruly students interrupting the solace of the night disrupting her sleep. He told her he had to speak to the Owens because of a matter of the utmost importance. She nodded her head with approval and strode away like a soldier on a mission. While he waited, he wondered when he'd last seen a maid or housekeeper. A moment later another heavy door opened to show her long pale hand motioning him to get in the other room quickly, while the iron was supposedly hot.

She turned to him with excitement. "I told them you're here for a grave matter, a man with a smart suit I said, not an average policeman. When they asked if it could wait I told them absolutely not because of the stressful situation."

Before Deville could utter a word or thank her for her delivery, he had to think for a moment if this constituted an urgent death-defying situation, as his new best friend had predicted it to be. He almost hoped she'd be pleased to learn about the murder and couldn't wait to see her harrowing expression when she found out the news, if she were to hang around. He truly found her entertaining. "The family is having dinner," she said, as if to prepare him for a threatening mission. "A pork roast with sweet potato and cabbage. I told them you wouldn't mind talking to them while they dined." She didn't miss a beat and he couldn't have felt more important when she announced his name when they entered the dining room.

The large room had an equally large dining table, where three figures dined. Only the man stood up to greet him. Roger Owen appeared to be a stylish man in his early fifties with a receding hairline. Tall, slim, suited, with small gray eyes and a thin-lipped mouth. He'd already heard the news from his winemaker, Ryan Ferris, and guessed Deville came because of it. "We get police in our neighborhood more often than you think but it's usually about the college kids."

Speaking about kids, or teenagers rather, Chloe Owen sat at the center of the table, staring at her food. She held her fork almost as if it were weighted. Deville noticed her moving food about like a bored child who couldn't wait to get up and away from the grownups. He could tell she was tall, even though she was sitting. Her long fair hair, oval-shaped face and eyes, which were staring directly at Deville, were just as enchanting as the rest of her.

Roger Owen began. "Detective, how could anyone, a stranger, go about wineries killing people? Was it a robbery of some sort? These tourists nowadays don't have respect for anything not even a human life. I don't understand what they would have gotten, a few measly dollars or credit card numbers, I imagine."

"It wasn't a robbery," a voice said from the end of the table. Kelly Owen took a sip of wine and continued. "Stop wasting the detective's time. I'm sure Monsieur Bellamont died for a reason other than money. At least not the readily available cash in his wallet." She picked up her fork and knife and continued eating. "That's what I called him, Monsieur Bellamont. It was different to have a French man in our midst, even if he was a prick."

"Kelly, please," Roger said.

"Shut up and let me talk for Christ's sake! Having a murder here is the most excitement this woman's seen in 20 years." Her husband opened his mouth and she lifted her knife to hush him. She looked at Deville and smiled. "Now let's offer the detective a drink or some food. I'm sure he's had a long day and must be hungry." She was dressed in a silk ensemble. Her skin glowed from a golden tan and her matching jewelry sparkled. Her gray hair had blond streaks with a trendy style and her face showed the anguish of someone forced to make the major decisions for many families, not just her own. "Mrs. Bumgarden, I know you're eavesdropping behind the door. Please give the detective a cup of hot tea. You're always drowning us with it anyway."

"Yes, ma'am" could be heard behind the door.

"Would you like some food, Detective? She may have an inquiring mind but she does make a mean pork roast." He declined but thanked her. "Just as well. She's done something to this. Too much garlic. What does she think? I'm a vampire?"

No one dared reply. Roger Owen offered a chair and moments later the dishes were cleared. Mrs. Bumgarden served tea and Deville swore she was enjoying his visit. Chloe asked if she could be excused and her mother blatantly told her no. Kelly Owen added, "You have to experience the trials and tribulations of life, my dear, Chloe. Besides, the detective may want to ask you some questions." She added two sugar cubes to her cup and stirred the tea. "Go on," she said, as if she expected to hear some gossip. "Ask away."

Deville cleared his throat. "Thank you. First of all, I'm not a detective but an investigator. I know it's confusing but we don't have detectives on our team, which is called Violent Crimes Investigation." He realized they didn't care and looked back to his notes. "Yes, well, how well did you know the victim?"

It was Mr. Owen who broke the ice. "Not a very nice fellow. Didn't seem to appreciate good wine or company for that matter. Such a miserable chap."

"He had balls," Kelly Owen said. "He said what he thought. Upfront, like a man." She shot a disapproving glance at her husband. "Roger here likes to dwell and hesitate. Can't make a decision to save his life."

"Kelly, stop comparing us. He was a complete fool."

She took a sip of her tea. "My dear Roger, I agree. I was just stating the attributes that probably got him killed. A vicious man like him doesn't make friends easily, only enemies. It doesn't surprise me if he's a womanizer, too. Poor Jan, his wife, or widow I should say. She is so oblivious. Takes enough prescription drugs to knock out a race horse."

Chloe asked, "May I be excused now?"

Kelly turned to her daughter. "Tell the detective about Wyatt, Chloe."

The glowing princess kept her sad gaze on the table, appearing to study her cup of tea. Deville couldn't help but think of Alice's Adventures in Wonderland. She would make an exceptional Alice. "Wyatt hated his father," Chloe began. "His mother doted on him. He didn't care for either of his parents." Then, she looked at Deville. "I don't think he did anything—I mean kill his father. He just didn't understand him."

Deville wanted to ask her about the night Bellamont died. He had heard Chloe and Wyatt were together in the cottage but it didn't seem appropriate to ask at the table. She stood and asked again if she could be excused. Her mother waved her away, as if she were fighting off peasants at a public bazaar. After Chloe had left the room, Kelly said, "Kids. Can't stop her yapping, can you? I have to beg for her to tell me how her day's going. I don't remember being like that when I was younger. As a teenager my mother would have to tell me to shut up."

Roger Owen grunted at this, which brought a look from his wife that could have been a criminal offense on its own. "I'm glad Bellamont is dead," he said. "Not happy, just glad. Maybe now Jan and the son can move back to the West Coast. I won't have to worry about Chloe and that street urchin."

Deville thought how easily they switch focus and avoid

motives or problems for another concern. Forget about the bad wine reviews Bellamont wrote, the book, the attempts to bring down Owen Winery and the possible affair between the victim and their manager, Stephanie Ferris. Throw in an interest in the children and the upbringing of Wyatt as their main concerns for the Bellamont family moving away.

Deville decided to play along with an interest in the kids as well. "So Wyatt Bellamont wasn't on your daughter's approved friend list?"

A brief silence made the room awkward. The only noise came from the clinking of the china as Mrs. Bumgarden cleared away the cups and saucers. Just as Deville predicted, Kelly Owen demanded another glass of wine and then continued the conversation. "Monsieur Bellamont and his son apparently did as they pleased. The child has a criminal past, I heard. Whether it's minor or not is of no importance to me. I just didn't like him. If he were like his father, he'd treat Chloe like the flavor of the week."

"Are you saying Gerard Bellamont cheated on his wife?" Deville asked.

"Let's not speculate my dear," Roger Owen said. "The investigator doesn't have time for that. Now about those kids. Chloe is different. I don't know what she sees in Wyatt. He barely says a word. He looks like a hobo and rides those skateboards."

Deville looked at his notes. "Why weren't you concerned about your daughter's whereabouts the night of the murder? Did you know she was with Wyatt?"

Mr. Owen replied, "You must be mistaken. She stayed home."

Kelly interrupted. "She had to work on her paper on global warming. That's why we didn't show concern. Who says we didn't? And who told you she was with Wyatt?"

Deville stood. "I don't want to speculate right now and spoil the rest of your evening." He thanked them for the tea and as he made his way out, he heard them begin to argue. Not only did he hate to be the bearer of bad news, he also hated the way they were speaking about Wyatt. No one would ever be good enough for their daughter. Many parents felt that way but they needn't be concerned. Chloe seemed far too sophisticated for her years; a young swan who seemed shy and could be very choosy about a suitor. Although she had been quiet, Deville thought she had many stories to tell.

Outside, he saw Chloe's silhouette in an upstairs window. Music could be heard playing and Deville recognized the kind of music but not the artist. She was brushing her long hair just as a guitar solo blared and drums filled the air like the amplified flapping wings of night birds. As Deville stared up at the clear sky, the stars seemed to twinkle to the music, which seemed a couple decades too old for the likes of Chloe's tastes. He needed to speak to her alone and ask pertinent questions but his mind and body were tired. He needed to come back soon, after the proper questions fully materialized, and his wit was once again sharp.

CHAPTER SEVEN

When he left the Owens he felt hungry and had an urge to unwind. The night was young and unwinding to him meant late night suppers. Although eating out was not as healthy as cooking one's own meals, cooking and eating alone seemed far worse. He found himself in downtown Geneva, where bars and restaurants were plentiful. Kings Cross, a pub only a stone's throw away from the vineyards on Route 14, looked hopeful. The sign in front promised lite fare and even better company. The present clientele consisted of a handful of patrons, one of whom Deville recognized.

He'd recognized Paul Shepard by the broad shoulders and smooth voice. Shepard seemed to be preoccupied with flirting. He sat on a bar stool chatting with the bartender, who just gave him a glass of wine. Laughter occasionally ensued when the clatter from the kitchen didn't disrupt. Kings Cross resembled an English pub with a cozy number of tables and benches of wood and artificial flowers in plastic vases. Lilies bloomed even in the fall. As he walked to join Shepard at the bar Deville discovered that Shepard must have depended on his charm and looks because his attire was not in the least engaging; sweatshirt and jeans stained with a full day's work. Not a great impression to woo the bartender, a busty woman who seemed to float on air when she delivered a plate of rigatoni. Her smile disappeared when spotting Deville, as if he'd crashed the party.

"Detective," Shepard said, acknowledging his new company. "Come sit next to me. Have no foes, drown your woes." He patted the stool, inviting him to sit.

Deville did. "The Prince of Palermo. Nice."

Shepard smiled. "You don't disappoint. I pegged you for an opera fan."

"It's investigator, not detective."

Shepard waved away the informality. He took a swig from his glass without delay, like he wasn't a winemaker. No swishing the contents. No nose, just downing the contents like a thirsty wino. He motioned the bartender. "Give my friend here the Pinot from France. From my special stash."

Deville smiled. "Your own stash? Thank you, Shepard, but no."

"Still on the job? It's after eight. I daresay you're working overtime."

"I'll have a seltzer and that tantalizing dish Mr. Shepard is enjoying." The bartender took the order, gave a frown and walked away. There were no flowers on the bar, only unlit tealight candles in clear glasses. Deville hoped the food made up for the ambiance. Much to his surprise it did. The meal was as close to Chicken Riggies as one would hope for. The original dish was famous in the Utica-Rome area of Central New York. Some restaurants in the Finger Lakes served their version or a mere comparison.

Neither spoke much during eating, except for the unexpected weather, fear of frosting for the grapes and the general business of wine. Shepard didn't bring up why Deville didn't order wine or any alcohol. Thankfully, the subject seemed closed. He hadn't expected to see anyone he knew at King's Cross, especially someone from a murder investigation.

It was after his third glass that Shepard asked, "You married, detective? No? You seem the married type though. You appear as if you already belong to someone. It's not a bad thing. I didn't notice a ring but I almost expect you to answer your phone at any time, telling your lovey you'd be home."

Deville smiled. "That's why you're not a detective."

"You mean investigator?" Shepard laughed. "I certainly would do a bad job, wouldn't I? Getting everyone's profile wrong, forgetting people's name. Hell, I already forget things like dates." He pushed his empty plate away. "Used to forget me and my wife's anniversary all the time."

Deville could feel the sadness of Shepard like quiet wind passing through the walls. He almost wished his phone would ring and his imaginary wife would summon him home. "Have you thought about marrying again? You're young"—he made sure the bartender was out of earshot—"and seem quite comfortable with the ladies."

Shepard gave a thin smile. "There's more to life than marrying or sharing your life with someone, detective. There's work, your pride. Never forget who you are. No one should take precedence over who you are."

Although he heard what Shepard said, Deville wasn't sure if he believed it. He didn't see Shepard spending his days alone. A handsome man fond of opera, a craftsman and winemaker, all alone? A wife dying years ago seemed not enough of an excuse for him to remain single. Shepard seemed to know what he wanted in life and Deville thought if Shepard wanted to find another partner he would. Although living the life of a widower may seem sad, it gave an air of substance and depth. Shepard wouldn't want anyone to feel sorry for him but some people, especially women, are drawn to emotions, such as sadness and despair, and this is what Shepard had, in spades.

"Mind if I bring up work?" Deville asked.

"Can't we just have a meal together? You always bring up work." Shepard gave a short laugh. "How about dessert? After a wonderful meal I can use a dessert wine. How much do you know about wine? In your opinion, what makes the best dessert wine? I love a late harvest Malbec." After he drank a small glass of dessert wine he closed his eyes, like he was drowning out all the noise from the bar and wished he were somewhere else.

Deville left the question unanswered. The last thing he needed was Shepard to discover about his past with wine. He knew more about wine than the average person. He'd studied the history of wine, particular grapes known to grow in France and the Finger Lakes and its effect on the body. It was time to bring Shepard back to the present. "Tell me more about that night when everyone heard about the kids going missing."

Shepard turned his head to look at Deville as if he'd had enough questions. "What about the kids?"

"Who was concerned about their whereabouts?"

"Jan was a little hysterical, yelling about teenagers. Bellamont said he'd check up on the cottage and I offered to go with him."

"What about the girl?" Deville asked.

"Chloe?"

"Yes. Who offered to go look for the girl?"

Shepard considered for a moment. "I don't remember anyone getting upset about her. Roger and Kelly Owen, Chloe's parents, no one seemed worried."

"Don't you think that's odd?"

"Maybe she goes missing often. Who knows?" Shepard paused. "Now I remember something. The Owens didn't seemed concerned at all. But someone else was."

Deville remained quiet.

"Ryan Ferris seemed concerned," Shepard continued. "He stood up and talked to the Owens and then I think he made a phone call."

"A phone call? To Chloe?"

"I believe he went into the office to make the call. Why would he have a sixteen-year-old girl's number?"

Deville thought about Ryan Ferris and Chloe Owen. If Ryan had called Chloe why go into the office at Allenwood? Everyone had cell phones. Couldn't he have stepped out or even messaged her? "Do you remember Roger Owen leaving to get more wine?"

"Yes. Didn't we already talk about it?"

"Perhaps. Was that when Ryan was making a phone call?"

Shepard shrugged. "Could be. I don't remember."

"Don't you think it odd that Roger Owen left to get more wine when his employee, Ryan Ferris, was there?"

Shepard pushed his empty plate away. "Why didn't he ask Ryan? It seems odd. Unless he went to get a certain vintage or his own personal stash. Are you suggesting Roger Owen killed Bellamont?"

Deville didn't reply but his silence may have said more than any words could. They both sat still until the bartender came back. Shepard offered to pay but Deville refused.

"It's the least I could do for your company," Shepard said. "I hate to eat alone."

They had that in common. The bartender made a grunt and took their money but not before leaving Shepard a note; her last desperate attempt to get his attention. Outside, the deserted street welcomed them in the cold. Shepard followed Deville to his car. "It seems you have an admirer," Deville said. "I think she left you her phone number."

Shepard laughed, placing his hands in his pockets. An

icy wind blew from the lake making them both shiver. "I don't even notice anymore."

"You need to take notice when someone is flirting with you."

Shepard shrugged. "My days of being with someone else are over."

Deville remembered Sydney Keller. "You'll have a lot of disappointed females in your future."

"So be it," Shepard retorted, as he strode away on the cobblestone street, waving goodbye, looking as if the wind was carrying him.

CHAPTER EIGHT

The new day brought much promise and spirit that Deville could attribute to a good night's sleep. The night was filled with dreams of Chloe Owen falling down a rabbit hole. Instead of meeting creatures from Alice in Wonderland, a set of large manly hands was waiting for her to land, ready to catch her fall. He couldn't understand why this young woman left such an impression in his mind nor could he explain the sense of urgency he felt developing. Just what was she doing with Wyatt Bellamont the night of the murder? Was she tangled in the arms of the streetwise Wyatt that night, as Paul Shepard had told him, or was she home or even at someone else's house? Was this even related to the murder of Gerard Bellamont?

The morning meeting with his fellow agents lasted five minutes. They acknowledged the Owens as suspects and more information about the Bellamonts was revealed. According to Gerard Bellamont's will, he left his wife, Jan, everything: a modest bank account, two properties, including a timeshare, and two cars. There was no business legacy to leave. Nothing she could fall back on since her husband's sole income was his writing. The new book could bring ongoing royalties but Deville couldn't imagine it would be enough.

He noticed there was a note on his desk saying he needed to see Jessica Malone. The station was a little smaller than the average bingo hall. Its clean interior and updated computers served them well. The station stood near Farmington on Route 332, an easy trip from Interstate 90, which ran from Buffalo to Syracuse. Deville liked being here, working here. It was calm with a laid-back atmosphere.

The investigative officers in the Violent Crimes Investigation Unit (VCIU) spread their expertise around, from Rochester to the southern western tier, including Bath, Corning and other neighboring towns. Besides the investigative officers, there were the senior officers, which included sergeants, lieutenants and captains. Although investigating crimes in the Finger Lakes may be an investigator's dream, having superiors in the State Police who didn't see eye to eye made up for it.

Jessica and Deville had a past. Not the usual throes of passion with your boss past, although it had happened. Besides being a senior investigator and holding the rank of sergeant, Investigator Malone was also a clinical psychologist, which made their relationship truly complicated. Deville wasn't a patient. He thought of himself more like a "case study" because whenever they spoke of his past she offered unofficial advice and counseling. Her office was open and visible to everyone. Deville imagined stares and whispers from fellow officers whenever he was with her. The glass door closed so they couldn't be heard and Deville always made sure he never stayed in the office with her longer than anyone else. He hoped they wouldn't be a subject worth talking about for the other officers. He could almost feel eyes spying on them, but whenever he looked no one was paying attention. His imagination was getting the better of him.

Their brief affair ended less than a year ago. She was

ten years older. Her wisdom and experience had told him the affair had to end. He agreed and could distance himself. He moved on but lately her light steps and passionate eyes told him she thought otherwise. They were trying to stay on friendly but professional terms but it proved difficult.

The relationship started with her fascination of him. She was drawn to his individual case, although it had happened years ago, supervised by doctors she'd only read about. Deville arrived as a comatose teenager from France, sent by relatives who decided the States would give him a better chance. He'd stay in a coma for months before he emerged, not knowing who, what or where he came from. The doctors in Rochester had studied amnesia cases like his before but not to that extent. Deville's coma and amnesia were due to toxic shock from alcoholism. The doctors were baffled. His case was severe and after several treatments, Deville waited for the memories to kick in. They didn't. His name was discovered due to papers and a letter found on his person. There also were instructions and pleas of mercy. The family listed on the release forms could not be reached. He always suspected this family had strong ties or was well connected to have shipped a body overseas. So Deville was put up for foster care as someone with special needs. He spoke his native language but learned English with ease, causing everyone to believe he was intelligent. Certain traits from the first 12 years of his life in France remained, including his mannerisms, inquisitiveness and love of nature. He learned new lessons and a different lifestyle from his foster parents, an older British couple in their sixties living in the Finger Lakes region. They taught him how to dress, stressed how important it was to be polite and gave him a reason to go on living. Few families would foster a teenage boy who already had a history of alcohol abuse, especially one who's almost lost his mind. He often thought the reason they took him in was because they, too, were outsiders. Europeans helping their own.

Jessica motioned Deville to sit. "Close the door." She seemed concerned. Her dark hair, pinned up and away from her face, showed her proud streak of gray. The officers at the station called her Mrs. Frankenstein but Deville didn't think she minded. She had a sense of humor. She was no beauty queen but she possessed a respected elegance men found attractive. A picture on her desk showed her son, who was just ten years younger than Deville. Jessica was divorced. "How were the Owens? Anything you want to add that you didn't tell us at the meeting?"

"Unusual. The father seems oblivious to things. The wife, Kelly, seems to run the family." He wasn't sure if he should mention Chloe. Somehow he wanted to keep her to himself, knowing she didn't have the strength to strangle anyone. There were other reasons. Dreaming about Chloe Owen left him feeling uneasy. He almost felt guilty such a dream stayed with him while other memories kept their distance.

"How are you handling it?" she asked.

Deville sat and crossed his legs. "Fine. I'll have a brief report on your desk before I leave today."

"I didn't ask because of a report, I asked how are you handling it?"

"Again, fine. Why wouldn't I be?"

He knew her concerns and decided it was best to ignore the elephant in the room. Having a murder at a winery was unsettling. She'd read all about him—having had access to all his personal files made his past an open book so natural concerns were obvious. From what he remembered, he lived in France for an undetermined time near or on a winery. He believed his mother worked at this winery and he had drank wine from a young age. The doctors couldn't believe he survived with such alcohol abuse. But from agony comes irony, as his new found home across the ocean also had the perfect climate for growing grapes.

"You know what I'm concerned about?" she asked into the stale air of the room.

He swallowed. "I have no wish to drink wine or any alcohol. I know what my body's been through and because of that I don't think about drinking." The last part was a lie, he told himself. He paused for a moment. "My past wasn't me. I don't remember that part of my life so I believe I never had a problem."

"All the more reason you may want to try drinking wine. You've disassociated yourself with your past and you may feel it's okay to start drinking."

"What if I do? What if I believe it wasn't me? Because this is what I feel. Do you think it's okay to say have a glass of wine or a margarita or go with my co-workers to the pub for a lousy freaking beer?"

"If you feel you aren't that person maybe it's okay to try but alcoholism is serious. You almost lost your life. Your body can't handle alcohol. Do you really want to black out again?"

"There's a chance I can start casually drinking. That was in the past."

"So was your coma. If you ask me as a professional then no, you shouldn't risk it."

"What about as a friend?"

"Still no. This is why I am asking about this case. If you'd liked to be taken off…"

"I'll do no such thing." He stood. "So what would happen? When would the protection end? We've stopped seeing each other because of this. It's not fair. You like an occasional glass of wine but you don't want me around." She tried to speak but he held up his finger. "I don't go to parties or events because of alcohol. I stay clear away from fundraisers, go to AA meetings, speak at schools and wake up every morning trying to remember what happened to me. Why did my mother let this happen? Where is my father? Why was I abandoned?"

She looked away with glassy eyes. "I'm sorry to bring it up."

He leaned on her desk. "It's okay. You're concerned. But don't do this. Don't bring it up and treat me any differently. I didn't come here on my own. I was brought here. I choose to stay here because it is beautiful and I can take care of my foster parent's home. They left me that home, Jess. Should I just move?"

"No. No, you shouldn't. You should do what makes you comfortable." She took a moment and tried to compose herself. He could see he caused quite a stir with her. He could imagine how he looked now, a tall, pale foreigner with a bony frame and a face that always showed his emotions. Right now it showed despair, abandonment and confusion with a hint of anger. Those emotions were just the beginning. He had to control his temper. He was distressing Jessica and that wasn't polite.

"I'm sorry. I have to go," he said.

"But Louis…" she said to the ghostly whisper of the man who had just left her office.

Gerard Bellamont's laptop revealed little. It had a draft of the book he'd been writing on Finger Lakes wineries. Plus emails to publishers, contacts and an address book. The book was more than just in its beginning stages. It was scheduled for publishing. Deville wondered if the book had a contract before its completion. Difficult to believe some publishers accepted books before they are finished but it had a lot to do with who you knew. Sleeping with Stephanie Ferris, the daughter of the publisher, might have had its privileges. Deville had Investigator Reginald Scudder assist him to organize the electronic files while he made phone calls and finished a written report for Jessica.

While he was typing, he thought about his supervisor. She still loved him. He could feel it but there was so much going against their relationship. There was no use trying to make it work. He remembered the touch, the embrace, the feel of her body close to his. He missed the warmth but beginning a relationship on the fringes of his perplexing past would fail. Her intriguing thirst of his sad life and her deep-rooted issues of wanting to help or save him from what he didn't know, was their typical date. Deville thought it was just a twisted version of a bad boy complex, seeing someone you know is bad for you, thinking you could change them. This analogy of Jessica Malone was something he'd conjured up one frenzied night while trying to fall asleep. His ideal relationship would be different.

Deville longed to meet someone who would just see him for who he is now. The past was a part of his life that made him who he was today. He would, however, love to have an engaging conversation for once with a woman who didn't involve his amnesia, alcoholism and longing for a sense of purpose.

He handed the report to Scudder to give to Jessica, put on his coat and left the station feeling that the day's events will flow as they may. He didn't want to rush around today and speak to as many people as he did yesterday. The only risk right now would be for Jan Bellamont and Wyatt to leave town and move back to California. He decided to check up on Jan. The last he saw her was when he left her lying on her bed, out for the count, from pure shock. Or a reaction brought on by enough pills from her medicine cabinet that could pay for her son's college tuition.

The cottage the Bellamonts rented looked different than the day before. Either the structure itself knew and felt for losing one of its inhabitants or the sun hiding behind the clouds made everything seem melancholy. There was a small garden near the front with chrysanthemums and blue asters lining the cottage, adding a splash of color. The garden, unlike the vineyard, looked well kept. He wondered whose responsibility it was to maintain it. He knocked on the door and waited, breathing in the air, wondering if Mrs. Bellamont was here.

Jan Bellamont opened the door looking more like a cook than a mourning widow. She wore an apron, her hair was up, but tousled, and he could see white powder on her face. She saw him staring and wiped her face. "Investigator, please come in. I'm baking. I do it when I don't know what to do. So far I have baked a cake, six dozen cookies and I'm debating about some cupcakes. You can follow me if you wanna talk. I don't want to burn my snickerdoodles!" He followed her into a small kitchen. The room smelled divine and felt warm. As she kept busy, Deville could see a sadness around her but it was a different sadness. A "what have I done?" sadness one asks after learning news that disproves something you invested everything in. Bad stocks, wrong car, dead husband. He could tell she was having a hard time focusing.

Deville hoped she would offer a treat. He spotted a peanut butter cookie with his name on it. "Please, have some," Deville heard, wondering if he'd imagined it. "I have to drop cookies off to the arts council. I know I have too many so take as much as you'd like." He grabbed one and ate. "I remembered I promised them baked goods this weekend," she continued, "and I know I can say no but it keeps my gears going and my mind occupied. The arts council needs help. I get bored easily so I've been donating some of my time there." After placing all the new cookies on a plate she turned off the oven and took off the apron. "I've been on the phone for three hours. It's sad when one has to deal with lawyers, jobs and other stuff before calling one's own family." She paused. "The bastard didn't leave me as much as I thought he would."

"Excuse me?" he asked, grabbing another cookie.

She crossed her arms. "Wyatt is taken care of because of my parents. Gerard's death means Wyatt can't go to the college I planned. Not that Wyatt cares. He'd be happy living on the street with his skateboard."

Deville asked, "What will happen to you?"

She shrugged. "I'll go back to work, I guess, I haven't thought about it. He had little to leave me. I told him to start a blog, with ads or something to keep money coming in but he didn't listen. We just lived job to job but he was always busy so I never complained about money. In case you haven't noticed, I'm easy to please." She poured water in a large glass and drank. "You know, it's funny. I left him a few times but never divorced him. Even after I found out he was sleeping around. I thought he would forget about his girls but he didn't. Then Wyatt came along and much to my dismay, it didn't make us closer." She sat on a stool and grabbed a cookie too. "The bastard is dead. I know he was a horrible man but he was my husband. He lied, cheated on me and made enemies every day but something about him kept me believing it was still possible, that we still had a chance."

A chance to fix a relationship that probably wasn't meant to be, Deville thought. Gerard Bellamont seemed to be a man who wanted things or people he couldn't have. Perhaps it was his philandering or conquests, such as Stephanie Ferris, that kept him going. Why couldn't he see what he had? It was a common problem: man overlooks wife for someone else, usually the same time the wife falls into a comfortable but humdrum life. Jan Bellamont didn't seem like the typical wife of a famous reviewer or critic. He speculated she had a liberal personality and maybe she'd played the role of a decent wife well. Did her husband's infidelity cause her to escape from reality with pills or did she have a problem before they met?

"Mrs. Bellamont can you tell me what happened the night your husband died? Especially when you were looking for Wyatt?"

Her thoughts seemed scattered and she stuttered before she spoke. "Wyatt? Where is he? Where was he that night? I don't remember what happened. He wasn't at the party. He wasn't around."

"You looked for him? Or did you send someone?"

"Yes, that's right. I sent Gerard, my husband. He went to go look for Wyatt."

"Why?"

She looked at him dumbfounded. "What do you mean?"

"What would a teenage boy, want to do at a grown-up party? Besides the alcohol, he'd be bored to death wouldn't he?"

"We were there, his parents. And the Kellers, our landlords. It was their party. I told him to come out of respect for them! He listens to his mommy. Sometimes."

"Could he have met someone, planned to meet someone?"

She stood and began packing trays. "I guess you've heard he has a thing for the Owen girl, didn't you? They're friends. They weren't dating."

"What makes you so sure?"

"A mother knows these things. Wyatt's different from other boys. When the time is right, he'll find someone. And I'll know."

"And you'll approve?" He was almost sorry for saying it aloud.

She looked at him. "Do you think I'm a horrible

mother? Chloe Owen is beautiful, even I acknowledge that. But she is seeing someone else I think. Oh, believe me, I've teased Wyatt about her over and over. I know my husband had differences with the Owens but it was about their wine, not the family. We would never stand in the way of romance. My father warned me about Gerard, tried to stand in the way of us, and I said I would never let my children endure that." She paused and went to the sink. "Even though he may have been right, I still stood up for what I believed in."

It seemed Jan Bellamont's past suddenly came to visit. As she looked out the window Deville thought she was popular when she was younger. She seemed to have her own identity, even though her husband had been the breadwinner. She took the role as the loving wife willingly. Playing the part of a dutiful spouse while following her husband and his career may have seemed an easy choice to many, but for her it was considerably the most difficult decision in her life. More so even than her marriage. What was her life before she married Gerard? Had she been a rising ballet dancer destined to be famous? Or maybe an actress whisked away from the stage before her big break? The life before Gerard Bellamont was definitely what she was thinking of. He would bet his life on it.

A loud thud and mumbling sound came from the other room. Then a door closed and heavy footsteps could be heard going to the second floor. "Wyatt, I have to drop some cookies off. I'll be right back." She grabbed a plate. "I'll give him these before I leave. They're his favorites."

Deville stopped her and grabbed the plate. "May I bring these to him?"

Her saddened eyes blinked and she sighed. "Yes, you may. I know you have to ask him questions. Just remember, he's a young boy."

"I know he is." Deville took the plate from her and watched her leave. After climbing the steps to the second floor, he walked to Wyatt's closed door and knocked. He could hear music playing.

"Come in."

Deville opened the door to see Wyatt folding clothes. He wore jeans and a skateboard shirt and looked like he needed a shower. Deville thought this look was common now. Teenage boys looked scruffy, often adding hair products to make their do look like they just woke up. Before Deville could compliment Wyatt for folding his clothes with such expertise, he noticed a knapsack on the far side of the bed. Wyatt kept his room organized, unlike his parents. No clothes lay on the floor, the bed was made and the room uncluttered. Besides noticing dust on the cupboard and mirror, the boy displayed some appreciation for his dwellings and clothing. However, he may have been planning an escape. Deville placed the plate of cookies on a dresser. "Your mom gave you these. She'll be right back."

"I heard her." Wyatt sat at the edge of the bed between his uninvited visitor and the clothes he was packing a moment ago. "What are you doing here? Wanna give me more bad news?"

Deville asked, "Are you going somewhere?"

"What's it to you?"

Deville walked closer and kept his hands in his pockets. "You won't be accomplishing anything by leaving. Your father will still be dead and the investigation will continue until his killer is found."

"I thought you would find him fast. What's taking so long?"

Deville sighed and knew the question was coming. "It's a process but we are working very hard."

"Will you find the killer soon?"

This time Deville thought for a moment. "I promise I

will." He told himself he meant it. "Don't leave. If you do, you will be considered a suspect."

Wyatt's eyes widened. "But I didn't do it. Don't you believe me?"

"It doesn't matter. If you leave it won't look good for you or your mother."

"She doesn't care. She never did. I told them I didn't want to come here, to the East Coast. I left my friends, my old school and they don't care."

Deville asked, "Were you planning on going back to California? How? Hitching, taking a plane?"

Wyatt Bellamont stood, rubbed his face with his hands, as though he were wiping off a mask, or giving himself a face massage. "I hate this place. It sucks! Been saving some money. Going to hitch a ride to the airport and fly."

"How? Do you have a job?"

"Nope. I'm earning a little money by helping people."

"Catalina Winery?"

Wyatt nodded. "And Allenwood. They have me move cases around. I'm their gopher, whatever that means. That's what they tell me. I miss the West Coast. This weather sucks."

"You'll be back sooner than you know," Deville said. Unless you or your mother killed your father, he almost added. Then you might stay a while. "Is there anything you want to tell me?"

"Nothing."

"Who in California do you need to see? A girlfriend? Other friends?"

Wyatt took his clothes from the bed and opened a drawer to place them back. "I don't have a girlfriend. I have regular friends, few, but some. It's what I'm used to."

Deville continued, "And familiarity is what you need right now. Going through this in a different town is horrible, I can understand but you have to bear with me. Do you think you can, just for another day or two?"

"Why? You don't need me. Whoever did this has to screw up. Don't you guys get calls or tips or something?"

"It doesn't always work out like that." After a few moments, Deville sat on the edge next to Wyatt but respected the other's space. "Can you please help me with a few questions? It's important." Wyatt nodded, with his elbows on his knees, his hands together. "The night it happened, you were here. There were witnesses. Were you alone?"

"I was."

"Are you sure?"

"Yes. Why? Who says I wasn't alone?"

"Paul Shepard from Catalina Winery. He says he and your father walked here from Allenwood Vineyard. They said they were looking for you and Chloe Owen. Was she here?"

He looked uneasy again. "She stopped by."

"So you and her? Are you a couple?"

With the typical response for someone his age, he delivered with credibility: "Who? Me and her?" As if the idea came from left field. "No way!"

She wasn't some two-headed monster. "Why not? She's young, attractive, good parents."

"Parents are losers. Especially her mom. She talks too much and doesn't like me."

"Let me tell you something," Deville said and leaned closer to him. "They're not supposed to like you. It's your job to scare the crap out of them."

Wyatt looked up and gave a slight smile. "Yeah but she needs to like me?"

"Chloe doesn't like you?"

Wyatt shook his head. "I thought about giving her time but now I don't think she's worth it."

"Why doesn't she like you?" The question was touchy.

Wyatt didn't say a word and let the mood of the room grow dull. "Let me guess," Deville said. "She thinks you're immature, doesn't care for the way you dress or this music. Maybe you're not sophisticated enough?"

Wyatt turned to him, "Why even ask me if you know already?"

Deville cautiously asked the next question. "Who is she seeing? Did she say anything about someone? An older man? Is it Paul Shepard? Is that why I saw you at Catalina Winery?"

His eyes flashed to Deville. "No. It's not Paul."

"Then who Wyatt? You can help me."

He shook his head and took a moment before he spoke again. "She said nothing but I felt it. I tried some moves on her but she's been used."

"Used?"

"You know, she's no virgin. She told me so herself. Not that it matters. I'm not interested in her. I don't know who's been intimate with her. Whoever she's with, I hope he appreciates her. Not that she's all that or anything."

"Do her parents know she is seeing someone older?"

He shrugged. "They don't care. She's adopted, you know."

"Does it mean they love her any less?"

"I don't know if they even love her. She's like their robot."

Deville thought about Wyatt and Chloe. After knowing the two were together and his talk tonight, he may mentally remove young Wyatt as a suspect. He could almost swear Wyatt had been innocent all along but one never knew. Different generations, abuse and drugs meant different outcomes—motives considered once surreal. "Tell me about your dad and his work."

Wyatt shrugged. "It's the reason we're here. The reason he's dead."

The boy was no fool. Getting his perspective on things could jog his memory about his father's business and personal affairs. "Why do you say that? Who has he made angry?"

"Who hasn't he pissed off? Authors want to kill him and artists have stopped working because of him. This painter who used to have a gallery now sells insurance. Another painter died. I heard she killed herself. A winemaker in California stopped growing grapes and now raises pigs. All because of my father's words. I know he's a famous critic. I understand that. But don't honor him for hurting people. He's ruined enough lives."

"What about here, Wyatt? Whose life has he ruined?"

He stood and went to the doorway. "I'm sorry I don't know." His mood changed. He appeared to be hiding something. Did he know about his father's alleged affair? "I'm sorry. I need to get some stuff done before my mother comes back."

Deville left his card and thanked him. No matter what or who Wyatt was protecting, it was keeping him in a shell. There was hope for the boy beyond the typical teenage angst and acts of aggression. There was a young man who had a good heart and a somewhat balanced head. He knew his father's work caused great pain but he also knew any suggestions would fall on deaf ears. How can you change or disapprove of the occupation that pays for your meal ticket? The many reviews Gerard Bellamont gave were harsh and not for the weak at heart. But if creative people or winemakers didn't prepare themselves for this, who was to blame? They should expect people to criticize their work, welcome positive feedback and respect constructive criticism. No. Gerard Bellamont didn't deserve to die, even if he had given poison pen press reviews that had ruined several careers.

CHAPTER NINE

The cloudy skies hovered above the hills and winding roads like smoke from an invisible muffler and the air smelled of rain. November rain was dangerous. In the hills it could push cars into the wrong lane or even off the road.

While walking past the vines of Allenwood Deville wondered what Frank Keller was doing. Leaving the vineyard this way should be a crime in itself. He remembered a vision of his mother picking grapes. He had enjoyed picking them himself, feeling that he'd helped her. Watching her during harvest time made him smile. Sometimes she would put him to bed after working 12 or more hours straight. Her clothes would be filthy, her face ashen and her hair oily. He remembered holding his mother's rough, cracked hands and telling her that her skin felt like a lizard. She called him silly. He wouldn't have known the texture of a lizard's skin because he'd never encountered one. After taking a beating from a long day picking grapes under the sun, she would tend to her hands with olive oil. She claimed it was a "miracle oil" and healed all wounds, not to mention it was great for dry skin. His mother seemed the happiest when she crushed grapes. If he'd try to help by jumping in the vat he would surely drown. He was too young to be doing this work.

The memories had surfaced because he was walking near the vineyard itself. He told himself this was a good thing. A warm feeling erupted in his chest. His mother loved him. He hadn't always been neglected. She had made a difference, even if it was only temporary.

His father was like an unseen energy or an orb floating just past his arm's length. He surmised something terrible must have happened, besides his coma, for him not to remember anything about his father.

He reached the car that he parked at Allenwood Winery's lot. It seemed strange to Deville that Jan Bellamont would go on about her business though she claimed it was the only thing keeping her from losing it. Baking, he decided, was similar to gardening in that respect. He had no inclination to garden or bake. He enjoyed jigsaw puzzles and tried his hand at crosswords, as most detectives in novels did, but he lost interest. But Jan Bellamont sure enjoyed baking. Her sudden exit didn't seem unexpected. It was almost as if she'd wanted to leave him alone with Wyatt.

Wyatt had not revealed much about what happened on the night of the murder but Deville learned something. Chloe Owen was seeing someone older. Were Chloe and Ryan Ferris public knowledge?

He also learned Gerard Bellamont had ruined several lives because of his occupation or negative reviews. He was a womanizer and had affairs that didn't stop on the West Coast. Stephanie Ferris seemed to have been his latest conquest. This made him consider his next destination: Owen Winery. The Ferris duo had a lot of explaining to do.

Before Deville left, a young woman met him in the parking lot of Allenwood Winery. She was medium height with dark shoulder length hair, wearing tight jeans and a perfect fall sweater. He recognized her as Sydney Keller, the person who'd discovered Gerard Bellamont's body. She gave him an uncomfortable smile. "Sorry. I crashed into your car."

"Excuse me?"

"My work shift just started and I was running late. I banged into your car. You don't recognize me from yesterday?"

"You are the Keller's niece from the big city? I remember." He paused, closed the door and looked around to spot the ding. She had parked her older Ford a little too close to his Honda Hybrid. The ding could be easily fixed but the time and effort required made him grimace. He looked around in the tiny lot and then asked, "Miss Keller, there are only four cars in this lot, did you have to park this close to mine?"

"My horoscope predicted something bad would happen today."

"All the more reason to…"

She went around to inspect the damage. "It's not too bad. Can't they take a plunger and…" she tried demonstrating what an auto body shop might do to repair it. "Shouldn't take longer than an hour with the right person. All they would need to do is push out from under." She extended her hand under the fender to elaborate.

Deville would have found it funny if he hadn't noticed the tattoos on her wrists. He despised tattoos and didn't understand why anyone, especially a striking young woman, such as Sydney Keller, chose to brand her body that way. "And that would be that," she said, finishing her easy one-two-three instructional crash course of auto body repair.

"Excuse me?" He hadn't heard the last of her rant but didn't want her to begin again. "It's fine. I'll take care of it." He headed back to the driver's side door.

"Come in. I'll give you my insurance info," she insisted, grabbing his elbow. "My aunt and uncle are here and I'm sure they'll want to say hi. You'll want to question us again, won't you? It is a murder investigation and I'm aware you aim to question us at least a few more times. We are suspects aren't we?" She said this as if she'd be disappointed if she wasn't.

"Of course," he said, following her into Allenwood Vineyard. The place seemed almost empty but the atmosphere seemed sunny and spirited. Great karma in the room, he imagined Sydney Keller would say.

"Look who's here!" she announced to her aunt, who was at the opposite corner of the room. Sydney grabbed his arm again and asked in a whisper, "Do you expect we'll have another murder on her hands?"

"Oh, dear God. I hope not!"

Marianne Keller came over to shake his hand. "You hope not what?"

Sydney replied, "I was asking if he thought another murder is in our midst."

Marianne said, "Sydney, please don't. The officer needs to do his job. I'm sure he doesn't consider your behavior appropriate. You must excuse her. She doesn't take things seriously."

"Yes, I do," Sydney said. "I was telling Uncle Frank when he was fixing the wires today that the new moon hasn't brought us anything good. The murder is just the beginning of something more ominous. That's why there will be another crime. It may not be murder, a fire or even a robbery."

"Sydney!" her aunt exclaimed.

Sydney went behind the bar and poured a glass of water for Deville.

Marianne watched her. "Why don't you ask him if he'd like a glass of our wine?"

Sydney waved her hand. "He won't drink. He's

scarred."

Deville and Marianne looked at Sydney, waiting for an explanation.

Sydney sighed. "You can tell by his eyebrows, the way they slope the sad eyes plus the way he looks away whenever he sees a bottle of wine. Oh, I'm not psychic, I realize you can't drink on the job either."

Deville took a long drink of water and sat on a stool.

Sydney placed her hand on his. "It's okay. We all have our own pain and suffering."

Marianne left the two of them to go back into her office. Sydney continued to hold his hand, on the bar and he saw her tattoos more closely. He pulled his hand away. She turned the conversation to her tattoos. "It's the sign of Mercury, my rising sign. My friend Clarisse designed it. She owns a tattoo parlor in Geneva. She also does readings, as I do. I never like doing my own readings. I'll take you to her sometime." She looked eager to take Deville anywhere. He realized he started to be an impressive figure in Sydney's life. At least the stars may have been telling her this because she couldn't keep her eyes off of him. "Yours must be Saturn."

"A pretty planet," he said, not understanding what she was talking about.

"Pretty but destructive. It has so much conflict." She sighed. "I have a tendency to be a loose cannon. At least that's what my aunt says. I talk a lot. When people come in to taste the wines they buy them but sometimes I expect it's because they want to escape from me. Don't you expect people would want to be informed about their destiny?"

"Do you give fortunes to everyone who comes in?" he asked.

"No. Who has the time? Just certain people; the ones who stand out. Last week a married couple came in to taste wine and she asked some questions about the wine.

She tried to engage her husband to be more romantic. I tried to tell her it was no use." Deville looked at her. "Well, he would leave her," she said. "I could tell by his face. And their love signs weren't compatible. I try to help as many…"

"What about Gerard Bellamont?" he interrupted.

She reflected silently and at that moment Deville realized how quiet Allenwood Vineyards could be when Sydney wasn't around.

"Unfortunately," she said, "he, too, having an affair. I could tell the way he and his wife were acting, his stares and his cologne."

"Cologne?"

"It was too strong. I saw him before that night and I remembered no scent on him. Plus Jan, his wife, said she didn't like what he was wearing so why would he wear it if she didn't like it?"

"Sometimes couples do things that cause petty arguments," he said.

"I know," she agreed. She poured herself a glass of water and continued. "When women spend too much, or when men invite friends over to watch football, but this was different. It wasn't an 'I-told-you-not-to' kind of thing. Jan Bellamont is very emotional. She stayed away from her husband almost the entire night. It looked as if they weren't a couple at all. Then she went on about Wyatt."

Deville considered this to be an odd way to describe the Bellamont's attitude the night of the party, saying they didn't look like a couple at all. Sydney Keller, despite being a true believer in the stars and the fortunes they told, could be an accurate judge of character. At least she seemed to pick up on emotions and problems with relationships and could sense when something would happen. Now if she would stop with this impending doom that she claims follows her everywhere.

He remembered yesterday's encounter with her and her ravings that the murder was her fault. "What else can you tell me about Mrs. Bellamont?"

Sydney looked away. "I don't know what to say about Jan. She doesn't like other women. I guess she thinks everyone is after—or was after—her husband. She's paranoid. I tried to be friendly, even talked to her about her pills, to find a common interest. She seems to be amicable but I don't suspect it's genuine. Wyatt is such a dear. I can imagine the pain he must be going through. I tried to offer him some companionship, that is Paul Shepard and I. We want Wyatt to feel welcome."

"Are you and Paul Shepard close?" he asked.

She straightened her shoulders. "We are friends, that's all." She took his glass away without asking if he was finished. The subject of her relationship with Shepard seemed to cause a reaction. She no longer was her bubbly self.

He changed the subject and asked, "You said Bellamont was gazing or staring at someone the night of the party?"

She nodded. "It was Stephanie Ferris, another lost soul. She isn't conscious of which side of the tracks she belongs on. Just when I thought we could become friends she does something that makes me back away."

"Like what?"

"She said she doesn't set foot in any independent stores. She shops at malls or outlets. She has to get the best of everything and there's nothing for her in the local shops. I told her we have to support local places or else they'll go out of business."

"What did she say?"

"She said she didn't understand and I was stupid. So I asked her what would happen if people stopped coming to our wineries and just bought mass produced wine from another region. Someplace where they pay laborers pennies an hour." Sydney shook her head. "She still didn't get it." She circled her index finger around her temple. "I don't have time for people like that."

A man who looked to be in his forties came in. Sydney leaned closer and said to Deville, "Excuse me, but I have to tend to him. See you around." She went to greet the wine taster and Deville walked to the office in back, where he greeted Frank and Marianne. She was on her computer and her husband was stacking boxes. They both greeted him and she motioned him to sit in a nearby chair.

"How's the investigation going?" Marianne asked.

"Did you catch our man yet?" Frank interjected, not giving Deville a chance to reply. He wore a red cap to cover his bald head and looked unshaven but dressed to work in the vineyard.

"We're following some leads. I was hoping you could help me with a few more questions?" She nodded while her husband remained silent. "Can you give me a rundown where everyone was the night of the party? Who went outside, who stayed inside?"

Marianne shrugged. "Everyone stayed here mostly; some went out and came back." Her husband came over and stood behind her, placing a hand on her shoulder. "What do you remember, dear?" she asked.

This seemed staged to Deville, as though they had practiced in a mirror. Frank Keller stood dutifully behind his wife, as though he had coached her to say what was on his mind. It didn't seem right. She was the more knowledgeable one, the one who made all the decisions, the one who "wore the pants in the family." Frank Keller shrugged. "Don't remember much. I told you everything when I saw you the first time. I talked about sports, even to that Bellamont fellow."

"Frank, although a winemaker, doesn't have much knowledge about wine," Marianne said. "Gerard found it refreshing that someone talked about sports and other things."

"What other things?" Deville asked. They both looked puzzled, as if the question came out of nowhere.

Frank cleared his throat. "Cars, collectibles, golf but that would be sports and I guess horses."

"My husband likes a lot of things," she said.

Deville pulled his notebook and wrote. "Horses. To ride or to bet on?"

"Does losing money count?" Frank asked.

Deville looked up and saw Marianne's eyes go back in her head. She pushed her husband's hands off her shoulder. "Oh, Frank, you might as well tell him everything." She looked up at her husband, who went back to stacking boxes. "Frank, you poor dear. I'm not convinced the investigator cares."

"May I be the judge of that?" Deville asked.

Marianne explained. "Frank owed Mr. Bellamont some cash. Horse racing. He wasn't getting any money from me but he had a hunch so he went with Mr. Bellamont to the track and bet with his money."

A low moan could be heard from Frank. "Anyway, now that Bellamont is dead, Frank doesn't know if he still owes him money."

Frank turned around, took his cap off then wiped the sweat from his head. "I don't want anyone to think I killed Bellamont so I wouldn't have to pay him."

"So I guess your hunch didn't pay off?" questioned Deville.

A sad shake of Keller's head answered his question.

"How much did you owe him?"

Marianne answered. "Ten thousand. It so happens they drank a lot at the track and Mr. Lucky over here persuaded Bellamont to loan him some money."

In his defense, Frank replied, "I didn't force him. I wouldn't force anyone to do anything."

"Pipe down," she said. "He needs to know everything. I would have told you but I just found out myself. I apologize for his behavior."

"No need to apologize for me, Marianne," he said to his wife. "You don't have to do all the talking for me. I know what I did is wrong and I'm sorry. I'll work extra hard and pay Mrs. Bellamont back every penny. I ain't the smartest person and I thank the Lord I have you, Marianne, but I am honest. Unfortunately, I may have a problem, an addiction."

"He's been playing the horses, the slots, the lottery. He works hard on the field but spends so much of his earnings on gambling." She sighed. "He's willing to go to a program and Sydney and I will support him."

Deville stopped writing and wondered if Frank Keller's gambling and recent transaction with Bellamont warranted enough to be a motive. If Keller wanted to rid himself of the debt why come clean, especially to an officer investigating the murder? No. He decided the gambling debt wouldn't constitute motive. He felt safe with both the Kellers. The only way Keller could have done something like murder was if his wife ordered him to. But Marianne had no motive to kill Gerard Bellamont. At least none had materialized yet. He flipped a sheet over and said, "Just know I will keep tabs on you. I will have to report this but I hope you pay Mrs. Bellamont back, for your sake."

Marianne replied, "Sydney will be pleased if you keep tabs on us. I think she really likes you, keeps talking about your love signs. Are you single?" After Deville straightened his posture and said nothing, she continued. "Oh, well, I guess it's not my concern. We'll save that conversation for another time, perhaps with dinner."

"Marianne makes a mean meatloaf!" her husband said.

Deville smiled. "Thank you for the invitation but what

else happened that night? Who stayed here? Who left your winery, even for a break?"

According to Marianne, "Some people went in and out. Gerard and Paul Shepard went to the cottage to find Wyatt. Stephanie Ferris went outside several times. She smokes, you see. I think her husband, Ryan, went out, too. I don't think he smokes though."

"Why would he go out?" Deville asked.

"I don't know, maybe to relieve himself? Men do that. It's horrible. They say they're being 'one with nature.' I don't understand it."

"I hope he didn't go on our vines," Frank said.

She rubbed her head, looking tired of Frank's ramblings. "I don't think anyone else went out. Maybe Sydney. Sometimes she and Paul are inseparable."

"Are they a couple?" Deville asked.

"I don't know. Sydney is friendly to everyone. I think she likes to keep him company. You know his wife died in a car accident and he seems much happier whenever she's around. I'm not sure if Sydney is ready for a relationship with him, or anyone, but Paul doesn't seem like he wants to be in a relationship either. Is Paul a suspect? Why would Paul want to kill Bellamont?"

"What about the California grapes or juice?" Deville continued. "Bellamont sold to many wineries but he refused to sell to Shepard at Catalina Vineyard."

"That doesn't seem like Bellamon. He seemed shrewd."

"Shrewd enough to loan someone ten thousand on a bet?" Deville questioned.

Marianne didn't seem to know how to take the response. "What I meant to say is Bellamont didn't seem like he would turn down a deal. What he and my husband did was between the two of them. I don't know if you realize but we were his landlords while they were living here. Since then, my husband and Bellamont seemed to have forged some kind of male bond."

Frank chimed in. "Sometimes Bellamont would stay outside with me, write away on his laptop, typing away at his new book, while I worked on the vines. He taught me some things and didn't treat me like I was an idiot."

Marianne stood. "Frank, no one has ever called you an idiot."

"No one has to say it. I can feel it. Some looks are like daggers! Just because I don't say much doesn't mean I don't think about stuff."

There was an awkward silence. Deville could sense the tension in the room. He watched Frank go back to his boxes while Marianne stared out the window at the impending storm.

"What about the Owens?" Deville asked. "Did they leave during the night?"

Marianne answered. "I don't know. I suppose they both stayed indoors all night."

"Roger Owen went to get more wine," Frank said, turning his head. "He left while Bellamont was out, too. Roger went to get more wine and said he'd be right back."

"Why wouldn't they send Ryan Ferris?" Deville asked.

"I don't know," Marianne replied. "That would seem logical. Ryan has the keys. He could get more wine so why didn't Roger send Ryan? Maybe Ryan wasn't there at that moment. Perhaps that's when he went to relieve himself."

"So Roger Owen came back with wine?"

They both nodded but Marianne spoke. "He wanted desperately for us to like the wine. I considered it okay but Bellamont didn't agree. I guess they don't have to worry about bad press anymore, at least from Bellamont."

"How long was Roger gone?" Deville asked.

"About twenty minutes," Frank answered .

In those twenty minutes Gerard Bellamont could have died. If Bellamont wasn't being killed was this when Paul Shepard caught Gerard and Stephanie together? Deville asked another question: "Do you remember Paul Shepard and Gerard Bellamont coming back from the cottage together?"

Marianne nodded. "I reckon so. That's how we knew the kids were okay."

Deville stood, thanked them and left his card again. As he walked out, Marianne said, "Make sure you say goodbye to my niece, Sydney. She finds you fascinating. Something about a 'walking time bomb of defaulted destiny.' I don't know what the hell she's into; all poppycock to me. Star gazing she calls it." She looked at her husband. "Why couldn't she have predicted a winning horse for you, Frank?"

CHAPTER TEN

Sydney Keller watched Deville leave the winery and was upset that he didn't even say goodbye. Indeed, she was busy with wine tasters but a glance back would have acknowledged there was something, a spark if she dared to call it, between her and the investigator. She knew his type though; always avoiding what was in plain sight, ignoring the signs and often fate itself. Generally, just being a guy. She wouldn't let it upset her. She had more important things going on. She didn't know how to get this wine taster to stop.

Pouring wine to drinkers already intoxicated wasn't something Sydney had bargained for. Helping wine tasters get happy by creating a positive aura in the room, however, was in her element and helped sales. She lit a candle that promoted happiness, helped purify the air and strengthen the positive mood but recently whatever she did felt useless. There was definitely something wrong with the air. Could it be the storm weather forecasters were predicting? Or maybe it was a sinister force threatening the area? She made a pleasant face and told the person who was tasting she couldn't serve him anymore. The gentlemen didn't argue. He walked away with his friends helping him. She could see they had the foresight to rent a limo for their wine tour. Drinking while driving in this part of the state was not tolerated, and Sydney was glad for that.

Allenwood Vineyards drew many tasters. She wasn't sure if it was due to the wine or the recent story about Allenwood that was in the news. Her Uncle Frank could have thrown the reporters off the property but they were smart and stayed on the roadside, not trespassing. The piece promising more at eleven showed a smart looking African American woman in a suit reporting how the wine "left more than just a bad taste in Gerard Bellamont's mouth."

At least there were a few cars parked in the driveway. Sydney thought it would look bad if the parking lot was empty. That could mean the premature death of this winery.

The news reporter also commented on how the murder appeared to be a robbery but no other motives were ruled out. As Sydney cleared her area, she thought how silly the robbery motive was. Why would anyone kill a famous critic for what he had in his pockets? She didn't know if Gerard Bellamont's wallet had been with him but she remembered seeing him with a decent wedding band and wondered if it had been taken. People did anything to avoid the motive of love, she thought. Dying for love was ever so common, more than one would think, and killing for love went hand in hand. She remembered seeing Jan Bellamont and her husband arguing when she was out helping her uncle re-attach the trellis wire. The Bellamonts were on the cottage porch. She could hear Jan yelling to her husband that he was back to his old tricks again. Sydney moved closer, trying to hear more but her uncle stopped her. Best to mind your own business, he said, urging her to go back to the winery. She could remember feeling guilty and dissatisfied. Eavesdropping, like gossip, was something she did so seldom it had never been an issue.

Now, after the death, everything came to light. It became a job to discern what was important and what wasn't. Sometimes a different light or angle was needed to see things more clearly. It was probably nothing. Her untrained eye seemed to pick up on the wrong things. That's why she turned to the mystical for help. She couldn't make sense of it all herself.

She concluded that the Bellamonts private conversation needed to stay private and she was making too much of it. If the handsome but awkward investigator asked, she would tell him. Otherwise it was none of her business. She thought the odd statement Gerard Bellamont made the other night was nothing either. Even though he made the statement here at the winery, Gerard may have let it slip because he'd been drinking. People said the strangest things when they're drunk. She remembered reading somewhere that the truth came out when one was inebriated. She believed it because her ex-boyfriend was rude and nasty when he was drunk. She didn't need the stars to help her on that subject.

Someone entered the winery and she looked up to see Paul Shepard with Wyatt. They were here to pick her up for lunch. She yelled across to her aunt she was going on her break and went from behind the bar to where Wyatt was, looking more distraught than usual. His father's murder seemed to weigh on his mind. He seemed to be aging prematurely by the lines on his face and under his eyes. Stress could kill you.

"Wyatt, you poor thing," she said, giving him a big hug. She reached in her pocket and pulled out something she'd created the night before. "Here's an amulet made with a tiger's eye. It's for protection." She placed the amulet, around his head and fought back tears. The innocent needed to stay innocent.

Wyatt gave a wry smile and a quick glance to Paul Shepard. "Thanks, Sydney. Are you hungry? I'm starving!" He turned away and entered Paul's car on the driver's side.

"Paul, do you think it's wise for him to drive? After what he's been through?"

Paul placed an arm around her as they walked. "He seems almost normal now but he needs a little more attention after what's happened. Look how excited he is."

"But we're not his parents," she said for what seemed the hundredth time. She loved Wyatt, or the young innocence he stood for, but couldn't quite understand Paul Shepard. As she entered the backseat, she moved some paintings and asked where they were going. As Wyatt revved up the engine, it was Paul who turned around and replied. "Fancy a drive to the gorges of Watkins Glen?"

She looked at her watch then glanced back at the winery. Her aunt and uncle wouldn't mind if she took a few hours off and some fresh air would do her good. But why did she feel so reluctant to leave the winery? She felt as though she was leaving all responsibility behind—as though she were back in the sixth grade—playing hooky when her father came around once every few months to have a play date. Was that what this was? A play date?

As they drove south on Route 14, she couldn't help but feel like it was. She heard the casual banter between Paul and Wyatt in the front seat and would have felt left out if it weren't for Paul's momentary glances and attentive winks. He had a way with people, she thought. She couldn't help but smile whenever he was around, even though she still didn't know what his true intentions were. How long would they be friends and is that all they'll ever be? She wasn't looking for a relationship so soon after her break up in New York. She didn't know what happened for them to be this close so soon but having a handsome older man dote on you and treat you with the utmost respect felt good. So what if young Wyatt trailed along everywhere they went? It was like a happy family without the legality of marriage or the pains of childbirth. She should treat it as just that. But she couldn't help but feel this family was destined to experience tragic events that would stop it from ever being truly happy.

There was hardly any traffic on the road to Owen Winery and the winery itself didn't seem busy. Deville noticed there was less wine around. Were they closing? Did the negative words of Gerard Bellamont cause this strain so fast? There were a few employees there and Stephanie Ferris was behind the tasting bar, appearing to take inventory. She looked up, pursed her lips and pretended not to notice him.

"Good morning, Mrs. Ferris."

"Oh, hi there. I didn't know it was you."

"Are you closing?" he asked.

She was wearing a lot of makeup, dressed in black with heels and her blond hair pulled back. "I'm sorry, what do you mean?" He mentioned to her he didn't see many bottles of wine and noticed missing displays. "Oh! No! We pulled the displays for a wine tasting event. It's at a ballroom in the next town. Can I get you something?"

"Just a moment of your time. I need to speak to you again."

She looked at her wristwatch, which had diamonds around the face. "Time for a smoke break then. Why don't you follow me?"

Outside she lit up and tried to act casual. He could see her fiddling with her nails as she tried to look in any direction except his.

"How well did you know Gerard Bellamont?"

Her gaze kept floating. "I told you. We were working together."

"Yes but you didn't tell me the book was finished."

She shrugged. "I thought he was still editing it."

"What about your relationship with Mr. Bellamont?" She pretended not to know anything, which made him angry. "Do you think the police are simpletons?" he asked. "There are witnesses who say you and he were closer than friends. They suspect you were having an affair."

"Who told you this? The Kellers? Paul Shepard? It's a total lie."

"Total or partial?"

She set her gaze on Deville, looking frightened and years younger than she was. "I don't know what they're talking about."

"Come to think about it, I almost didn't believe it either. Why would a bombshell like you see a miserable older man like Bellamont? Yes, he had money but not enough to risk everything. You were helping him get published so if he was getting a book deal already why sleep with you?"

"You're right about some things. He was miserable, stubborn, selfish and couldn't look past his own ego."

Deville continued, "Then I thought to myself, what would you possibly gain? It wasn't the book was it? I daresay the wines from Owen were receiving a bad review with a little help from Bellamont. Some may even wonder how Bellamont could have reviewed a wine before it was available? Bellamont knew these wines inside and out. I don't think the Owens were so forthcoming with information. I don't think they would even give him a tour, let alone allow him to taste a private stash of wine not released to the public. So tell me, Stephanie, what do you have to gain by this place closing down? You and your husband both work here—jobs are difficult to come by—so why would you jeopardize all this to sleep with a man?"

Her ash fell and so did her cigarette. She grabbed hold of a nearby rail, covering her face with her other hand. The sudden but true accusations must have come over her like a wave, engulfing her with unexpected despair, maybe even a touch of shame. Terror may have best described her emotion. The man or the love she got was not what she envisioned it to be, Deville thought as he saw her withering, still trying to maintain control. "Gerard was just a thing. What do you men call it—a phase? How can I lower my standards? My husband is a handsome man. Gerard was just a..." she broke off.

Deville waited a moment before saying, "Was it sympathy? Was it something that happened when the two of you had too much to drink? Wouldn't it be dangerous to sleep with a man who has so much against Owen Winery?"

She took a deep breath. "He said what he thought. He wasn't afraid. Maybe I found him attractive because he was so brash. Ryan, my husband, is quiet, always worried about what people would say, never opinionated about anything." Her face looked tired but Deville didn't think it was from manual labor. The lines and wrinkles around her eyes were from sleepless nights thinking about cheating on her husband.

"Did you even care for Gerard Bellamont?" he asked.

"Yes. I cannot just sleep with anyone. What do you think? I'm some tramp? Gerard made advances, flirted with me and I enjoyed it. He was miserable, and not the best-looking man but he wasn't ugly. I feel bad for his wife."

"A little late for that don't you think?"

She looked at him as if he'd just slapped her. "I wish you wouldn't judge. I didn't think that was the police's job?" She shook her head. "Fine. Judge away. Everyone else does without knowing the entire story."

"Who else knows about you and the victim?"

"No one. People just judge in general." She paused and looked at the sky. "He didn't deserve to die. I told you. I didn't do it."

"A witness places you with Gerard on the night he was murdered."

"And who might that be? It wasn't Jan. She was too busy popping pills. Could it have been the Kellers or Paul Shepard? He's one to talk, the way he's always lurking around."

"Describe lurking?"

"He hangs around Wyatt and Sydney Keller. It's like his own little family. They have picnics. They sail. They do everything together. I don't trust her. She's like a witch. Always knowing what the stars are saying It's all devil worship, messing with the future. God doesn't want us to know the future. We shouldn't be playing with dangerous forces."

Deville was speechless. The righteous Christian path of Stephanie Ferris was lucid by her opinion of witchcraft but the lines of adultery were a blur and okay to cross. "Is there anyone in particular out to get you, Stephanie, or is it just everyone in this county?"

She became livid. "So it's not her? She didn't see me with Bellamont?" Stephanie Ferris grabbed the doorknob. "Wait a minute. Are you tricking me? No one saw me. I just admitted to something you lied about? You're a horrible, horrible man!"

She went in and he followed her. "Mrs. Ferris, someone saw you. Please don't walk away from me. I can take you to the station."

She stopped and turned around. "You got what you wanted from me, now go. I didn't kill him. I don't have the strength to strangle anyone. If Ryan finds out…" she broke off and looked behind Deville, expressionless.

"If Ryan finds out what?"

Deville turned to see Ryan Ferris standing near the door holding a grocery bag. "Hi. honey. Back from the store?" she asked.

Ryan Ferris walked to them and gave his wife a grocery bag. "Out of the spray cleaner you wanted but I got the trash bags. So what were you two talking about?" His manner seemed normal and low key but Deville wasn't sure if Ryan heard anything. What did his wife say about him? That he didn't have an opinion or he was reserved, and worried what others thought? Deville thought maybe Ryan Ferris was one to watch out for, maybe a ticking bomb. So many years of harboring emotions could lead to violent episodes. Ferris could fit the part but there were other concerns Deville needed to talk to him about.

Stephanie marched away with an angry stride and Ryan turned to Deville.

"Geez. What's up with her?"

Moments later both men were in the winery's office on the other side of the tasting room. This was the furthest from the back door. Ryan Ferris sat on one side of a desk writing in a notebook. "Sorry. Just have to jot things down in my log."

"Is this for winemaking?" Deville asked.

He nodded. "Check the temperature, tasting notes, a bunch of things. Sometimes we may think a wine is ready but it isn't. Trial and error can get you so far, but a log," he indicated his notebook, "is a recording."

"Mr. Owen must be proud of you."

A short laugh erupted from Ferris. "The Owens don't care about this log. I told them about it but they weren't thrilled. As long as my wife and I give them the reports they ask for, they're happy. The finances and such. I want this business to grow, to have more than just tastings. It was my idea to build up this place, have a bistro, merchandise. Sometimes I think I'm the only one with decent ideas around here. They agree but it's like they don't even care."

"Maybe they just don't appreciate you?" He was hoping for a response of some sort but nothing happened. Deville noticed a chair by the door and took a seat. Apparently Ferris had too much on his mind because his manners went out the window.

"Sorry. Have a seat." He took a deep breath and added, "No, I think the Owens know we can handle it."

Ferris filed his notebook away in a cabinet while Deville studied him. Someone so dedicated, so good at what he does and someone who has brains to build a business. What was holding him back? Where did it go wrong?

Or had it? Who was to blame if the wine wasn't worth a beggar's sip? Ryan Ferris or the owner? Maybe the wine wasn't appealing. Deville couldn't try it but why would others continuously buy it? If Gerard Bellamont was the only person who wrote a bad review for Owen Winery, it might mean sabotage. Deville recognized music playing as something he heard the night before when Chloe Owen was brushing her long hair.

Deville remained calm but the thought of Ryan Ferris and Chloe Owen together engulfed him. This idea made him think about what kind of monster Ryan Ferris was or could be. "Tell me, Mr. Ferris, about the night the kids went missing."

He looked at Deville blankly. "You mean when that fellow got killed?"

"Isn't that what I said?"

"No you mentioned the kids being missing, which they weren't. They were safe. You didn't mention about Bellamont being killed. I just thought it was peculiar you said that instead of the murder." Then, after a pause, "Is it still a murder? He didn't kill himself?"

Deville shook his head, "Oh, no. It's much too difficult for anyone to kill themselves like that. I apologize. I guess I've completely skipped over the killing. So much going on that night. I guess I was concerned about the children. It's funny how fast kids grow up these days. How old do you think the boy, Wyatt, is?"

Ferris shrugged, "Sixteen, seventeen, don't know. Can't tell because I can't see his face. His hair is always in it. Don't understand styles nowadays."

"I agree. They are such an enigma. And Chloe, she's such a looker for a child. She'll break some hearts when she gets older. Don't you agree?"

Ryan Ferris leaned back in his chair. "I don't know what you mean."

"I think you do. Your wife is very beautiful. Blond, tall, kind of like Chloe."

"Chloe is just a kid. Like you said, just a child." He stood up. "She has a lot of growing up to do."

"Let's just make sure she grows up. Especially with people her own age." Deville stood and leaned toward him. "Tell me, how well do you know Chloe?"

The words weren't there but Ryan Ferris's face turned pale. He took a few moments to digest the question. "Chloe is just a girl. I don't know what she's been telling you or anyone else but nothing has, or ever will happen, between us. She's a child."

"You say that as if you're trying to convince yourself more than me. People say you were concerned when she went missing. In fact, you were the only one concerned."

"I care for her."

"And she cares for you?"

He looked at Deville. "It's not like that."

Deville replied, "You can get in a lot of trouble for this or have you already? Maybe someone found out about your little infatuation? Someone like Gerard Bellamont?"

"Please leave now. I have nothing else to say." He strode to the office door and opened it. "It's not what you think."

"I will be watching you, Mr. Ferris. Every move. And just how much influence do you have with the Owens? Bellamont was a sore subject for them wasn't he? His words had the power to close a winery. There was much at stake. Too much for you not to do anything about. Tell me, where does your job end? Here at the winery? Or do you indulge in extra activities for them?"

"Now you're suspecting me of killing Bellamont for my employers? You have a lot of speculations but no proof. I'm a winemaker and I'm good at what I do. I can go somewhere else and make wine. It doesn't matter."

"Then why don't you?" Deville asked. He turned to go but before he left he said, "But how else could you keep the fair-haired Chloe on standby, waiting for her eighteenth birthday?" Ryan Ferris still stood, holding an open door. He didn't say another word but his face was had turned red. Deville had hit a nerve. "Good day to you, Mr. Ferris. Don't leave town. I will speak to you again."

Outside, the storm clouds were moving in, covering this area of the Finger Lakes. The dark gray of the day was creating more than a mist. Deville felt a few raindrops. The weather, just like his case, was getting darker and just as threatening by the minute.

CHAPTER ELEVEN

The next day Deville received a phone call from Paul Shepard. He wanted to speak to Deville and asked if he could come to Canandaigua, where Shepard was ready to launch his boat. Deville said he'd be right over. The traffic was heavy for this time of year with more tourists than Deville expected. This meant the leaf peepers were out enjoying the wineries or the last bit of fair weather before the frost. Canandaigua's architecture ranged from a Swiss-type building on Main Street to several brick and stone edifices, including a new handsome structure toward the lake front that housed the New York Wine and Culinary Center. Although Deville had his demons preventing his partaking of wine, he had enjoyed several trips to the Center, where he'd taken a few cooking classes.

He drove to the marina, where the lake began, and parked the car. While walking on the dock, he searched for Shepard's boat, wondering why Shepard needed to see him. He had written down specifics about the boat's location and found it without a problem. Paul Shepard emerged from the cruising thirty-foot sailboat with a rope in hand. Deville noticed the name "Danielle" on the front of the boat, named after Shepard's late wife.

Visualizing him getting ready to sail was like an advertisement for cologne or aftershave.

"Good afternoon, investigator," Shepard said, jumping off the boat and onto the pier. He was wearing khakis, a Polo tee and a sweater tied around his neck. He shook Deville's hand with a sturdy grip.

"Nice sail you have here," Deville said, not knowing if it was the correct jargon. He didn't just want to say "good looking boat" and hoped it was passable.

"Thanks. It's called a Catalina sailboat. Some may consider it a yacht but I don't."

"Catalina. That's fitting."

Shepard nodded. "I brought it here from California. Traveling with these things was quite a challenge but I didn't want to sell it. It has a lot of sentimental value. It was Danielle's boat. She loved sailing. She loved wine. I'm just a wood worker."

"Isn't it too late to sail in November?"

Shepard outstretched his hands, "Sunshine is all I need. I like to keep sailing until the first snowfall. Although we're supposed to get rain tonight." He offered Deville a hand to step aboard. Deville accepted gingerly and they both walked down below. Deville stayed near the open doorway that led to the busy pier. He watched Shepard with caution, making sure there weren't any weapons around, like a loaded gun or sharp knife.

The death of Gerard Bellamont seemed unplanned not premeditated. The killer finding the trellis wire meant just that but one could never be too cautious. Once they were inside, Deville noticed the boat's tinted windows, the clean and unused state it appeared to be in and wondered how often Shepard used the vessel. The surroundings were simple—wood paneling, vinyl seats—and the cabin appeared organized. Shepard moved about as if he were at home, trying his best to make his guest feel comfortable. But Deville wasn't a guest. He wondered why Shepard was so intent on being nice. It could just be his nature. "I don't have many people on board. I'm kind of a loner. I have nothing else to offer you, sorry. Then again, you're not a drinker are you?" He motioned Deville to sit. "Sorry if I seemed extra gregarious last night, must have been the wine."

"No need to apologize. You seemed at ease." Deville sat, trying to adjust to the movement of the boat on the lake.

"How is the case going?"

"Moving along," Deville said, glad Shepard brought it up. "Why did you call me?"

"I thought I would come clean."

"Come clean?"

"About Bellamont. How he refused to sell me grape juice from California or anywhere." He sighed. "I don't want you hearing it from anyone else, although you might have already. He supplied other wineries but wouldn't do it for mine."

"Any reason he wouldn't?"

"I don't think he wanted anyone else to succeed. He said there were too many wineries up here and wouldn't mind seeing a few close."

"Which ones?"

Shepard shook his head. "He was strange, saying things that made little sense. He argued with me about it but I searched on my own for another distributor. I've talked to some but I don't hold a grudge. I'm not that type."

Deville took notes and wondered if this was the only thing Paul Shepard was harboring. "Anything you can tell me about the party?"

"I already spoke to you about it."

"You remember Gerard Bellamont acting unusual or saying anything? Do you remember him saying something he didn't care for? Or that he didn't like the first time he saw it?"

Shepard turned away. Deville couldn't decide on any reaction because the boat moved and he had to steady himself. When he looked back he saw Shepard grabbing things from the cabinets. Sunblock lotion, whistles and ropes. "Like I said, Bellamont was always saying freaky things. Must have been talking about the wines."

"Can you tell me your whereabouts that night again?"

Shepard turned around and crossed his arms. "The party was for Allenwood Vineyards. We all stayed until around eleven."

"When did you hear the kids were missing?"

"Wyatt and Chloe? Around ten, I think. We found them though. They were in the cottage."

"Bellamont's cottage?"

"Yes. Music was blaring. They both were there but they were kind of busy, if you know what I mean. Bellamont and I didn't want to disturb them so we walked back."

Deville thought for a moment. "The kids were getting busy? I thought they were just friends?"

Shepard shrugged. "Could be but friends can mean different things to different people. They are both young, full of hormones, anything could have happened."

"How did Bellamont react when spotting his son with Chloe?"

"He seemed happy about it, almost proud. You know how it is. Girls aren't treated the same as guys. I almost think Bellamont would have given his son a high five if they had seen each other again. Then again, they weren't doing anything too serious and we didn't want to disturb them."

"What time did you get back?"

"I guess around ten thirty, maybe later. After we saw the kids we came back and then we left. Well I left anyway."

"So Bellamont came back to the party with you?"

He nodded. "Yes. We came back together but I don't know if anyone saw me coming back. I don't think I went back into Allenwood."

"So let me get this straight. The people at the party didn't see you come back but they did see Bellamont?"

Shepard looked confused. "I guess I don't remember what happened. It would give me an alibi? I'm sure everyone saw him or both of us come back from spotting the kids."

Deville took a deep breath and continued writing in his notebook. Shepard watched him but didn't stir or seem nervous. "Better hope someone saw you and him, Mr. Shepard, otherwise, if you didn't kill him, you were the last person to see him alive."

At this, Shepard showed concern. After a pause, he shrugged. "That's ridiculous. Why would I want to kill him?"

"You tell me."

"You've been talking to the clowns at Owen. Ryan Ferris? He told you about the California grapes? That's nothing. Deals go sour all the time. I didn't care about that. I don't know why he wouldn't sell to me."

"Maybe he didn't like your wine."

"Bull."

"What did he say about it?"

"He said the quality wasn't there. He said I could do better so I believed him."

Deville continued. "You mentioned that you argued with Bellamont. The victim didn't sound like he'd squash his own deal, some would say he'd sell his own mother."

"Bellamont didn't care about anything. Like I said, he thought the Finger Lakes had enough wineries and he would be happy seeing some go down. Especially the ones that produce mediocre wines."

After a moment Deville raised his eyebrows. "I'm

waiting."

Shepard swallowed. "Owen Winery. There's no hope for them. If you're looking for motives, there's plenty there. Roger and Kelly Owen know their wine is no good and they're not doing anything about it."

"What about Ryan and Stephanie Ferris?"

"Ryan is an imbecile. He's a hard worker and if Owen Winery goes down, he'll have nothing. No job. No wife."

"Do you think Stephanie Ferris would leave her husband if the winery went down?"

"She would leave him in a heartbeat. Poor Ryan needs to get his act together and prepare himself. He's good at what he does. He's learned from the best. I have to hand it to the Owens. They treated Ryan to a trip to Europe to learn about winemaking."

"Did it include France?"

"I don't know. You'd have to talk to Ryan." Then as if he'd read Deville's mind, "Wasn't Gerard Bellamont from France? I think I remember him saying that." Shepard connecting Ryan Ferris and Gerard Bellamont by a suspicious trip Ryan made to Europe wasn't as far-fetched as it seemed.

Deville was waiting for the inevitable, waiting for Shepard to ask him about his own origins. He changed the subject, leading to the more likely connection between Ryan Ferris and Gerard Bellamont. "Where did you see Gerard Bellamont and Stephanie Ferris? It was dark, and sometimes at the vineyard the shadows can cause illusions."

"Geez, it was so unpleasant I have to think for a second. I went to relieve myself when I spotted them. I wasn't looking for them. It was just behind the vineyard. I think they saw me because they started talking and I went back. I felt embarrassed.

"Does anyone else know what you saw?"

"Like I said, it's not my thing. Jan Bellamont was so

drunk or drugged all she did was smile and laugh at everyone's jokes. Ryan Ferris just sat at the table speaking to the Owens. They were clueless about what their spouses were doing."

Deville thought about Stephanie Ferris. Why did she risk anyone spotting her and Gerard? She admitted to seeing Bellamont. The reasons were still unclear but Deville thought it had to do with the book. He didn't think the affair was a long one. Stephanie seemed like she would only bed him just enough times to get what she needed.

Deville continued writing while asking, "What about Frank and Marianne Keller?"

"What about them? They're great. They made sure everyone had plenty to drink and eat. Sydney, their niece, is from New York City. She did all the cooking that night. Great appetizers. Frank Keller doesn't know much about wine. He and I sympathize with each other. Although his wife runs the show there. Surprisingly, they have decent wine. Guess it's the climate. We don't grow our grapes at our winery. We have another property."

Deville asked the next question with reservations. "Are you and Sydney Keller close?"

"As close as friends can be." He looked up and they both heard footsteps walking toward them and voices from outside. Both their heads peered out to see two figures coming closer. The woman was dressed in a wide brim hat, a tight sweater and jeans that showed off a small but shapely figure. Her dark hair seemed to blow from the cool wind of the lake.

"Hello Paul," Sydney Keller said, setting foot to come aboard. Both men reached out to assist her. Her wide smile showed almost perfect whites. "Hi, again, detective."

"Investigator," he replied.

"Nice to see you again," she said and put on her

sunglasses. Before hiding her eyes, Deville thought she looked glad to see him. While fussing with Sydney Keller, both men seemed to have ignored Wyatt, who was carrying two bags. He threw the bags on the deck, jumped aboard and Deville noticed Wyatt seemed a little troubled. He didn't like Deville being around. After he gave a quick nod to Shepard, Wyatt walked toward Deville. "Shouldn't you be trying to catch my father's killer?"

Sydney, who had raised the mainsail, chimed in. "Wyatt, he is doing his job. He's asking more questions."

"How many questions does it take?" Wyatt sighed. "Oh well, guess we all work in our own way." He strode away, holding the boom with one hand while whistling. He reached Sydney and helped unroll the mainsail.

Shepard came from below with life jackets. He began throwing them. "One for you my fair darling. One for you young man and one for me." He had an extra one. "And one for the investigator, if he's able to sail and if he trusts us enough." A slight smile appeared on Shepard's face. "If you don't want to, I'll understand. Although I am sure you'd want to speak to Sydney again."

Sydney slid her sunglasses off her nose partly, showing concerned eyes. "Oh, please do. The waters should be calm because of the position of the moon. There's more I need to tell you." She gave a forced grin that made Deville wonder if she was playing a game.

Was the invitation a welcome one to sail or was it a cry for help? Did Sydney think she was in danger by having Wyatt and Shepard along or was it all a front? Maybe she was concerned about Deville himself joining them, ruining the party. After all, she arrived with Wyatt, she accepted an invitation from Shepard. She knew what she was getting into didn't she?

For the first time, Deville thought there was more to Sydney Keller than her thirst for danger and all too many flirts with disaster. The enigma of her and her relationships in this case made Deville think of former heroines in history who fell into widely public but suspicious roles, such as Tokyo Rose or Mata Hari. She seemed to play the part fittingly: a woman in distress who feared for her life or for the people around her. But she had a choice. She placed herself in the eye of the storm and thought nothing of it.

Deville took the life jacket. "It's been awhile. Can you help me put this on?" Sydney helped him fasten it. He tried to look into her eyes but she turned away, not wanting to see him or show any concern.

Sailing on Canandaigua Lake was new to him but he knew it was something he'd enjoy. The brisk November wind made it challenging to maneuver the boat but with everyone in place, it moved with ease, a controlled device on restless waters. Wyatt held the tiller with a nervous hand but with the guidance of Shepard, who was always near, there weren't many sudden movements. The surroundings were marvelous when out in the open water. The blue sky showed patches of gray and looked more like a border, ending with a thin line of colored trees, homes and boats. Though they could see the shore from a distance, it was as if they were in a much larger body of water. At times, even the faint signs of life seemed miles away.

Paul Shepard and Wyatt Bellamont continued to take control of the rudder by the tiller, while Sydney Keller held on to the boom. "It's so beautiful out here," she said, staring out into the water. "One can forget how cruel the world can be."

"Do you sail with them often?" Deville asked, moving closer to her with caution. The winds picked up and he found it difficult to keep his balance.

"Not often enough. We started this summer. It was a fairytale summer. At least it seemed so to me. Living here, having friends."

"It's new, and exciting? Didn't you have a lot of friends in New York?"

She turned to him. "Depends on what you call a lot. New York is not as rude as people say. There are some great neighborhoods but I didn't happen to live in one of those." She told him to watch the mainsail while she grabbed a basket. She brought out sandwiches and offered him one, which he accepted. Egg salad with dill pickles. "It's not gourmet but it's fun to make."

"You made the food at the party as well?"

She nodded. "I would hardly call it food. It was scallops wrapped in bacon, stuffed mushroom caps and a veggie tray. Just appetizers. Uncle Frank thought I spent too much, even though I hadn't. He meant time, not money. He thought I'd spent all day preparing."

"How did you learn to cook so well?"

"I helped a friend who caters. Believe me, there's a lot I don't cook."

"Everything she makes is delicious," Shepard said.

Deville turned to watch the others. Shepard was showing Wyatt the basics of sailing and sailing upwind. While Deville watched them he thought how they got along so well. However, being on the force and his cynical eye made him question everything. What was the motivation for the relationship? Why would a grown man spend so much time with a troubled soul like Wyatt? This wasn't the only relationship that was troubling him. Ryan Ferris and Chloe Owen also left him with many questions. Was it just mentoring or the worst-case scenario, lust, the base of it all? Could these grown men be treated like pedophiles, shunned by society, without facts or evidence?

Watching the two laugh and speak to each other as though they were old friends made him feel uncomfortable. He wondered if there was anything happening. Maybe his own troubled past gave him a sordid outlook. Deville could not live with himself if there was even an ounce of jealousy. His own father was missing from his past, taken from him as though a storm came and swept him away. No images of sailing along the Atlantic, playing sports or doing anything a father and son do. Real relationships like that don't exist, a part of his cynical self said. Just like this one isn't real. Someone is taking advantage of someone and it may not be the person you think. He glanced back to Sydney and asked, "What is it with those two?"

She followed his gaze. "Paul and Wyatt? What about them?"

"Don't you find it unusual how well they get along?"

"Not really. Paul does so much for us. He helped my uncle with vines in the beginning, when they were just starting. Ryan Ferris helped my uncle, too. It seems ridiculous why we even have a winery because we need so much help. Paul helps Wyatt by giving him companionship. Somehow I don't think Gerard was a good father."

"What about your aunt, Marianne? Does she like Paul?"

Her face turned pale and she seemed uncomfortable. "I've not offered you anything to drink. How silly of me." She went down and left him holding the boom. The wind picked up and he heard Paul Shepard say the gusts were reaching around 20 knots. Sydney came back with some bottled waters. She gave one to everyone and sat down again with Deville.

Deville took a sip and decided to be blunt with Sydney. He spoke to her in a low voice so only she could hear. "I can't help but feel that you are in danger and you don't want to listen. Stop ignoring the facts. There is a killer out there. I don't know who it is but if you know something more than what you've told me, then please speak up."

"I've told you everything. At least I think I have."

"Well then, you need to be cautious and for once, listen to your horoscopes. If you feel unsafe for any reason, you need to call me. Don't feel pressured and do things you don't want to do just because someone asks you."

She took a deep breath. "I do what I want. No one pressures me. My life is filled with unhappiness. Some of us are just dealt that. I'm sure you of all people know what I'm talking about."

Deville stood and couldn't decide if he felt angry or confused. He walked over to where Wyatt and Shepard was and offered to help. Shepard told him to take over while he used the head. Deville did so, asking more questions than any neophyte would. Wyatt looked to be in his element. He studied the mainsail and the water, giving Deville little pointers and directions along the way. Whenever he told him what to do, he was polite.

The boat continued to move but it felt like they were more in control. "So are there any leads of who killed my father?" Wyatt asked. "Can you tell me who's in the running? I heard ten percent of police work is investigating and ninety percent is proving your man did it."

"What makes you think it was a man?" Sydney asked from a few feet away.

"Has to be. It would have taken a lot of strength to squeeze the life out of my dad."

"Actually, a woman could have committed the crime," Deville said. "It doesn't take much strength with the wire that was used. Just a good grip and a woman who's as tall as you," he motioned to Sydney, "with some moderate strength, could do the job with little difficulty."

Paul came back and Sydney told him she was considered a suspect. She was smiling.

"That's nice," Shepard said. He then asked if she needed help with guiding the rope. Since the wind was becoming stronger they decided to turn around. The boat took them on its own course, following the trail of rising waves. The choppy water nearly caused the boat to capsize several times. Deville cursed himself for deciding to join them. Sydney Keller and Paul Shepard laughed. Wyatt, who seemed a bit shaken, showed no fear but rather amusement. He listened to the orders Shepard gave and delivered them with accuracy and ease. Wyatt's attention and ability to learn things so fast impressed Deville. When they were on the right course, Deville's terror eased. He tried to keep his mind busy ignoring the developing nausea. He couldn't imagine how anyone would find this relaxing. It wasn't at all how he imagined it to be.

By the end of the trip, Deville could feel his head spinning. While the boat docked, he jumped off and gave a sigh of relief. He almost wanted to kiss the dock itself. There were other boats docking and everyone was talking about how much the weather had changed for the worse. Deville noticed the others on the pier were calm and couldn't help but feel silly. When he turned to see his other three passengers, he noticed all eyes were on him.

"We hope we didn't shake you up too much," Shepard said.

Sydney gave a slight smile and Wyatt seemed in better spirits. It appeared Deville was the subject of ridicule and this seemed to have caused them great joy.

Wyatt jumped to the pier and helped Deville out of his life jacket. After, Wyatt made a small fist and patted Deville's shoulder. Deville recognized this as a sign of acceptance. "It's okay. I was scared for awhile, too," Wyatt said. He then moved the hair away from his face and stepped back on board to help the others finish docking.

"Thank you for joining us," Paul Shepard said, wrapping a rope with his arms. "It's not every day we have a man in blue question us on the water."

"They usually question you somewhere else?"

Sydney wrapped her arms around Shepard. "Paul means it's not often he gets questioned. Period."

Shepard released her embrace and gave a curt order to rush the packing. She did so reluctantly. Did Shepard always dismiss her advances or was it because Wyatt was around? Or maybe it was Deville who made everyone uncomfortable. He left feeling like he was observing their staged show—the witness to their deception—and the reason their make believe family would come to surface and show the world the sham it actually was.

CHAPTER TWELVE

Deville arrived back at the station and searched for pills: ibuprofen, acetaminophen, anything to help the pounding in his head go away. His body felt like it had been through the eye of a storm. His hair, usually groomed to perfection, was now untamed and wild, like it had rebelled against all the products he'd used the past decade. There were a few stares from the officers when he came back, including Investigator Reginald Scudder, who was the only one who had the nerve to ask what happened. Deville was vague, and said he'd been in a minor fender bender. He had his car and the ding from Sydney Keller to prove it, if need be. There was no way he was telling anyone a weather-beaten sail on a rocky lake caused this. They'd never believe him. Scudder offered pills but they were for indigestion. He thanked him and asked how he was doing on the case.

Scudder replied, "All right. I've been working with the computer lab."

"Can I have a copy of Bellamont's book?"

Scudder nodded. "We found a printed manuscript. It's on your desk. Wolanski is working on the victim's other writings, reviews and such. What would you like me to do in the meantime?"

"Find out about the victim's haunts, here in the Finger Lakes. Where did he enjoy dining, drinking, hanging out? Also, check into the horse track. It may lead to nowhere but try."

The young officer seemed ready to jump through fire for his job. He nodded and turned away.

"Scudder, thanks." Deville always thanked fellow officers. Being polite was something he held in high regard. His foster mother taught him to have manners. She had been from British Royalty, raised by her uncle, who had been a duke.

Walt and Lenore Fitzhugh raised him as their own and never asked for anything in return. They decided not to adopt him, knowing when Deville was old enough he may want to discover his true family. The subject of adoption never came up. Growing up in a house with two strangers was one thing. Taking their name is another. Perhaps the thought of giving up something from his past, even if was just his name, was silly on their part. They kept their distance, never getting too close, never acting like actual parents or any kind of blood relative. The word "love" was never uttered. He read in books from a classic library about such fancies but emotions were always distant, as if they lived in some other solar system.

Walt Fitzhugh had been in the service, remaining a police officer until he died. He was hardly ever at home, which left a lot of time with Lenore, who did her best raising him. She taught him how to dress, how to respect one's clothes and how important it was to be polite. It was more than just saying please and thank you. She taught him how to respect life itself. Deville's gratitude extended more than just to people. He was earth conscious, too, and recycled as much as possible. He was the first one in his department with a hybrid car and tried to use as little electricity as possible. Jessica Malone, who once saw where he lived from the outside, asked him why he kept the house so dark. He said it was because he was energy conscious. That was partly true. There were some areas in the home he never went to and thought he never needed to. Some rooms were as alien to him as the new world was when he first arose from his coma. Different parts of the house were like secret worlds to him—worlds only he could visit. He never invited anyone to his home. It was for him and the spirits of the Fitzhughs, whom he was sure were lurking around.

While trying to locate a first aid kit, he noticed a confused looking woman searching for someone.

Jan Bellamont saw him. Her face showed grave concern. When she spotted Deville, she placed her arms around him, as though he had already solved her husband's case.

"Oh, thank God. You're here." She looked frazzled, sleepless and worried. For someone who had enough drugs to kill an elephant, he thought she could use some. Maybe she had taken a wrong dose or ran out of something to make her look so worn.

Easy now, he told himself. She just lost her husband.

"If you needed me you could have called my cell," he said.

"I did. Maybe you didn't get it. Were you somewhere where the reception was bad?"

Deville had been on the lake. He brushed the back of his head with his hand, wondering if he still looked like he just woke up. He ushered her to his desk. "Mrs. Bellamont, what can I do for you?" He motioned for her to sit.

"Is this your police station?" She looked around. "It's smaller than I thought it would be."

Deville sighed. "We're not a major city." And it's not every day we get a homicide, he almost added. "What brought you here?"

She looked both ways before she leaning forward. "Pills. I'm missing pills."

"Pills?" he repeated. She nodded. "Do you know which pills?" he asked.

She opened her purse and searched, "There's a few missing, some anti-depressants, sleeping pills and others. Pills." A few bottles fell to the floor and she dropped down on all fours to pick them up. The other officers looked at her because she was creating a scene. Deville told her to sit and grabbed the rest of the bottles. After placing them on his desk they went through them, one by one. Her eyes were glassy. She was on the verge of tears. "I know how I look. Please don't judge me."

"It's okay. You'll be fine. Here's the rest." He gave the medication back to her and fought the urge to ask if she had anything to work as an anodyne for his pain. He couldn't believe how many bottles he saw go back into the purse. He thought about people like Jan Bellamont and the doctors who prescribed to them. When is it enough? When the patient dies of an overdose? It must be a job in itself, mixing the right drug cocktail to get you where you think you need to be.

She took out a tissue from her large purse and blew her nose. She looked around then back to him. "I'm sorry. I know I had more. More powerful ones. I looked for them yesterday and today. It's not like me to lose pills. I usually store them in my purse or medicine cabinet."

Her son came to his mind immediately. "Mrs. Bellamont did you ever wonder if your son, Wyatt, has taken anything? I can't tell you how dangerous it is to keep those pills around a boy your son's age. Especially in the fragile state he's in."

"Are you telling me how to raise my son?"

The accusation startled him. "No. No. Not at all."

She sighed and waved her hand. "I'm sorry. Why not you as well? When we were young Gerard used to threaten to call social services on me. Everyone thinks I'm incapable of raising Wyatt. Well, I've done an okay job so far." She searched for approval, such as a nod from Deville. When none came she looked down. It was as if she received the message, not just from him, but from many years of suspected glances. "Wyatt's a mess, just like me. I can see the writing on the wall. Gerard was no help. None whatsoever. Ignoring Wyat. He didn't try to hide his disappointment with him. They were opposites. Never had the same interests, always disagreeing with one another. They didn't even share the same diet."

Deville remembered something Kelly Owen had said. "Mrs. Bellamont was Wyatt ever in trouble? What would I find if I dug in his records?"

She fidgeted in her chair. "He's a kid. Just like anyone else's kid. They all get into trouble." After a moment of silence she sighed. "Oh, stop looking at me like that. Wyatt is a good kid. He just got into trouble in the past."

Deville noticed she was clenching her purse. "Did it involve your medication?"

She nodded. "Wyatt got into his head he could make some money by selling. Do you know the street value of Valium?"

Deville wondered what had kept this family together. Gerard was a womanizer, the son sold his mother's prescription medication and then there was Jan. How much could a woman like her take? A thought occurred to him. How was she involved and did she inadvertently cause this? Years of shutting down and turning away from your husband and son could devastate her. He watched her looking ahead in a dead stare, lost in thought. She was probably thinking the same thing. How could a family fall apart? Deville believed in the idea of marriage—knew it could work well for others—but he also believed sometimes things just didn't work. When a relationship reaches an impasse there's no climbing over it. "Mrs. Bellamont, back to your missing pills."

"Maybe I gave them to someone or someone grabbed them from my purse. I wouldn't think anything of this, except when I awoke today the front door to the cottage was open. Wide open. Wyatt never leaves it open because of the animals roaming around. I would never do it. There's only one explanation. Someone entered the cottage." She looked hopeful. "Could someone be looking for something? Is the killer coming back?" Her inquisitiveness turned to fear. "Oh, no. What if he's after me or Wyatt?"

He patted her shoulder and asked if she would like someone to watch the cottage. He didn't know who he could find, acknowledging it would probably be himself.

She seemed relieved. "Please. Just for a night or two. I know I seem paranoid but I can't help thinking of Gerard. He didn't see it coming did he? It must have been sudden. I've read about those crimes, a spontaneous killing. He was wearing an awful cologne. I thought he might meet another woman that night and I got upset. I feel so bad because now he's dead."

"Who did you think he was meeting?"

She blew her nose again. "I can't do this. It's my paranoia growing. He probably wasn't seeing anyone. He was just so charming." She looked at Deville. "I know you think he was a monster but you only saw a part of him. He wasn't always horrible." She said the next few words as if she were trying to convince herself more than anyone else. "He wouldn't do that, not after his father did it to his mother. He knew the grief it would cause." She stood. "A person couldn't be that cruel." She turned away, leaving the station in somewhat of a hurry, bumping into other officers, apologizing as she went.

CHAPTER THIRTEEN

The rising concerns of Jan Bellamont were not as far-fetched as he would like them to be. The danger of a killer coming back was real and one could never be too cautious. There were many questions Deville needed answered about this situation. He allowed himself to write them down. Why would someone enter the cottage and leave the door open? To frighten Jan and Wyatt Bellamont? Haven't they been through enough? Maybe someone came in to search for Gerard's records or the book he was writing? Was there anything else Gerard kept from Jan?

Jan Bellamont had stated Gerard was wearing a cologne she vehemently despised the night he died. He'd also heard this from Sydney Keller. Perhaps he wore it to attract Stephanie Ferris? Although Deville couldn't think of any cologne that *wouldn't* attract Stephanie Ferris. One only had to bathe and she'd be ready to rumble. He shook his head and couldn't believe how inappropriate it sounded. Gerard Bellamont was seen kissing her right before he died. Poor Gerard. He got all dressed and scented for his killer.

Deville checked on Investigator Christine Wolanski. She was at her desk, typing away, looking more like a secretary than an investigator. She looked up and smiled.

"Looks like you had a rough night. What was her name?"

He gave a wry smile, deciding to come clean. She thought it was funny.

"My first husband had a boat, practically lived on the lake. Didn't want to come ashore. We stopped vacationing and doing everything else except sailing."

"I can see how it can become addictive," Deville replied, although after this morning's excursion on the lake, he deduced one had to be healthy to take on the water.

Wolanski continued on about boating. "Addicting is right, however, owning a boat is not what it's cracked up to be. All the taxes and fees. It doesn't pay to have a boat here and not use it. Not unless you already have storage and live right on the water. Which you and I know can be expensive."

Christine loved to chat and often pulled up her chair and asked Deville about France. She always seemed disappointed with the few bits of memories he had. When she found out he'd never been to Paris or didn't remember ever going, she stopped asking. That was when she realized he wasn't like any of the other officers. Shame, she had said to him once, to live abroad and not remember any of it. All the beauty of a world one could dream of going to, wasted on someone who couldn't remember a thing.

He looked at the time and cut her off to discuss the case, knowing she'd go on with irrelevant babble. "How is the case coming along?"

She pursed her lips, getting the message. "The man was like a demon with words," she said, going back to her typing. She moved her head. Her mousey hair danced while she spoke to him while finishing a report. "A few wineries had little to say about him. Some even hung up when I mentioned his name." She stopped to give him the list she'd been typing. "Here are the ones who agreed to speak about Bellamont."

Deville counted 18 wineries. Christine had her work cut out. "When are you planning on questioning them? Do you need someone to assist you?"

"I didn't expect so many. I'm planning on taking Jerome tomorrow, if he doesn't mind parting with his desk." She yelled out to Officer Miller, "Hey, JM, why not give that chair a rest from your big ass?"

Officer Jerome Miller looked up from his desk and readjusted his glasses. "I'd be honored to accompany you, my dear."

"Gotta love him," she said to Deville. "I'm compiling a list of all the wineries the victim sold grape juice to. I think I'll head home, if that's okay with you. Got to pick up my son at lacrosse before the storm."

He nodded and thanked her. He knew her son was her top priority. She was a single mother and the office sympathized but respected her. After her promotion to investigator, she told a few of her comrades she wasn't looking for sympathy. Yes, being a single parent was difficult but having a no good bastard as a husband or a father to her son was worse. She had friends who helped her when she needed it and the Finger Lakes proved to be a safe place for her son to live. However, she still monitored his friends. Dangerous people live in the best of neighborhoods, she once told him.

He walked over to Officer Jerome Miller, hoping he wouldn't hear a complaint. Miller handed Deville some info and motioned him to sit. Deville did so. Despite being equal officers, Deville always felt as though Miller held a higher rank, partly because of the other's age. Miller's presence demanded respect. His balding gray hair surrounded a round patch of forehead. His inquisitive eyes looked larger because of his small spectacles and his burly figure made any assailant shrink with fear. Any time they needed someone to confess, Miller was there. A closer who got people to divulge their darkest secrets. Miller was good. This talent overshadowed his shortcomings with the physical demands of the job.

"I hear you and Wolanski will pound the vineyards," Deville said. No response. "It's not the pavement but the wineries. Get it?" Again, his sense of humor only seemed funny to him. He rubbed his head, the pain now a dull throb.

Miller placed a bottle of aspirin on his desk. "You look like shit."

Trust him to say exactly what's on his mind. Deville thought. "Now, about Bellamont," he said, as he grabbed the bottle. "What have you found out?"

"Bellamont moved to California from France about 20 years ago," Miller said, eyeing his handwriting. He dared not use a computer. "He had a father with the same name, who had moved to California. It seems as though our victim was following his father's footsteps."

"His father had the same name?"

Miller nodded. "I did some research on Daddy Bellamont. Senior lived in France but moved to California after marrying his second wife. It was on a trip back to France when he died in a plane crash. The hijacked plane by Cubans, Flight 209. I remember hearing about it on the news. Years later Gerard Bellamont Jr. moved to the states, as his father had."

"When did he marry Jan?"

"Twenty-five years ago."

"They waited almost ten years before having Wyatt?"

Miller shrugged. "My sister didn't have her first born until she was 43. Tried everything. Thought the problem was her but it was her husband."

Deville thought for a moment about Jan's prescription

pills. "Find out about Jan Bellamont and her pills. Who is her doctor? See if there is anything that may cause her to have delusions." He paused. "She thinks someone broke into their cottage last night. I'm not sure if I should stay there tonight. Watch her. Do you think someone from…"

Miller shook his head. "The other stations are busy." He looked at Deville. "If you'd like me to watch her place for a few hours, I will but I can't stay the whole night." He looked over to Jessica Malone's office. "You'd have to clear it with her."

Deville couldn't believe what Miller was offering. Had Deville passed the test and won his approval? Or has he finally earned enough respect to be treated as an equal? He decided not to wonder. Some mysteries people just had to accept without speculating. He grabbed his coat. Before he left he thanked Miller for the aspirin and his help.

Miller gave him a slight nod. "Be careful, Frenchman."

It was a nickname Miller used for him. One that Deville didn't care for. The delivery seemed obnoxious the other times Miller had said it. This time there was a hint of endearment with the statement.

"Don't tell Malone. I don't want her to worry."

"That she does," Miller said, as he grabbed his coat. "Don't remember the last time I had a stakeout. I'd fall asleep after a couple of hours. I'd be no good to you. Truth is I'm no good at a lot of things." The solitary figure left the room in what seemed a saddened stride. Deville thought he was getting to know Miller and getting to see how hard it was to be in someone else's shoes.

After finishing some reports Deville called the other stations to see if they had anyone who could watch over the Bellamont cottage for the night. Jessica Malone left her office and waved goodbye. He waved back, thankful he was on hold. He didn't want to request another officer while she was in the room. It was enough of a challenge for their station to handle a homicide. While the other precincts pondered what the outcome would be, they may expect a call for help at any time. This case could be a turning point for the station, especially if he were to solve it without any help. He glanced at the window, watching the gray sky get darker by the minute. A light rain began when he heard the line crackle. This was the storm they were calling for, he thought. While he continued to hold, Deville looked for Bellamont's manuscript. Didn't Scudder say he'd left it on his desk? After a few minutes he stopped searching and the line went blank.

He checked his mail and looked at the notes left for him. Christine Wolanski left the report she'd been writing on his desk while he was speaking with Miller. The folder read "Bellamont." Inside were copies of news stories featuring the victim. Within these photocopies was a trail of Bellamont's career; when he was hired as a column writer, a feature writer and finally a reviewer. The folder also included samples of the victim's writing but didn't include all the reviews, just a few Wolanski found interesting.

Then there was another bunch clipped together with a Post-it note attached that read, "His wine reviews, ruthless!" This group contained all the wine reviews for the past year, which were over 100. They covered the United States, plus some other countries. She grouped the Finger Lakes together. As Deville read, he wished he could have a taste of wine. The reviews, at least the good ones, made one crave a glass. With words such as "notes," "bouquet," "dry" and "sweet," it's no wonder why wine tasting had become such a phenomenon. Deville wondered how one become a wine reviewer.

Could there be another job with so many wonderful benefits?

The craving for wine made him remember the first time his mouth encountered the delicious concoction. He was with his mother, who had just finished working in the field. She was enjoying wine straight from the barrel and already intoxicated. His uncle was smiling at her, brushing her hair with his small calloused hands. Deville couldn't remember much, but the image of seeing his uncle's fingers disappear in his mother's long black hair stayed with him. Deville had just finished his meal, pasta with homemade sauce, and he remembered reaching for a glass of the red substance. No one stopped him. In fact, his mother saw him reach for her own glass and smiled. Her thoughts were on other things, he decided, not on her son. There was no way of knowing if this was wrong or right. Everyone at the table was drinking. There were three of them, him, his mother and uncle.

His father was nowhere around. Did his father know that his brother was here with them?

Suddenly, he heard a whisper. "Louis, go away," an urgent, but soft voice said. "Leave from here."

Just then the lights flickered. He thought he heard the voice again.

Lightening flashed, bringing him back to the present and the station, where the room felt sinister. He was alone now and could feel a chill in the room. The storm was playing tricks on him. A moment later, the lights flickered then turned off, leaving him in darkness. The only light now was from the street poles outside, which gave a shadow of tree limbs, windowpanes, and birds in flight.

Louis.

The voice seemed real and so did the terror. He bit his lip. The shadow seemed to grow, taking a wider shape, reaching towards him. He moved in his chair, rolling it backward in a slow, steady pace.

Save yourself. Forget about me, the voice continued.

He grabbed another phone from a nearby desk, feeling a moment of ease when he heard a dial tone. Before he could dial, the lights came back, glowing brighter than ever. He stood, looking around him. No more shadows. Humming from the ventilation system became louder and a voice on the phone asked him to either dial a number or hang up. He did the latter, sat back in his chair and wiped his brow for the second time that afternoon. This time it was from the nervous sweat of the demons from his past.

CHAPTER FOURTEEN

Outside the dark clouds opened and rain fell on the hills of the vineyards with a force that unnerved him. The winds reached over 40 miles per hour and the traffic had everyone swerving like a wet snake uncoiling on the road. The headlights of other vehicles were blazing. Deville tried to keep his vision steady while the winds and rain were doing a number on his vehicle.

The storm continued but soon the rain turned steady and the wind calmed. Deville was on his way to the Owen property. On the way, his thoughts were on what he'd just read. The reviews of Finger Lakes wine were almost all positive, with just a few moderate critiques about how previous year's varietals were superior. He searched for any bad reviews that stood out—one that could damage a winery to the point of paralyzing the business but there was none. Well maybe one. Deville thought this review was more like a warning to Owen Winery that their focus had to change. It seemed the recent emphasis was to be a destination for "everything wine" but not quality. The latest review dated, almost a month ago, stated that the winery was "too busy expanding their retail to notice their recent Merlot was so sweet it could have come with its own sippy straw."

The final review was just a few weeks ago, when Bellamont wrote about Owen Winery's latest release, their new Riesling that had notes of green apple, pear and peaches. This review suggested the winery "give up." Deville noticed the date of the review and when the wine was released. It was suspiciously close. Was this the review Ryan Ferris had mentioned to Deville the first time they met? How could anyone review a wine before its release? How can anyone have access who wasn't an employee of Owen Winery?

Could Ryan or Stephanie Ferris sabotage their place of employment by giving Bellamont bottles of wine before their release? Deville wondered if anyone could just make up a wine review without tasting it, which may have happened in this case because of the release date and review. Could someone pay Bellamont enough to drive a nail in the coffin of a competitor's wines?

Back at the Owen residence, the housekeeper, Mrs. Bumgarden, was pleased to see him again. Her eyes lit up when she opened the door, as though Deville was a nephew returning from the war. She ushered him in and closed the door, remarking on the terrible storm outside.

"Traveling in this weather will get you sick, sir. Haven't you learned anything from your youth? Don't you dare set foot on the carpet. Take those shoes off now. I'll have tea for you in fifteen. Who do you want to speak to? Mr. Owen is away on business, something about a wine festival in Buffalo. Mrs. Owen is here. She's in the study writing out invitations."

"Invitations to what?"

"A party to celebrate their new Riesling. Launched three weeks ago. The missus likes to host parties. A new wine is just as good as any other reason."

"Were you familiar with Bellamont, the wine reviewer?"

"I'm afraid I wasn't." She held her hands in front of

her. Her long and steady gaze told him she was deep in thought. "I know they didn't want to speak about that gentleman because every time someone mentioned his name they stopped talking. Especially when I entered the room."

Deville thought it was a wise thing to do.

"However," she continued, her head cocked to one side, as if she'd remembered something, "their moods are a little brighter now that he's dead." She walked away. "I daresay the party could also be celebrating his death but you didn't hear that from me." She left the room, eager to start on the tea, leaving Deville alone. No announcement. No showing him where the study was. He imagined it to be on the main floor but Deville didn't go searching for it. Instead, he climbed the steps, in his socks, for his shoes were by the front door and searched for Chloe Owen's room. He guessed the room's direction and found a closed door that faced the front of the home. He knocked. There was no answer. He knocked again and heard a shuffling of noises.

"Chloe. It's Investigator Deville. We had tea last night. Do you remember?" That's right, he told himself, announce that you had tea with her so she won't think you'll be grilling her for information. Just a friend coming over to talk about your infatuation with older men. He heard a stir then the door opened slightly. He could see from a sliver of light that the inside of the room was colorful. Not like the rest of the house. Pink walls, he deduced, plus there was a fruity candle burning. Her head appeared but he only saw half of it; one eye checking him out.

"Who? Why are you here?"

"I just have a few questions. I need your help. Please."

She continued inspecting him with the one beautiful eye. After a few blinks, the door opened to show her grappling with a sweater. One arm was in and she was forcing the other through. She succeeded, lifting her hair out of the sweater, which was pink too, and sparkled with a few rhinestones. Here she was, in all her beauty, doing what most teenage girls did, listening to music, trying on clothes. Who had the nerve to rob or deprive her of this youth? If not Ryan Ferris then who? Were there other men in her midst, waiting for the next opportunity to pounce? She looked troubled. Her colorless face showed a furrowed brow but her lips shone from the light of a nearby lamp.

"Does my mother know you're here?"

"The housekeeper does. She's letting her know."

"I don't think Mom's home. Her car is out of the garage. I don't have a car. I wanted to use it."

"Where were you going?"

It would be far too easy for her to tell Deville. He wondered if the question was too frank.

"Just to see some friends. Are you coming in or are you just gonna stand there?"

"Would it be okay to come in if neither of your parents is home?"

"Don't worry. They don't care." She went to her dresser by the window and began brushing her hair. This was where he'd noticed her the night before. She looked at him through her mirror. "Go ahead. Ask away."

"Did you know Mr. Bellamont?"

"Not really. Just Wyatt, the son. Wyatt said his father didn't treat him like a son. Too worried about himself. Not everyone needs their parents. I'm doing perfectly fine." As if she were all alone on a desert island. "I mean, I have them but I don't need them. They need me more."

He waited for an explanation.

"They have me do things, silly things," she announced.

"Like what?"

"It's nothing really. Just ask some questions, be friendly. Listen to people."

"You mean Wyatt?"

She nodded and continued brushing. "I tried to be his friend although I think he wanted more."

"Did your parents want you to become Wyatt's friend?"

She stopped and turned around to face him. "I don't know. I just assumed. They wanted me to ask him things." She paused then said with a concerned voice, "I don't want to get my parents in trouble."

He walked to her and almost ran his hands down her hair. It wasn't an urge but an automatic response. He felt ashamed and awkward, stepping back. This young creature, he decided, had a way with gentlemen. Even though there wasn't an attraction, there was a sense of caring, consoling or nurturing. The kind of consoling one wanted to give, even if it was uninvited. He could see how anyone, especially older men, could misuse these emotions and do horrible damage. "No one is getting in trouble, Chloe. Just tell me what happened."

She was biting her lip. "Mom and Dad wanted to find out more about the Bellamonts and asked me to talk to Wyatt, you know, become his friend. I told them I made my own friends but they insisted. They said they would pay me a little more than my usual allowance." She looked down, as though she'd done something wrong. "I did what they suggested and asked the questions."

"What questions?"

She shrugged. "About some book Wyatt's dad was writing. About some reviews."

"How many times did you speak to Wyatt?"

"About his dad? A few times. My parents said it had to be natural. They told me there was no harm in it. So when I found out what happened to Wyatt's dad, I freaked."

Deville thought Chloe's story fit with the events and her emotions. Being quiet and reserved meant she felt somehow responsible for what had happened. Common sense was something so elusive to so many but here was a teenage girl who understood her role—and the consequences she may or may not have caused. Being a messenger of vital information was not an easy job. Chloe Owen didn't ask for it. Somehow with her beauty and smarts, she'd accomplished her mission. The Owens had sent their daughter to do their dirty work. To collect information about the winery and Bellamont's book with Wyatt to help execute their plans. What else did they tell her to do? Wear skimpy clothes? Add a little more blush? Pretend to like the music Wyatt liked?

"What happened the night Wyatt's dad died? Were you at his place?"

"Yes, we sat and talked and that's when he told me his father was writing a book. I asked him what it was about and he said, 'Wine. What else?' We both laughed." She paused and said, "We drank some wine. I know we shouldn't have but we did. After a while I stopped and got up. He continued to drink and drink and I didn't want to anymore. He got angry because I didn't want to drink with him. I don't like the taste of wine or beer. Sometimes we just drink because of everyone else." She placed her head in her hands. "He changed. He was a different person, a mean person and I began to worry."

"About what?"

"About what he wanted. He wanted me to kiss him and I said no. He raised his voice and asked why. I just didn't want to," she cried. This time Deville patted her back.

"It's okay, Chloe. You did the right thing. He wasn't his normal self. I'm sorry you had to see that part of him." It made sense now why the Owens didn't show concern about their daughter's whereabouts the night of the murder. They'd already sent Chloe to do their deed. They knew perfectly well where she was at the time Jan Bellamont wondered what had happened to her son.

Teenage drinking was a huge problem. Deville himself had firsthand experience with underage drinking, wine to boot. Memories fluttered in his head again but he didn't have time to deal with them now. There were still a few more things to clear up with Chloe.

"Have you seen Wyatt since then?"

She shook her head. "What if he has no one? What if he needs me?"

Wyatt Bellamont was still a suspect and allowing her to go to him, or consort with him in any way, would endanger her. Wyatt could have killed his father in a drunken state, for motives he wasn't aware of yet. Besides, Wyatt seemed to be an alcoholic and needed help right away. "Don't go to him. I'll speak to him and his mother about his drinking."

For the first time that night she looked hopeful. "Please do. He isn't a close friend but I do worry about him. He's a nice guy, like I said. Just not my type." She sighed. "Besides, I don't think I'm his type."

"Please explain."

She looked reluctant and thought for a moment before answering. "Like I said, he wanted more than just being friends but I really don't think he's interested. He wanted to kiss me but it was the way he asked. Like he was testing himself. I don't really think he was interested."

Deville sighed. Wyatt Bellamont seemed confused about his sexuality. So confused he almost forced himself on Chloe to prove he was straight. He wondered how hard it must have been for Wyatt having Gerard Bellamont as a father. Bellamont didn't seem the type to approve of homosexuality and probably condemned it. Deville thought this provided a motive for Wyatt to kill his father.

He cleared his throat and asked, "Are you seeing anyone now?"

She looked at him and didn't seem to know where he was going.

"Do you have a boyfriend in your class? Someone your age?"

She turned around again and stared in the mirror.

"Chloe, I know you might be confused and you may have feelings for certain older men. These men may not be the right age for you. You may think you're in love but I'd like for you to speak to your parents about this person."

"What do you mean? Who are you talking about? I'm not seeing anyone."

She would say that, he thought. "Any special friends who might want you to keep things a secret, a special relationship perhaps?"

He obviously hit on something. Her face turned crimson and she looked on the verge of tears again. "Please leave. I don't want to talk anymore."

"Chloe, please speak to your parents. Don't make a mistake." He turned and left the room, closing the door. In the hallway, he could hear her crying. It was a slow, steady whimpering with sharp intakes of breath. Deville looked at his wristwatch and heard more thunder outside. The night was getting long and he was no closer to solving the case. In fact, he felt more challenged with these troubled teens. He didn't need more staff to help him solve a murder. He needed a psychologist to help keep them from ruining their lives. First Chloe, sent by her parents to find out information, little as it may have been, to help keep their winery from going down in ruins. How could she do anything when her emotions and hormones were on overdrive from a man who had no right being with her? An oversexed man; a predator who may or may not be taking over the winery. Was this Ryan Ferris's way of getting even with his wife for having an affair with Bellamont? Or was it the other way around? Maybe Stephanie Ferris jumped at the chance of hurting her husband because she knew what was happening.

Then there was young Wyatt Bellamont, who was looking more and more troubled. Falling into a pit of alcoholism by drowning himself with wine while his mother was in her own pit with prescribed drugs. This was no way to start your life in adulthood. Deville thought one of the hardest things about this job was trying to save the living while serving justice for the dead. Veering off course from your investigation could lead to a cold case or worse, your offender escaping because you were too busy salvaging what remained in someone's life. For Chloe Owen and Wyatt Bellamont there might not be a second chance to save their lives.

Deville had his second chance when he transferred to a medical facility in the States. He could have been left to die in France and the world would never have missed him. But an angel, or God's own mysterious design, had something different planned. Before he could think any more on the subject, he heard the front door open, letting in the wind and rain. He walked down the hall, went downstairs and saw rain boots, still wet, lying next to his shoes.

Someone had come inside. It could be either of the Owens but the boots seemed too small to belong to a man. Thunder continued and there was an ominous silence in the room. He heard a door slam and turned but saw no one. Should he continue roaming about the Owen estate, waiting for Mrs. Bumgarden to deliver her promise of tea, or just leave? Before he could decide another door opened and Kelly Owen appeared, wearing what appeared to be an Asian silk robe. Her smile was deliberate.

"Detective. There you are. Mrs. Bumgarden brought tea into the study. Care to join me?"

Deville didn't correct her this time and decided tea sounded good. As the storm continued outside, he followed her into the study with uneasiness. It wasn't because of his host—or suspect—Mrs. Owen or her daughter, Chloe. It was because of someone else. He knew those two were safe tonight. The uneasiness came from inside the pit of his stomach, a twisting dark feeling that didn't seem to go away. In his heart there was a fear of another victim. If Sydney Keller's fortune came true, another was to die tonight. It seemed silly. Sydney Keller was young and working at Allenwood Vineyards with her relatives kept her out of mystic mayhem yet Deville couldn't help but think maybe the fortunes will come true. Something didn't feel right. How was he to stop danger if he didn't know who the next victim was? How could he check on everyone this moment or call to see if they were okay? What would they think? If what he suspected was true, that there was a killer amongst them, how would the culprit act?

"Did you say something, detective?"

Deville was sitting next to a lit fireplace with tea already in hand. "No, Mrs. Owen and it's investigator, not detective."

"Oh, hogwash, whatever it is. I should just call you dick, that's the term for law enforcement, you know." She was in slippers that matched her red robe and the flicker of the fireplace made the dragons and symbols glitter. Her hair seemed frazzled but dry, as if she'd just taken off a hood.

"Where were you Mrs. Owen? Mrs. Bumgarden said you were in here writing invitations."

"I went to mail them because I didn't want to wait. They'll go out first thing in tomorrow's mail. Mrs.

Bumgarden is a little deaf and maybe a little blind. She couldn't tell you if we were having a rave in the basement. I don't know why she's still here. I hardly pay her anything. The damn woman has so much pride in what she does, so hard to find nowadays. I could do better but it's a question of loyalty."

Loyalty, Deville repeated to himself. He thought Mrs. Owen came from the "old school" line of thinking. A woman who warranted and demanded respect. He decided she also was the stronger of the two. Just like the Kellers. No one could tell these women what to do or where to go. They seemed to come from money and made all the decisions. As if she'd read his mind, she spoke about her life.

"I've married three times. The first one cheated on me, the second one died and then there was Roger Owen. I'm from the Crenshaw family. My grandfather built the plastic company. They made storage containers, food bins, and a lot of other things we use every day. He sold it to my father, who was ruthless; it's where I get my attitude. I inherited the business when he died. No sons. I was their only child. I hated running the business but I learned fast." She stared into the fireplace and took a sip from her glass. Deville noticed it was a hard drink, not tea. Her tea was still on a nearby tray. "I married young. I just needed someone to help me run the business but he was an asshole. Frederick Simpson. A playboy if I ever saw one. As soon as I heard he was embezzling money, I divorced him."

Deville took a sip of tea. Earl Grey, his favorite. He listened to Mrs. Owen and wondered where her story was going. He thought he should write something down so took out his notepad. When he heard her next few words he almost dropped everything.

"That's when I met Gerard Bellamont, the first."

"Excuse me? You knew the victim?"

"The father. He was my second husband." She watched as he scrambled for his pen and notepad. She picked up a piece of pastry and swallowed it whole, like a lion would devour a small defenseless animal in the wild. Her gaze told him she seemed to be troubled, remembering the past. "I want to tell you upfront. That's the way I am. Don't want you to find out later and harass me about it. The first Gerard Bellamont was a gentlemen. He had some knowledge of running a business. That was part of it. He also worshiped the ground I walked on. Loved me to the fullest, just like he loved his life."

Deville knew the answer but asked anyway. "He died, you said?"

She nodded and her eyes became glassy. "In a plane crash going back to France. You see I met him in France while he was still married to Gerard Junior's mother. We met at a party and had an affair. He fell head over heels. It was wrong." She looked at him. "Sometimes good things come out of bad. He left his first wife for me and we moved to the States. The divorce was a nightmare. Just as difficult to get remarried to a foreigner as it was for him to get divorced and then remarried. The first wife and son blamed me and never forgave him for what he did. Gerard still went to visit his first wife and child and it was on one of these trips that the plane was hijacked. Do you remember Flight 209? Cubans? The passengers tried to take over the flight and the pilot was shot by accident?"

Deville remembered reading the report. The coincidence of Kelly Owen knowing Gerard Bellamont was remarkable. There was no way of knowing whether she was the stepmother of Gerard since she didn't have the name Owen at this point in her story. "Gerard Bellamont, Junior, our lovely critic, stayed in France, even after his mother died. I guess he moved to

California because of the wine. It was because of my second husband we built this winery. I sold the plastic business and now this is all I have."

She stopped for a sip of tea. She took a deep breath and said, "That's why we don't mention his name. Gerard. I told Mrs. Bumgarden we couldn't mention it."

"So that is why Bellamont was eager to ruin Owen Winery?"

She closed her eyes and nodded. "Doesn't matter how good the wine is. He had it in for me from the beginning. Closing the winery would have been revenge for me and his late father."

"What about the age difference? You both have children the same age."

"I married his father at 43 and Chloe is adopted."

He'd heard this from Wyatt earlier and remembered the discussion with the young man. How young Chloe seemed like a robot. "Mrs. Owen, your daughter Chloe…"

"What has she done now?"

"She seemed to think you've asked her do some things."

Kelly Owen frowned, "What do you mean, do some things? Clean her room? She is supposed to do that!"

"No, other things. She told me she'd been assigned to ask Wyatt questions."

"Is that what she's told you?" She looked around and then leaned forward. "She is a compulsive liar. Always has been. The orphanage warned us but Roger insisted on her. I was an only child so I thought it wouldn't be so bad since I turned out all right." She looked at him as if he were ready to challenge her statement. "It's hard. I know. We told her she was adopted because others were wondering how old we were when we had her and the kids picked on her. Anyway, if lying is the worst thing she can do, that's fine by me."

He wrote in his notebook someone was definitely lying. It could be Mrs. Owen herself—for different reasons now. Maybe it wasn't information on the book or the winery she was seeking. Maybe it was about her past. Her marriage to Gerard Bellamont Senior meant new motives. As if the Owens didn't have enough. On the night in question it seemed everyone saw the Owens together at Allenwood Winery. Paul Shepard had left, along with Bellamont and Ryan and Stephanie Ferris. But the Owens seemed to have stayed put. Except when Roger went to get more wine.

Just then Mrs. Bumgarden came in with a cordless phone. It was so odd to see her with any device from the past few decades that Deville had to stop from staring. She seemed at ease and walked halfway into the room to announce it was Mr. Owen on the phone.

Mrs. Owen said, "It's Roger. He's coming home from some wine event in Buffalo. If you don't mind, I need to take this." She grabbed the phone from Mrs. Bumgarden, who didn't seem to know how to put the caller on hold; she had been covering the mouthpiece with her long boney fingers. Mrs. Owen talked to her husband and Deville left her to follow Mrs. Bumgarden into the hallway.

He said, "Thank you," as she helped him with his coat.

"Mrs. Bumgarden."

"Yes, sir?"

Deville looked around before asking, "How would you describe Chloe? Has she told tall tales? You know, exaggerate, cause minor trouble with her words?"

Mrs. Bumgarden pursed her lips and looked as though she would not say anything. Then she cleared her throat. "Chloe needs attention, just like all girls do at that age. She's told some fables but not recently. Lately she's been well behaved."

He thanked her again while putting on his shoes. She gave him his umbrella and looked at him with concern. The storm was still doing a number outside. "Be careful. It's dangerous."

"I'll drive slow and be careful."

"Oh, yes, the weather, too, but I meant there's a dangerous killer out there. Even though some people may seem evil and lie through their teeth, it doesn't mean they're guilty of murder. Sins of the guilty do not always fit the crime. It's those quiet ones or those who seem friendly you may have to worry about." She opened the door as the rain and wind came in.

Deville noticed someone above the staircase, watching them. Chloe Owen stood, hands on the banister, with intense eyes. Her face told him she'd heard everything.

CHAPTER FIFTEEN

He wished he hadn't told Jan Bellamont there would be an officer on the lookout tonight but he felt it was his duty to keep his word. If the intruder made another appearance at their cottage, he would witness it. After leaving the Owen residence he stopped at a convenience store, picked up an apple, a ready-to-go sandwich, more pain relievers and a large coffee. He was already growing tired, hoping he would be fine tonight.

An ominous fog rolled in, leaving the air with a hefty weight he could feel on his face. It was more than just dampness. The skies still bellowed with flashes of lightning. Deville couldn't imagine a worse night for a stakeout.

The last time Deville took part in a stakeout was his rookie year in Rochester, New York. He and his partner were assigned to keep an eye on an older gentleman. This gentleman, by the name of Maxwell Starks, had been known for money laundering in the past but was trying to keep his nose clean. After many years on the wrong side of the law he opened a legitimate business when his family was threatened. It was a low profile shoe repair shop. He helped the police by offering the names of a few more wise guys in exchange for his safety. Deville could remember the actual stakeout location. It was an old brownstone on Park Avenue, one of the better neighborhoods. His partner, an officer who smelled peculiar and needed to wash behind his ears, kept busy by telling stories of how old neighborhoods were becoming less safe.

Deville remembered sitting in the unmarked car watching the brownstone, waiting for anything to happen. After three nights of boredom, the stakeout was called off. Sure enough, on the fourth night Maxwell Starks was gunned down in front of that brownstone, groceries in hand. Deville was called to the scene of the homicide to investigate. He thought how ironic and tragic the circumstances were.

After three years he became a state officer. He requested a transfer when he heard of an opening in the Finger Lakes region, knowing the scenic beauty, low crime rate and fresh air would do him good. Besides, his psychologists told him his mind couldn't take inner city violence much longer. The episodes in his past, which still remained a mystery, had caused him to abuse alcohol, go into a coma and trigger amnesia. The doctors suggested his position should be reconsidered: maybe switch to light desk work or a call operator. They even suggested he seek employment somewhere else and leave law enforcement entirely.

Choosing to be a policeman was easy for him, following in his foster father's footsteps. He had been a retired soldier, a decorated war veteran with ruddy skin, serious deep eyes and a mouth that always seemed to frown. There wasn't much laughter in Deville's teenage years. Growing up in a serious household with a quiet and reserved elderly couple made him who he was today. Because of his upbringing, he didn't have many friends and was unsure of himself with women. His past hurt the situation. He often dreamed of a time where he could have guests in the house, maybe a small party, but found no one as intellectual as himself. He needed to liven up the house and his life but fear turned to reluctance. It seemed nothing would ever change. The house left to him was hidden from the main road, surrounded by weeping willows. Deville didn't use three-quarters of the old Victorian, keeping to himself in his bedroom. His window gave him a view of a copse of woods that surrounded the side of the house. When there was a new moon the top of the woods looked more like a sea of green, tempting enough for a swim. The bedroom was the first room he'd ever had to himself. Night after night, with some exceptions of a few semesters of college, he stayed in this room, closing out the world and all the uncertainties it held.

He arrived at Allenwood just after nine o' clock. He pulled into the driveway, past the tasting room and followed the path to Bellamont's cottage, which loomed in the distance like a beacon in the dark. The inauspicious grapevines on his right looked like twisted limbs of tortured souls. If it weren't for his headlights and the light of the moon, he wouldn't be able to see the driveway. The rain turned into a slow, steady patter. After finding a suitable spot, about 30 yards from the cottage, he turned off the ignition. There were two lights on in the cottage; a lamp in the living room and one on the second floor, which would be Wyatt's room. The front door was closed and other than the rainfall, there was complete silence.

Deville surveyed his surrounding and waited 45 minutes before he went to work. He took out his recorder and viewed all the videos he had taken of the case from the beginning. Watching the videos took all of 20 minutes. Then he looked at his notes. He glanced back at the cottage periodically. After an hour he ate the sandwich and apple, taking sips of the coffee for the caffeine.

There was nothing he could do at the moment, which was almost a relief. No calls to make. No one else to interview. Just him and the cottage. He thought about Jan Bellamont. Why was she so troubled and who was threatening her and why? She was just a widow who depended on her husband for financial support, put up with his adultery and did her best to mother a troubled child. With all the traveling the Bellamonts did, how could anyone make a proper home for a family? Was it even possible? Be part of the community, donate your time, be social? Deville remembered she had baked cookies for the arts council and wondered what else she did for the community.

His eyes felt like weighted windows and the notes were blurring his vision. He couldn't stop yawning. He put away his notes and continued staring at the cottage while telling himself this wasn't an official stakeout. Moments later, when the yawning stopped, his eyelids closed and he fell asleep while listening to the melodic rhythm of rainfall on the hood of the car. It sounded like a sweet ballad of soft percussions.

He awoke to the screams. He opened his eyes and saw the cottage with more lights on than before. He jumped out of the car and ran to the cottage. As he got closer, he noticed Wyatt's bike at the foot of the entrance, blocking the open doorway. He heard the scream again, recognizing Jan Bellamont's frightened cries. He moved the bicycle out of the way, entered the building and called out for Jan. Her voice could be heard from her room. He climbed the stairs two at a time, reaching her room to see her sitting in the corner. She held a lamp toward him, aiming the light from the lit bulb.

"Who is it?" she asked with a shaky voice.

"It's Investigator Deville." The light from the shadeless lamp was bright. He came a bit closer. Now she was sobbing. "It's okay. I've been outside. Are you all right?"

She lowered the lamp she was holding and he could see the fear on her face. A moment later she ran into his arms. He told her to calm down and explain what happened.

"Someone was at the doorway of my room. I just saw a shadow. At first I thought it was Gerard." She clawed Deville's clothes, as if to prove he was real, and looked into his eyes. "I thought it was his ghost! I couldn't move or find my voice."

"Were you asleep?"

"I don't think so."

"Could it have been a dream Mrs. Bellamont? You're under a lot of stress. Sometimes it can transfer in your dreams."

She sighed. "No, no. It was real, I tell you. As real as you standing there."

Deville heard a sudden noise in the distance—a shattering sound of glass. He listened further, wondering if the intruder was still inside. She gave out another scream and a few moments later they heard footsteps.

Wyatt appeared in the doorway, dressed in sweats, wearing his usual headphones, loud music blaring. "What happened?"

Jan Bellamont jumped and after noticing it was Wyatt, went to him. She put her arms around him. "Oh my God. You're safe."

"Why wouldn't I be?"

Deville noticed Wyatt looked damp. "It appears your mother thought she saw someone."

Mrs. Bellamont looked at him. "Appeared?"

"Yes. Can you confidently say it was a person?"

She nodded. "Yes. It was a figure. He ran away after I

screamed!" Her hands shook. "It was the most terrifying thing I've ever seen. He could have killed me or Wyatt, right here."

It was Wyatt who sat her down on her bed. "Were you sleeping?" her son asked.

She nodded. "Yes, before. But I heard a noise and woke up seeing him at my door. I thought it was your father at first then I remembered he was dead. Then I thought it was his ghost. But if it were his ghost, why did I fear it so?" She gave her son a look of bewilderment. "How could you sleep through my screaming?"

"I was downstairs. I noticed the front door was open and my bike was out."

Deville went to the doorway and searched around. There was no carpet in this section of the house so there were no visible footprints. He walked into the hallway, noticed the door to Wyatt's room ajar then walked down the stairs. After doing a quick search he called for backup. "Don't touch anything," he yelled out to them from the bottom of the stairs. He went outside, noticing the rain still falling. There were also trees down. Strong winds must have done some damage while he was sleeping. He walked back to his car, wondering about what had just happened. He'd call for a crime scene unit, just to appease Mrs. Bellamont, but in the back of his mind he thought it would be a waste of time. There was no telling what prescriptions she was currently taking. He believed the whole intruder thing was just a ruse for attention. She was just like some of the cases he'd read about—a woman who achieved fame when in distress. Being a grieving widow wasn't enough. Now she stayed in the limelight by producing phantom intruders.

He changed his tune when he reached his car, where a sense of dread and fear invoked him. He'd let Mrs. Bellamont have her time. Her imaginary intruder might very well be real. Judging by the smashed windshield of his car, which had happened while he was inside, her intruder didn't like being watched.

CHAPTER SIXTEEN

The crime scene officers arrived in record time. Before being questioned, a medic checked Jan Bellamont and her son. The officers dusted the cottage and Deville's car for prints. The rain had turned into a drizzle and the tireless team worked hastily to escape the weather. Deville was anxious and asked Jan Bellamont if it was okay to use her kitchen. He brewed coffee and waited there, where he could still smell the faint aroma of cookies. He knew Jessica Malone would speak to him soon and possibly reprimand him somehow for partaking in a stakeout without her permission.

While waiting, he thought about the intruder. The possible suspects were many. It was unfortunate Jan Bellamont couldn't make out which sex the intruder was. Maybe Jessica would get more information from Mrs. Bellamont than he did about the intruder; even a specific height would help. There *was* someone here. He was ashamed for doubting Mrs. Bellamont at first. There was no way she could have vandalized his car. She was in her room. Who scared the Bellamonts? Mrs. Bellamont's frightened reaction to the intruder made him believe her terror. He still remembered her shaking with fear in her eyes. He couldn't imagine waking up to a ghostly figure standing in the doorway. It was something that could cause nightmares for months, even years.

Malone entered the kitchen. He stood and pulled a chair out for her, handing her a cup of coffee. She looked at the chair then back at him. "Being polite will not help me forget what you did."

"Jess, I'm sorry."

"Don't ever do a stupid thing like that again. Did you think I wouldn't find out about a stakeout?"

He bowed his head and pushed the chair further.

She sighed. "Always a gentleman, aren't you?" She grabbed the cup offered to her. "Do you ever stop being polite?"

"No. It's part of who I am."

She leaned to look at him. "You look horrible."

"And you look like you've been interrupted from a wonderful slumber."

"I almost thought about coming here in my pajamas and a trench coat."

"I don't think anyone would have noticed."

She took a sip of her coffee. "Thanks for the coffee. This case is getting on my nerves."

"You haven't said that in a while."

She smiled. Her hair was pulled back to show a pale face without makeup, somber and tired. The lines around her eyes made her look hard but the rest of her expressed a softness few had ever seen. It was difficult ending the relationship with her. She still cared and so did he.

"You screwed up. Did you think it was okay to make your decisions without consulting me?"

"I'm sorry. It was a sudden thing."

"Sudden or not, you can just call. What do I have to do for you to follow the rules? I can't authorize overtime without you telling me."

"It was my own time. She was frightened."

"All you had to do was call. I know you don't want to call me..." she stopped and looked away.

There it was again. The past always came up. Whether they liked it or not, it still interfered with their police work. The reason he didn't call was because of their illicit past. Part of him wanted to break all ties, anything that still kept them connected. Leaving the station was an obvious choice but he enjoyed working there so he did everything else to maintain his position, including avoiding contact with her after hours.

"This has nothing to do with you or me," he said. "Mrs. Bellamont was frightened. I just wanted her to feel safe."

She tried to keep her composure. "How is your car?"

"I'll try to salvage it."

She shook her head. "It's evidence now and it's not safe. Drive a rental. I'll authorize that. We'll have it returned soon."

He sat with his head down, elbows on his knees. "I'm sorry, Jess. You're right."

She took another sip. "Well, I guess something positive came out of this." He looked up. "You finally admitted I was right about something."

He cracked a smile.

"There. I don't remember the last time you smiled. You're so melancholy. With good reason but it's time to put it all behind you. Remember, I was a psychologist and laughter is great for your body your mind."

"There's not much to laugh about," he replied.

"A smile is a good beginning."

He took a deep breath. "How can I put everything behind me? It's coming back." He noticed she leaned back, a sign the doctor side of her was showing. He swallowed, nervous because he was eager for any help. "The images," he continued, "a vineyard. I think I'm coming closer to what happened to my father. It could help me find out the truth."

"You're having a breakthrough, Louis. Soon you'll get to close that part of your life and you can move on." She took his hand. "These images or dreams. They just occur when you sleep?"

"Yes. No daydreams yet," he said, lying. "Just when I sleep." He feared she would take him off the case if he said yes. Walking along the vineyards and being around the wine stirred things up. Smells, images, sometimes even noises were triggering his memory. Enough about me, he thought, while taking his hand away. "So what do you think happened here?"

"I was about to ask you."

He spoke softly, remembering Jan Bellamont's state. "She was scared. If I hadn't arrived, if I wasn't outside watching, I don't know what would have happened." He paused and wondered if Jan Bellamont had a bad heart. If she did, this could have been a murder attempt. Scaring someone to death happened more often than people think. "I'll take inventory of all her medication. If she has a bad heart, this could have killed her."

"What about her son? Where was he when this happened?"

He stood up. "In the next room, with these." He produced Wyatt's headphones and an MP3 player. He pressed a button that displayed the artist he had been listening to. Ironically, it was The Killers. He turned it on, raised up the volume and said, "Let me know if you can hear anything I say, okay?" She nodded and continued to take part in his experiment. After placing the headphones on her, making her grimace, he went in the other room. He shouted her name, causing other officers in the next room to turn and stare. Then he recited a line from a nursery rhyme, "The cow jumped over the moon!" He passed the crime scene officers, who may have thought he had lost it, and went back to the kitchen, where Malone was sitting, swinging her crossed legs, as if she was enjoying the rhythm. She was oblivious to what had just happened.

She noticed him and almost yelled herself. "Did you start? Why don't you say something?"

He pulled her headphones off. "Maybe Wyatt didn't hear his mother screaming. I just yelled at you from the next room."

She looked disappointed. "I don't know what that proves."

"It proves he could be telling the truth. He may not have heard his mother."

"Or he could have done this himself?"

Deville nodded. "I think it's time we question him. Care to join me?"

"Let me grab another cup of coffee and you grab him."

Moments later, a very nervous Wyatt sat in a chair. Deville could tell Wyatt didn't sit in the kitchen often. He guessed the young man didn't have many dinners with his family. It was sad most teenagers didn't. He offered Wyatt a glass of water and asked how he was doing.

Wyatt stared out at nothingness. "How would you be if someone broke in your place? It's not even our place. We're just here until you guys find out what happened to my father. Then we can finally leave. I can't wait."

It was Malone who replied. "I would be angry. Furious." When Wyatt didn't respond, she continued. "Wyatt, I know it must be difficult to speak about this, especially after what happened to your father, but we need to ask a few things. Do you know who could have done this?"

He blinked a few times, the only movement in his blank face. "I've been thinking about that. I don't know anyone who would do this."

Malone looked at Deville and he could tell what her next question was. He shook his head as a sign suggesting: Don't ask him if he did it. She nodded and then asked, "I know you told Investigator Deville you didn't hear or see anything. I am asking you again because maybe you didn't remember then. Do you remember anything that happened? Did you see any shadows under your door? Maybe you heard someone downstairs and you thought it was your mom?"

Wyatt's slump figure made him one with the chair and it looked as if he'd slip off any moment. "I didn't hear nothing," he said. "Earlier my Mom was messing around here, in the kitchen. Asked me if I wanted cocoa. I said no."

"And when did you hear your mother? When she was screaming?"

He nodded. "I wasn't listening to my player then, I was—doing other stuff."

Deville wondered what other stuff kept Wyatt this busy. He pulled up a chair to sit eye to eye, although it was an effort to see where the young man's gaze was going. "Wyatt, I had a great time on the boat with you. You were remarkable guiding us home." Deville caught a glimpse of Wyatt's eyes.

Wyatt brushed his hair away from his face and pulled himself up. He gave Deville a shy glance. "Thanks. You were funny."

Deville spotted Malone looking perplexed. He gave her a reassuring look and turned his attention back to Wyatt. "Wyatt, you knew I was outside watching didn't you?" Wyatt turned away and said nothing. Deville continued. "When I arrived, your bike wasn't here. When I heard your mother screaming, I rushed in and practically had to jump over it. Did you know it was in the front doorway? Did you leave it there?"

He turned to face Deville. "Of course not. Why would I do something like that?"

"Well, where were you? You weren't here when I arrived."

After a pause Wyatt replied. "With Paul and Sydney."

Deville took a deep breath. "You hang with them often?"

A soft shrug of the shoulders. "Yeah, so what?"

"Tell me about them. I noticed you were at Catalina Winery when I first visited there. What do you do there?"

"Help Paul with moving stuff. Cases of wine, his wife's paintings. We hang out. Sydney comes along too."

Deville waited a moment before saying, "She tags along, does she? Uninvited?"

Wyatt sighed. "Paul invites her. She's okay, I guess. She's nice to me. I know she isn't interested in me, she's into Paul. Sometimes I feel like I'm tagging along. But it's different. They respect me. They don't treat me like a child."

"So what happened tonight?"

"Paul and Sydney dropped me off. I told them I wanted to go with them, wherever they were going, but they didn't want me." He frowned and gave a short grunt. "I don't understand. I've been with them all afternoon and then they ditch me. I know. They need some time alone, I guess. I'm not an idiot. I just wish I could be with them. All the time." His gaze trailed along to the other room, where his mother sat on the couch surrounded by other officers. "My mom's not herself. I just want a normal family. They keep moving me around, like I was some pet, and I never have any say. I'm expected to just agree with everything."

Deville thought for a moment about what he'd heard. Wyatt actually made sense with almost everything he said. However, there were some things he was definitely hiding. Sense of normalcy could very well be what he was craving but companionship and intimacy might be something he got. He wondered how deep Wyatt was involved with Paul Shepard and Sydney Keller. How much did he know about the other two? Wyatt would definitely protect them, especially Shepard, where there were other possible interests.

Wyatt gave a long yawn, which made Deville want to do the same. He told him to go to bed. When the young man left, Deville asked Malone, "Care to give me a quick analysis?"

She placed the cups in the sink. "I think there's a lot of things happening with him. Abandonment issues, lack of love. He doesn't know who he is. The normalcy he's craving is common with kids. Some people think kids rebel and want to live their own life but most of them desire a close-knit family. In this case it's to stay in one location." She motioned for him to get up. "I think he knows more than he's telling."

CHAPTER SEVENTEEN

Jan Bellamont entered the kitchen as if she was greeting adoring fans. Her robe covered her rigid body with a tight fit and a mess of frazzled hair topped a worried face. She declined coffee and asked for tea. After a few awkward moments Sergeant Malone went about looking for the tea kettle.

"It's in the cupboard below the sink," Mrs. Bellamont said. "I don't drink tea often but I can't fathom coffee at this hour. Not after what I've been through." She looked around the kitchen as if seeing it for the first time. "I wonder if he's been here. Looking in the fridge, handling our food?" She caught her breath.

Sergeant Malone found green tea and prepared a cup while Deville flipped over a sheet in his pad. "Mrs. Bellamont," he said, "you can't worry about where the intruder has or hasn't been. It's not productive and you need to relax. Any more strain can be devastating."

She nodded. "I need to stay focused. We need to get things in order." The order of which she spoke was more than just a widow preparing for a funeral. The body hasn't been released, calling hours unknown and Deville didn't know if family members had been notified. Mrs. Bellamont's life was much like that of her late husband's —in limbo. As if the murder wasn't enough there was now an intruder to haunt her dreams. She would always live in fear, Deville thought to himself. That is, if she wasn't involved in the crime. He asked what she remembered of this evening and little had changed since when he found her. She still couldn't make out who the trespasser was. The dark figure would always be a faceless intruder, standing by the doorway.

"Did you notice if Wyatt was home or had he gone out?" Deville asked.

Mrs. Bellamont looked confused. "I think he goes out often. Most boys do. They take advantage of the weather before it gets colder. I asked him earlier if he wanted some cocoa when he was home."

"Did you spend most of the evening in your room?"

She nodded. "I was making phone calls and suddenly got exhausted. Must be the pills. I could barely keep my eyes open." She took a sip of tea. "What do you think he wanted? Is it drugs? My pills?"

"It could be something of your late husband's. A file, manuscript. Can you think of anything?" She shook her head. Deville continued. "We have your husband's laptop. Maybe the intruder was looking for it."

Mrs. Bellamont frowned. "What would he do with it? And why would he come into my room?"

"Are you sure it was a he?" Sergeant Malone asked.

"Why would a woman do this?" She looked around and then said in a low voice, "My husband flirted like it was second nature. I'm sure women threw themselves at him." She paused and stared into her cup. "I'll never know what happened with whom. But if something happened, would a woman come back here to threaten me?" She took a deep breath. "It makes me remember something that happened a long time ago. It was over ten years and I can't help but think of it now. A woman came to our home in France. She asked if my husband lived there. I thought nothing of it at the time. People were always calling him or visiting. Once I answered the door and saw her smiling. She gave a brief nod and then left. I can still remember her deep red lipstick. She was so pale and her lips seemed to pop. She left and I thought I'd never see her again."

"What happened?" Deville asked.

"That night I asked my husband. He claimed he didn't know her. So I went about my business and tried to forget her. A week later I was going through my vanity and noticed something peculiar. I found a single sheet of tissue with a lip print. As if someone blotted their lips. It was the same God awful shade!" She gave a short cry. "It was horrible. I felt violated just like I do now."

"Did you confront your husband with the evidence? Did you call the police?"

"Gerard told me to calm down. I didn't call the police. He told me I had imagined it. Blamed it on the pills I was taking. Wyatt was a baby then and I had started taking medicine for depression."

"Mrs. Bellamont, I'm sorry this is making you remember things in your past. I have to ask about the lipstick. It's not a shade you wore?" Malone asked.

"People always assume I imagine things. Like I have nothing else to do but come up with stories of intruders and threatening situations. I didn't imagine the lipstick. It was there. It wasn't mine because I didn't wear lipstick. Still don't. I didn't imagine an intruder tonight and I certainly didn't imagine my husband's murder." She stood and everyone else did, too.

"Again, I'm sorry Mrs. Bellamont. You've been through so much," Malone said. "If there's anything we can do."

"Yes, I've been through a damn lot." She rolled her eyes and turned to Deville. "Please, you listened to me. You were here. Find out who killed Gerard." She turned to Malone. "Since your lead investigator will be so busy investigating you can follow up with me. I expect to hear from you several times a day with any information about my husband's death. That's what you can do for me, sergeant."

Malone nodded and exited the room in a despondent manner. She encountered officers along the way, requesting one to stay in the cottage. As Deville watched, he felt sorry for her. Murder has stirred a multitude of emotions, disrupted many schedules and has transformed many lives. Jessica Malone wasn't ready for this and the truth was clear. Though she was doing her best and trying to stay strong, she was struggling. Hopefully, it would not reflect on the other officers, especially those few who looked up to her. The case was now top priority for the station and they may need help from another city.

Mrs. Bellamont walked with Deville into the living room, where a few officers were dusting for prints. "I'm sorry if I offended your superior. I'm just not myself lately."

"It's quite all right. We can arrange something if you don't want to stay here."

"Thank you but we will be all right. Sydney Keller invited us over for the night." She looked over to where Wyatt was sitting on the floor in the corner of the room. "Wyatt is smitten with her, I imagine, and she's been kind to us." She left Deville to go to her son. After a moment, Wyatt stood and they embraced.

"Sometimes a crisis will bring a family together," Malone said, appearing next to him. "I hope it brings them closer."

"One can hope," Deville replied.

They walked out of the cottage together, Deville feeling restless and uneasy. The rain continued, creating puddles and mud. Neither were dressed appropriately so they quickened their steps. Deville knew any prints outside may be washed away by the storm.

"I don't think we've heard the last of this intruder," he said.

"Who do you think it is?"

He raised his voice so she could hear over the storm. "Ryan Ferris comes to mind."

"Would he be doing this for Owen Winery?"

"Perhaps or maybe because of his amorous wife. It's difficult to see through him. He has an obligation to the Owen family, his wife, who was friendly with the victim, and then there's his own passion." He thought about Ryan Ferris and Chloe Owen. "One can imagine what's going on in his head." They made it to her car. Both were soaked and shivered from the cold and dampness.

"Why don't you ask him on your next sailing adventure?"

He smiled. "I never sailed on a lake before." He summed up his adventure with Sydney Keller and Paul Shepard. "Seeing them together was enlightening. They treat Wyatt like he's a grown up. That's golden when you're Wyatt's age."

"Thanks again for the ride." He got in and fastened his seatbelt. As they backed out of the driveway, the cottage didn't look like a crime scene. Besides a few squad cars and his vandalized vehicle, it looked like they were leaving a party in the rain. "I fell asleep, Jess," he said, as they passed Allenwood Vineyards. "Whoever came in the cottage—I missed the opportunity. I tried not to fall asleep but I was so tired."

"The case is draining you, physically and emotionally. Be glad the intruder didn't try anything with you." She shook her head. "You were a sitting duck."

He thought about what she'd said. A sitting duck, floating on a pond with tall grasses, frogs and other creatures. A hunter was watching him—a hunter who had a chance to kill him while he was sleeping. He was incredibly lucky that nothing happened to him.

How unfortunate it was they passed Owen Winery and didn't know what was about to happen in the next few minutes.

CHAPTER EIGHTEEN

Deville had expected another night alone. A sense of despair, loneliness and familiarity were his usual company but when they pulled up to his driveway he invited Malone in. Her pale face and furrowed brow told him how troubled she was and she could use the company. After tonight's menacing events, he was far from tired himself. She stood by the doorway before entering "Are you going to invite me in or am I going to catch cold in the doorway?" He ushered her in, apologizing. It was so long since he had a visitor in his home he felt lost and out of sorts. He wasn't sure if it was because he hadn't had a visitor or because of the visitor herself. Now she was apologizing. "Sorry for letting in the wet. Somehow I seem more soaked than you," she said, taking off her coat, showing what looked like a flannel shirt and jeans. He knew she had a habit of wearing her son's clothes when she went out in the middle of the night to satisfy her ice cream urges or for an emergency. He imagined when she heard about the intruder and the possibility of Deville in danger made her rush over in a feverish haste. She seemed protective with those she cared about. These were some of the many attributes he admired. "Cozy place you have here," she said, ringing her hair. "It's kind of gothic. Thanks for inviting me in."

Their past interludes, brief as they were, involved her place. He never offered his place and she never pushed, claiming to understand and respect his decision. "Do you use the entire house?"

"No. Why? I expect you'd want a tour?"

"Not if you don't want to."

"I...don't know." He felt lost for words. "I don't want to...I mean." He looked around. "It's beautiful but I don't use most of it, just my room, the kitchen and the library." He watched her walk in the foyer in wonderment. "I can certainly show you around some areas," he continued.

She turned to look at him. "What do you want, Louis?"

"It's just a house. I'm offering a tour."

She came to him. "Again, what do you want?"

He let her come close. "I don't know why I asked you inside. You seemed troubled after tonight and Jan Bellamont made you uncomfortable."

"Is that why you invited me in?"

"I don't know. I knew you would try to comfort me if that happened, I guess."

"And how do you expect to comfort me?"

He took her into his arms and they kissed. The rain had left her body wet and soggy and made her shirt and pants cling to her body, accentuating her figure. He felt her shivering. He wasn't sure if she was shaking because of him or the rain. He felt on edge because he couldn't forget she was his superior and their history made their embrace uptight; an awkward act. This led to bitter thoughts and memories. He couldn't stop holding her. When she held him, he felt a temporary moment of peace.

Hours later, in his bed, they slept. It was an awkward

encounter having her here but tonight's choices were made with empathy and a little soul searching. He felt they both needed to talk. Neither could wrestle the right words so he turned to the physical side of communicating and she accepted. He couldn't forget her body. It felt nice to touch it again and make someone feel something again.

Lovemaking was something he could use a course on, or at least more practice, but when you're a conflicted detective with a tarnished past the opportunities were slim. Passion was not a standalone ingredient. There was too much emotion attached to lovemaking and developing a relationship was something he couldn't quite get used to. Not when there was so much tragedy in his past he couldn't share. He felt attached to Malone, even though their relationship was confusing. The feelings were still there but they were always in a state of disorder.

While lying in bed he thought about what she meant to him and wondered if he could separate intimacy from love. He decided he couldn't. So much for being a player, he thought. She sat up and looked divine. She moved closer and above him, covering her nakedness with a sheet. He held her face in his hands. She was beautifully aged and showed a soft, vulnerable side when she was fully exposed. Part of him wanted to tell her they belonged together, part of him wanted to show her the door.

"What are you thinking?" she asked.

He thought for a moment. "The case," he said, lying.

She climbed out of bed, rolling her eyes. Nothing could hide the disappointment in the air.

"Sorry. This is the part when I offer you a drink but I haven't a drop in the house."

She started buttoning her shirt. "Funny, Louis. It's a good thing you don't." She sighed. "I wish we could talk

about what you're really feeling and not lie to my face."
She looked up. "You can't hide forever."

He crossed his arms behind his head and stared at the
ceiling. "What happens now? Am I just a booty call?"

"I could ask you the same question." She sat on the
edge and continued dressing. "My socks are wet. May I
borrow some?" He told her which drawer to find his.
"Please," she continued, "I'd like to think you know me
better. Why invite me in? Don't you think I can handle a
demanding suspect such as Mrs. Bellamont? My feelings
don't get hurt so easily. I wouldn't have been promoted
to sergeant if they did."

"I'm not sure why I invited you here tonight," Deville
admitted.

His reply triggered something in her. "Sorry to disrupt
your evening. What plans did you have? Wallowing?"
She grabbed her shoes and headed for the door. "You're
impossible!"

He jumped out of bed and ran to her, blocking the
door. "Calm down, please. You just insulted me with a
reminder of my lack of a social life. I don't think we need
to get more upset than we already are."

She glanced at the bed and back to him, "I see. You
have a funny way of showing how upset you are." She
closed her eyes and took a deep breath. "I wanted to
come home with you. I miss you."

"We both know this is no good. For either of us," he
said. "I'm sorry. I know I seemed all over the place. I
didn't want to be alone either but I don't think ending
up in bed was something I wanted or planned."

She sighed. "I shouldn't have taken advantage of the
circumstance. You're going through a lot. This case, that
intruder. I understand how your feelings are all over the
place. I should have known better." She tried to get him
to move out of the way. He refused. "Louis, I don't want
to have a friend with benefits thing. I'm too old for that

and I don't deserve it. I need something more."

"It's not a good idea, considering we work together. Plus, you're my superior."

"Enough of that crock. I don't care if I'm your superior. I like you. I care about you."

"Do you love me?" he asked suddenly, surprised to hear himself utter the words.

She looked bewildered. "My, aren't we mushy? Get out of my way."

He let her go and watched her leave. "Where do we go from here?" he called out. He could hear the shuffling of her large feet descending the staircase.

"See you in the morning," she yelled out to him. "We'll see what develops."

CHAPTER NINETEEN

The Finger Lakes were not known to be kind with their storms. Occasionally, dangerous storms came, maybe even a twister, taking their toll on lakefront homes, condos, sometimes entire communities. The news of the storm and the thousands of dollars of damage it had caused filled the airways. Some schools closed due to floods, roads had to be cleared and there was debris everywhere. On average, storms didn't make the news much but when the wind blew most of the leaves away it caused quite a sensation. Citizens and tourists were now faced with empty trees, stricken and winter-ready, as though someone erased the leaves by hand. If that wasn't enough, the storm did a lot of damage to the vineyards— grapes and trellis wires scattered about, requiring a backup of workers to organize and assess the damage. This left tourists with no leaves to peep at and winemakers with little to harvest for their famous ice wines. Deville couldn't bear to think of the calamitous state Allenwood Vineyard was in. Poor Frank Keller. He couldn't take care of the vines when the weather was fair and manageable.

With the topic of the storm, plus the foreboding vision on everyone's mind of what it would do to the tourist industry, no one seemed to care about other news. One piece of news, which deserved much more attention than it did, was the discovery of a body at Owen Winery. Someone reported an unidentified body trampled by animals. The word "murder" was never mentioned but a body found in the office of a winery, apparently killed by wildlife, didn't seem to deserve as much media attention as the fallen leaves of autumn.

Deville got the call in the morning. When a car arrived to pick him up, he rushed to Owen Winery to arrive by nine. There were a few police cruisers in the parking lot, along with an ambulance and a few people curious to know what was going on. He met the medical examiner on the scene and asked questions. Ryan Ferris had been strangled the same way as Gerard Bellamont. The body was discovered in the office where Deville had last seen him. The victim sat in a chair, behind a desk, with blood everywhere. The wire used had cut through the skin of his throat, causing massive blood loss. The wide-open front doors beckoned animals to venture inside. The police reported to the media that animals were a part of the investigation. The full details were not known.

Animals had tampered with the crime scene. Bloodied paw prints stained the floor while other smaller prints, possibly squirrels, left their mark on the desk. Food was left out on a table; an open pizza box but no pizza. Several wine bottles were open but only one wine glass. Deville looked at the bottles. Owen Winery, Allenwood and Catalina. Those three together again, like a horrible sequel to the first death, representing pieces of a puzzle. The wire used to kill Ryan Ferris was gone. Sometimes, with thin wire, the killer bleeds from their own hands while strangling the victim, unless the perpetrator wore gloves. Somewhere in this bloodbath, there may be a different blood than the victim's. Deville doubted it.

There wasn't any other blood on the first victim, just Gerard Bellamont's.

Ryan Ferris's head lay on the desk. The wound was already hours old, thick and wider than a thin wire, but wounds expanded.

"So you're not sure it was a trellis wire?" No. Not completely sure. It looked like something like that, or similar, the medical examiner reported. Deville wondered how Ryan Ferris could let someone strangle him, given his strength, youth and agility. It couldn't have been a surprise attack. He was sitting at the desk. Ryan Ferris may have known his assailant not to have fought back, he could have been asleep or out cold. Judging by the opened wine bottles any of those scenarios fit. If he were out cold, the killer could have come around, trellis wire in hand, and strangled him. But Ryan must have woken up, maybe moved around, causing the skin to tear, blood vessels to rip, resulting in a nasty wet mess. He still wore the same clothes he'd been working in the day prior. He'd never gone home.

Deville dreaded finding out the time of the murder, knowing he'd been in close proximity watching Jan Bellamont's cottage. The break-in last night, the damage to his car and this murder could have happened around the same time. Whoever did all this was busy last night.

Photographers were taking pictures. Deville took out his video recorder while feeling an overwhelming sadness. Not just for the victim but for the situation itself. Again he wondered how he could have prevented this murder. Ryan Ferris had problems but could have been rehabilitated for any offenses he may or may not have committed with a minor—Chloe Owen.

He could picture Roger Owen coming in, talking about business then bringing up the subject of his daughter. Or maybe Ryan himself brought it up, saying he loved her and couldn't live without her—and Roger agreed that yes, Ryan couldn't live, period.

"Who found the body?" Deville asked the first officer on the scene.

"Stephanie Ferris, the victim's wife," he replied "She noticed he hadn't come home last night."

Deville asked to speak to her and found her in the back, almost exactly where he'd seen Stephanie Ferris the first time he'd met her. She was sitting on a stack of boxes, smoking. Her hair was pulled back and her eyes were red. She wore jeans, a sweatshirt and sneakers. No more black dress, makeup or high heels. He thought she still looked beautiful, even at her worst. She saw him come closer. Her lips trembled as she held back more tears. Deville never knew what to say to the grieving so he just stood there, hands folded, and waited.

"He never came home," she said, her voice shaky. "I waited as long as I could but he never came home. We have separate cars."

"Why didn't he leave work last night?"

"We argued and I left him here. Late afternoon."

"What did you argue about?"

She looked up. "Gerard. He knew about the affair because I came clean. I told him I was sorry." She paused and continued smoking.

"Did you say anything else? Or maybe he revealed something to you?"

"Just what do you know?" she asked in a low tone. "What did Ryan tell you?"

"I'm asking you that same question now," he said, knowing he had to be forceful to get the facts. "No more messing around or waiting for me to find out things. If your husband said something, if he confessed something, now is the time to tell me."

She didn't say anything but her face did. Offensive things Deville would consider rude and impolite.

"Listen," he said. "I will find out what happened to

your husband. It's my job but there can't be any more secrets." Deville thought this case had a bunch of secrets and they seem to compete with each other for a yet unjustified cause. Whether it's money, love or a little revenge, there were always secrets. If Stephanie Ferris had nothing to hide—and if she was innocent of both murders—then her walls had to break down. "I am asking you again. Then I will take you to the station. You need to go there anyway for a report."

She sat there silent, staring across the room, through a door where her husband's body lay, ravaged and left exposed to animals. And now by a different breed of animals: crime scene officers.

Back at the station, Stephanie Ferris sat alone in the interrogation room with a steaming cup of generic brand coffee that never made anyone smile. In the next room, Jessica Malone stood, pacing and biting her nails. Deville was with her going over his notes. They both could see Stephanie Ferris through a two-way mirror.

"I think she's ready," he said in a low voice. "Stop chewing on your nails," he told Malone but didn't take his eyes off Mrs. Ferris.

"You always hated when I did that," Malone said. "How can you just stand there? So cool and calm? The other sergeants, the city officials, and the press will be all over this. The Finger Lakes region is known to be safe. Now we have two murders within days of each other."

"We're lucky they're related," he said. "We don't want people to think this kind of stuff just happens at random."

"You think this is funny?" She went to him and placed a hand on his shoulder. "Louis, I don't know what to do. I'm glad you're cool about it but I have to think of the consequences."

"I didn't say I was cool about it and I don't think it's

funny either. She may be our killer. If not, then we have a bigger problem." He turned his head to catch a glimpse of her hand. "I can't think about what other officers or officials will say or do. I've got to stay focused." He moved her hand away. "I need you to stay focused, too."

It was tough for her, he knew, but this was no time to be messing with their emotions. What happened last night should stay in the past. However, he knew Jessica Malone dealt with stress and pressure in a different way. She reached out—wanting to talk or embrace—whereas he became introverted and lost in his world of notes, clues and theories. He couldn't talk about it with friends over a beer. He needed to get lost in the paperwork at home or his desk, going over countless play-by-play scenes. Finding different angles helped him crack the surface of a case. He walked to the door. "Take care of this, all the politics, and I'll find out the truth."

A moment later, he sat with Stephanie Ferris, his list of questions ready. He knew she would do her best to lie if it meant saving her own skin. Having given her time alone to think may have been a bad move, but her state of shock at Owen Winery would not lead to any productive questioning. Having her sit where she found her husband's dead body was too close for comfort. Bringing her back to the station didn't guarantee her cooperation but at least she could answer questions more freely. This kept her away from the job site, her dead husband and the part of her that kept secrets. He turned on a recording device and started. She answered with short, non-emotional answers.

"When did you last see your husband?"

"Early evening, right before six."

"You mentioned you argued with your husband. What caused your argument?"

"I told you. He found out about Gerard and me."

"Because you told him?"

"I wanted to come clean. I couldn't hide it anymore. Plus the affair was over."

"Over because Mr. Bellamont is dead?"

She turned her face away, as though she was tired of the questions. "No. I ended it before. I just wasn't thinking straight."

"What did your husband tell you, Mrs. Ferris? Did he confess anything to you?" There was a chance Ferris had mentioned an affair with Chloe or, if Deville was lucky, information about Bellamont's murder.

Having Ferris dead didn't rule him out as Bellamont's killer. A different hand could have killed Ferris. Making it look like a copycat killing was easy enough. Given the slight variances of the two crimes, it was possible it *could* be two different killers. After a long silence, he continued. "Mrs. Ferris, your husband is dead. Whatever he's told you cannot hurt him now." Any past sins may even be forgiven, he almost added.

"He was in love," she said, wiping tears away with her hand. "With Chloe Owen, the daughter. It made me sick when he admitted it, even though I'd suspected for a while. The way she clung to him, the way he looked at her, it's all so pathetic, even now. I didn't want to believe it. How stupid of me."

"Did they have an affair?"

"I don't know how far it went. He just told me he loved her. I didn't ask him if they'd been together or how long they'd been seeing each other. I just couldn't hear any more of it. After he told me I said would leave him." She covered her face and spoke in fragments. "I thought we would talk about it more but I was disgusted. That's why I started seeing Gerard. I knew he was slime but I couldn't stand imagining Chloe and my husband together."

So there it was, he thought. A reason to seek revenge

on her husband. She said she wasn't sure if Ryan had an affair but why would a man say he loved someone if all they had was a platonic relationship? It wasn't just the cheating, he surmised. It was the age difference between the two that infuriated Stephanie and which she may have found unforgivable. He wondered if such a romance could survive today. Besides the fact relations with an underage child is illegal, would it be ever accepted?

"Weren't you worried when he didn't come home?" he asked. "Why didn't you call the police?"

"He'd stayed overnight before filling orders or working on other projects. Once we had another argument."

Deville continued writing.

She watched him for a moment and sighed. "I wanted to leave Owen Winery. I thought the place was going down and it would get worse. The wines were not the best but I've had worse. It seemed Bellamont was merciless with the reviews of them—almost as if he had a personal vendetta."

Deville wasn't sure if Stephanie Ferris knew about Bellamont's history with Kelly Owen. He'd just found out himself last night. How would Bellamont benefit from telling Stephanie Ferris about his father's second wife? The wife who may have led his father to his death? "You mentioned you wanted to leave Owen Winery? And Gerard Bellamont could help?"

She nodded "Yes. He already seemed to have it in for the Owens so I thought with his connections I'd find other employment." She paused, looking with pleading eyes. "I wanted out of here. I hate winters here. They're so harsh! I wanted to move to California, where Gerard lived, seemed so perfect. I could find a job easily so could Ryan. It was perfect."

"What about the book Bellamont was writing?"

"It's done and scheduled to be published in the spring. It's about Finger Lakes wineries."

"Would anyone want to kill Bellamont so the book wouldn't be published?"

"That's silly. The book is very favorable, telling about the area's growing industry in wine. Many pictures of the vineyards."

"Even Owen Winery?"

"Not them but Allenwood is there. So is Catalina."

"Could Bellamont have written another review or a book? Something someone wouldn't want published?"

She shook her head. "Not that I know of." She looked drained of energy. Deville wondered if she would collapse at any moment. He gave her a bottle of water. She looked as if she needed nourishment. After taking a sip she continued. "I told Ryan we should move. The winery would probably close but he said he would sink with the ship if he had to. He had too much pride."

Deville wondered if it was pride that killed Ferris in the end. Pride as a winemaker, dedication to the Owens or was it the love of Chloe that kept him hanging on? It could have been all three and Stephanie would appear to be ruining his plans. Why then was he killed and not her? It would make more sense if he had killed his wife, take over the sinking ship of a winery and settle down with the young Miss Owen.

"Who would want your husband dead?" he asked.

She crossed her arms. "I don't know. Chloe's parents? What if he told the Owens he was in love with their daughter? What if they were planning on running away?"

"Who else could have done this? Did anyone argue with your husband recently?"

She shrugged, "I don't know. He was into his wine. He was quiet but he was a good winemaker."

A thought occurred to Deville. "Did anyone try to

court Ryan Ferris away from Owen Winery?"

"Sure, several, including Allenwood and Catalina. They said it jokingly, in front of the Owens, but I know they were serious. It wasn't Ryan. It was the grapes causing bad reviews. I know if he worked for another prestigious winery he would have been famous."

He dreaded the next question, though it was necessary. "Where were you last night? Any witnesses?"

"I told you. I went home. Didn't see anyone." She sniffed and then added, "So I guess I don't have an alibi or witnesses. I can't think of anyone who would want to kill Ryan. He wouldn't hurt a fly. He was just an average guy, nothing special." She looked at Deville and added, "You can't suspect me. Why would I kill him? Bellamont is dead, too. It's not like I'm after anyone. Besides, doesn't it take strength to strangle someone like my husband?"

"If he was out cold from drinking it wouldn't be too difficult to strangle him with trellis wire."

"So it was trellis wire? I couldn't tell with all that blood. Just like Gerard's murder?" Deville nodded. "Seeing all those animal tracks around the body was horrendous. Ryan loved seeing the wildlife when he was in the field. He called the animals his friends." She paused and wiped her nose again. "It's Mr. Owen. It has to be. Can you just arrest him now? Why are you standing here?"

"No matter who the culprit is, we need evidence." He asked her if she needed to call anyone. She told him no. She had family here and had called them earlier and they were on their way. After helping her stand, he handed her to another officer and they left the room.

A moment later Sergeant Malone came in and closed the door. She watched as Deville continued writing his notes. "Any groundbreaking news or clues? Do you think she did it?"

"Killed her husband, maybe, but not Bellamont. There was no motive I'm aware of. Her husband could have killed Bellamont but why? Ferris was having an affair himself. It makes little sense."

"Maybe he was so devoted to the Owens? Wanted nothing to jeopardize his job or his future mate?"

In a dry tone Deville said, "It could be but I'm not sure, at least not for that motive. This case is so emotional, so intense."

"Then the motive must be, too," she finished for him. "What motive fits this?"

He knew she was testing him. It was what she did to help him. Jessica Malone never seemed to give him any new slant or idea. However, she was good at making sure he dotted his i's and crossed his t's. "Passion," he said.

"Love always wins. Even when competing for motive. Consider the method of killing."

"The first murder, Bellamont, seemed spontaneous. The trellis wire was all around the vineyard."

"That doesn't mean it was any less passionate."

"With the second one, the killer had to have had the wire with him. I don't think it was spontaneous." He picked up his folders. "We were there. We could have stopped this."

"There was no way of knowing Ryan Ferris was in danger. You were trying to protect someone else."

"Fine job I did with that."

She walked closer. "Yes, fine job, indeed. Who knows what would have happened if you weren't there. For all we know you might have saved a mother and son from being killed."

"So we give Ryan Ferris as sacrifice instead? Someone had to die. If it wasn't one of the Bellamonts then someone else. So was Ferris there at the wrong time? Are we dealing with someone who just needs to kill?"

She crossed her arms. "No. I think Ryan Ferris was

planned."

"And the attack last night, the damage to my car. Just something to scare me off?"

She shrugged. "Maybe but what about the Bellamonts? Someone entered their home and from what she told you, it wasn't the first time." She stood and handed him keys. "Your car is ready, be extra careful."

He thanked her and stood. It was time to embark on the next journey of his investigation. Two murders had crossed his path and now he would have to interview everyone again for motive and opportunity. Even though it was early in the day, the recent murder and upcoming tasks felt overwhelming. He also felt anxious. He needed to think straight and keep his mind fresh.

They left the room together and as if she'd read his mind, Jessica Malone handed him a large cup of coffee while he was putting on his coat. "I know you get tired when you're anxious."

She showed a slight worried smile. Deville thought she'd be perfect in so many ways. This would be the moment he'd kiss her but he dare not, not in front of everyone (who were already staring) and not for his principal. He didn't want to fuel her emotional state. He imagined she was plotting to throw more fuel onto his fire, make him want to come back into her arms. Before she could say or do anything else, she turned and walked away, knowing he didn't like awkward moments.

CHAPTER TWENTY

His first stop was, again, the Owen residence. He almost knew his way by heart, he thought, as he turned into the driveway. He parked in front and walked into the attached garage, where he noticed a Lexus and Cadillac. Both were late models. While he took photos of the vehicles, he wondered if he was lucky enough to have a witness who could place either of them at the scene of the crime last night. The Lexus, he assumed, belonged to Mrs. Owen and the Cadillac to her husband. He opened the doors of each and did a quick study of the interior, the distance of the driver's side seat to the steering wheel and smelled each one. The Lexus smelled like perfume due to the air freshener that hung on the rearview mirror, whereas the other car had no scent. Both car doors were unlocked. While he was inspecting the interiors, he saw a shadow behind him. It appeared suddenly and before he could do or think of anything else, he grabbed the gun he kept on his holster to defend himself.

"Can I help you, investigator?"

Deville turned to see Roger Owen dressed in a robe, similar to his wife's, but blue. He had two cups of coffee and offered one to him. Deville shook his head and thanked him.

"Are you looking for something?"

"Have you heard about Ryan Ferris?"

"Heard what? What happened?"

"Do you mind if I call a few crime scene officers to take a look at your car?"

"Sure but why are you looking into my wife's car? I drive the Lexus."

Deville had been kneeling but now he stood, gloved. "This is your wife's?"

Owen nodded. "I'm average height but my wife is taller, if you haven't noticed. And I know, I have an air freshener and sometimes we switch. I had to have a Lexus but my wife, she loves her Cadillac but please, tell me what's going on with Ryan?" He had a blank expression on his face. His receding hairline was damp, suggesting a recent shower and the furrowed brow beneath could have been genuine ignorance. Deville told him about Ferris. Owen dropped his coffee cup, breaking it and spilling the contents on both of their shoes.

A moment later they were in the Owen's kitchen, a large, but well equipped room that held the latest appliances. Deville couldn't imagine Mrs. Bumgarden feeling comfortable cooking in here. She stood near the stove now, hands crossed and ready to serve refreshments. The Owens seemed too busy to ask their maid to leave. They sat at the kitchen table speculating.

Crime scene officers were in the garage. From where they sat in the kitchen, they had a great view.

"Are you sure it was murder, detective?" Kelly Owen asked.

Deville didn't bother correcting her. "Yes, we're sure. The death occurred between nine p.m. and twelve this morning."

"Roger wasn't here," she said. "He was just getting

home. You remember, he called while you were here."

Deville said, "That was after eight. Where were you Mr. Owen?"

Roger Owen looked like he'd lost a child. His pale face showed sadness when his nervous eyes weren't watching the crime scene officers go in and out of his garage. Deville knew of murderers who felt remorse and those who didn't. It was possible Roger Owen killed Ryan Ferris and felt sadness. He may have even considered Ryan Ferris one of his children. "I was on my way back from Buffalo. Didn't get home until ten-thirty."

"Did you stop by your winery?"

"Why should I?"

Buffalo was west. He would have to pass his home and travel another few miles to the winery then turn around to come home. "Did you stop anywhere or see anyone?"

He looked lost in thought. His robe came undone, showing his hairless chest. Mrs. Owen stood to go behind him to close it. "Roger, he's asking you if you saw anyone? Can you answer him?" Deville noticed Kelly Owen, as she closed her husband's robe. Her big and strong arms were around his neck, closing the flap. Deville thought she could have easily killed Bellamont and Ferris herself.

"No one," Owen replied. "I don't remember seeing anyone. I have friends who saw me at the show but no one on my way home. I had to stop for gas."

"Did you go to a wine show?" Owen nodded. "Did you do a tasting?" Again he nodded. "I suppose you didn't get rid of all the wine so you brought some back didn't you? Why were both cars clear of any wine? Do you usually bring back wine?"

Kelly Owen understood where he was going. "Roger, if you went back to the winery to drop off wine before coming home you need to tell him." She paused looking at her husband. "Roger," she said, with a sad frown."Now is the time to come clean."

Roger Owen kept watching the officers go in and out of the garage.

Deville asked with a gentle tone, "Mr. Owen, will the police find anything in your car?"

He turned to Deville. "He was sleeping with my Chloe. I killed him. I did it."

Deville brought Owen back to the station. Owen sat in the same chair Stephanie Ferris had just a few hours ago. He confessed to the murder of Ryan Ferris in a frenzied manner, with scattered thoughts, nervous twitching and brief pauses. Deville wondered if he had enough room in his recorder. Jessica Malone sat on one side of the table and Deville on the other. Roger Owen sat in the center, spewing out last night's events as though his memory was threatening to diminish them.

His story seemed plausible. He had gone to the winery last night where Ryan Ferris was still working. After helping Owen remove the wine from his car, Ferris invited him into the office to talk. "The rain was horrible. It poured and I—we—both needed a short break from bringing in the boxes. I only used one case of wine. I'd brought six. You never know with these things. Ryan wanted to talk in the office. I didn't know why. I told him I had to go. I needed to get home but he said it was important. So we went into the office and that's when he told me."

"That's when he told you what?" Deville asked.

"Don't make me repeat it. It's too awful. I don't want to think about it." He looked away, eyes closed, and took a few sharp breaths. "Poor Chloe. Our poor daughter. His hands—all I could imagine was his hands around her—touching her. I couldn't take it."

Jessica Malone questioned him. "What exactly did

Ferris say?"

"That he loved her. That he wanted to marry her. He said he would take care of her." Owen paused, noticing the cup of coffee in front of him. "I thought he was joking, a horrible cruel joke if it were one. Then I remembered. I remembered how he looked at her. How she acted whenever she was around him. I believed him then. This was something I couldn't let happen. I didn't want it to happen. She's sixteen. A baby!"

Deville asked, "Mr. Owen, what happened next? We need to know the details."

Owen grabbed the coffee with shaking hands and continued. "I thought I must end this. I must end it now, before he ruins her life. So I grabbed something, whatever I could find, and strangled him."

"What did you use?"

Owen looked at him with a nervous gaze. "Trellis wire, just like Bellamont."

"There was no trellis wire around. Did you take it with you?"

"No. I found it in the back, where Ryan worked. He had a little tool area where he kept the trellis wire for our vines."

"So you left Ferris in the office, went to grab the wire and came back?"

Owen nodded. "Ryan wasn't going anywhere. He wouldn't leave in that storm. He trusted me and knew we had to talk about it more. Ryan was like my son. I guess he thought I would approve of the relationship."

Deville frowned. "The bastard. I felt betrayed," Owen said. "All those years working for me while he lusted after my daughter."

"She was adopted wasn't she? Mrs. Owen told me that."

"That doesn't mean I love her any less," Owen responded.

"What happened next Mr. Owen?" Jessica Malone questioned.

Owen leaned back a little. "I left. I couldn't stay any longer."

Deville asked, "Did you take the trellis wire with you or leave it?"

Owen glanced at him with a bewildered look. "Did you find it?"

"I am asking you a question. Did you take it or leave it on the body?"

Owen waited a few moments before saying, "I took it. I guess I didn't want to leave any prints. I heard police can get it from almost anything."

Deville paused a moment, thinking. "Did you leave the winery door open or closed?" Owen looked at him while crossing his thin eyebrows. "A simple question, Mr. Owen. Did you leave the winery open or closed? The doors? Were they left wide open or did you shut them?"

"I don't remember. I was nervous. I don't kill someone everyday."

"But you should be an old pro at this now—after killing Bellamont?" Deville leaned closer to him. "Or did you actually kill Bellamont?"

"I did. That was different. It was spontaneous."

"So you say but was it? What did you say your motive for killing Bellamont was?"

"Gerard Bellamont was an incredible fool."

"That's not enough of a motive to kill a man."

"In case you haven't noticed, he's trying to bury our winery!"

Jessica Malone, who had been watching the two while turning her head, as though in a tennis match, stood up. "Deville, meet me outside!" She walked out of the office and Deville followed. As soon as she shut the door she yelled, "What the hell is wrong with you? What are you doing?"

"I'm just getting all the facts."

"The man is trying to confess and you don't seem at all happy about it."

"Why should I be happy? He's confessing to killing two men. Should I be thanking him?"

"That's not what I mean." She took a deep breath and crossed her arms. "I know you far too well to believe you're not satisfied with his confession. What is it? Why don't you believe Owen?"

Deville thought for a moment. "I guess he had a motive to kill Ryan Ferris and Gerard Bellamont but I'm not sure he did."

"What makes you say that?"

"Chloe Owen was adopted. I know it sounds awful but I don't believe he cared much for her. Even Wyatt said they treated her as if she didn't belong."

"I was adopted. My parents cared for me," Malone replied.

"Yes but I don't think they cared enough to kill for Chloe. The business, yes, but not her. She was their spy. She made them look like a family." He leaned on the door where Owen sat in the next room. He tried to keep his voice low. "Plus, the way he reacted when he found out about Ryan Ferris. He showed genuine surprise. If Owen is the killer in either of these crimes there must be a different motive. I don't think he cared for Chloe enough to kill for her."

"Maybe he was in love with her, too. You hear it happening all the time."

"I thought about that but I don't think so. I believe him about Gerard Bellamont. He could have killed him for a bunch of reasons but mostly because he was a thorn in his wife's side. Kelly Owen married Gerard Bellamont's father and was inadvertently responsible for his death. Gerard Bellamont was making their life miserable because of this, not the wine."

"So if he killed Bellamont, why not Ryan Ferris?"

Deville remained silent for a moment. "Leave him here. I need to find out if there was any trace evidence in Owen's car. I'll also check and see about the trellis wire." He walked away but she grabbed him.

"What are you doing?" she asked. "You can't just walk away while someone confesses. Are you mad?"

"It's not the first time someone has called me so," he remarked. "Book him and place him in a holding cell. I just need to make sure."

"If it's not him then who? Why would he confess?"

Deville decided it was time for him to quiz her. "Why would an innocent man plead guilty?"

Her mouth showed a glimmer of a smile. "Who is he trying to protect then?"

"If not Chloe then his wife, Kelly."

CHAPTER TWENTY-ONE

His next stop was Allenwood Vineyard and he had mixed emotions going there. The thought of Sydney Keller waiting for him was something he wanted to avoid. He liked her energy and exuberance and found her attractive but she could be too much for him. For a moment the thought of asking her out came to mind. It would be after the investigation and only if she was innocent of the crimes. However, there were a few quirks she had that bothered him. Her obsession with the mystical seemed silly and there were also those wretched tattoos.

He quickly dismissed the idea of courting her. She was sure to have other suitable men in line, especially those who would appreciate her dramatic flair and tolerate her eccentricities. Plus, he was sure something was brewing with her and Paul Shepard.

And why would someone as young and attractive as Sydney fall for a guy like Deville? His looks were nothing to write home about. He stood tall and thin with a thick-skinned face and crude looking ears that stood out from either side. Piercing brown eyes shone below a head of wavy dark hair. People had introduced him as a cousin to the celebrity Lyle Lovett because of the similarities.

He learned to live with the jokes from other officers because he had a sense of humor and knew they meant no harm.

If someone actually told him he was attractive, he wouldn't know what to say. He'd probably suggest they get their vision checked. Some days he couldn't bear glancing in a mirror.

He entered the building and Marianne was there waiting on someone who just bought a bottle of wine. It seemed business was stable, despite Owen Winery being closed next door with yellow crime scene tape streamed about like toilet papered homes on Halloween. Marianne Keller smiled when she noticed him and he smiled back. He didn't see her niece, Sydney, and felt relieved.

He told Marianne about Ryan Ferris and watched her reaction. She was dressed in blue again, which seemed to be her color. She seemed to show genuine sadness but kept busy labeling bottles lined on the bar. "It doesn't make sense," she said. "I imagine Ryan was killed the same way?" He nodded. "Poor boy. He worked so hard. He was a good winemaker despite everything."

"Despite what?"

She stopped what she was doing and continued. Her voice seemed a little more cautious. "It's nothing really. Just rumors but I don't want to say anything about Ryan."

"Mrs. Keller, please. I need to know everything. We want to make sure we stop this killer from striking again."

"So it is the same killer? Well, I guess it would be. Dear, I can't seem to think straight." She gave him a look that suggested he shouldn't rule out a second killer and then said, "Why would someone want to copy Gerard's death? For fame? It's not like the Boston Strangler or another serial killer." She paused, mouth opened wide. "Oh, no. What if it is a serial killer, like 'The Finger Lakes Killer?'"

He sighed and decided he knew where her niece got her wild and crazy notions. "Mrs. Killer."

"Keller."

"I'm so sorry."

"It's okay. You're thinking about the killings. It must be awful to have your job right now. I wouldn't want it for the world! Just wait until Sydney—where is she?" She looked around. "She must be in the back, I'll go grab her."

Deville stopped her. "No, wait. Please tell me, Mrs. Keller, what were you going to say about Ryan Ferris? Remember? You were about to say something. I need to know everything."

She dropped the labels and leaned toward him. "It's nothing really, mostly rumor, but it's about the book Gerard was writing. It was supposed to be published by Stephanie's family. They have a publishing company it seems. Ryan did the paperwork for it so the publisher made a pretty penny. More than the author."

"Who? Ryan?"

"Yes and now that he's dead, his wife will get all the profits. The book is destined to be a big seller, at least that's what I'm told. It's all about the industry and the Finger Lakes region. You see, Gerard Bellamont could write but he had connections in the newspaper world, not the book publishing world. That's where he needed the Ferris's. Personally I think they were taking advantage of Gerard."

Deville thought about what she'd said. The Ferris's working together seemed plausible. He wouldn't put anything past Stephanie Ferris. She seemed ambitious, cunning and was probably impatient with the wine business. She probably took advantage of many men in her lifetime. However, working as a team meant Ryan

Ferris was involved and took part in the deal.

Speculating Ryan and Stephanie may have been working together was a new angle. However, the character of Ryan Ferris seemed to shatter this notion. He was young, filled with respect and appeared to love his occupation. Deville couldn't see Ferris agreeing to anything underhanded like this. Everyone he spoke to said Ferris had pride and was good at what he did. Here was a loophole in Marianne Keller's story.

"Are you sure about this so-called contract?" Deville asked.

Marianne Keller nodded. "I can't believe Ryan would do that."

"Ryan? You believe Stephanie Ferris could do this but not her husband?"

"If he did, he pulled the wool over my eyes."

Deville agreed. But Ryan Ferris had an affair, or at least wanted to have one, with Chloe Owen. How can anyone so dependable and likable do this but not try to take advantage of Gerard Bellamont?

An image of Ryan and Stephanie Ferris came to mind, like a modern day Bonnie and Clyde but not to that extent. Perhaps this couple would try to take over Owen Winery or take advantage of every opportunity that presented itself, crushing anyone who stood in their way.

Now Ryan was dead. This left Stephanie to continue with any plans they had devised. He wondered what went wrong and what details led to Mr. Ferris's death. She admitted to her affair because she had a witness. She said she told her husband yesterday, which caused an argument, but no one could vouch for that. She said she left him at Owen Winery after hearing about him and Chloe, which left Ryan alone to meet his killer.

What if that never happened? What if the Ferris's made an agreement: she would sleep with Gerard

Bellamont and he with Chloe? An open relationship to further their goals; to help them succeed financially. This career course would veer, as most malicious plans fail, causing her to kill her husband. Thinking of this, he decided to ask Marianne Keller about love interests.

"Did you know that Gerard Bellamont and Stephanie Ferris were having an affair?"

She shook her head. "No but it doesn't surprise me. She looks the type to have probably done anything to get the book deal done, even sleep with him. Doesn't surprise me if Ryan…" She stopped. "Never mind. That's too low."

"Do you think Ryan knew about the affair? Possibly didn't care, maybe even helped make it happen?"

She shrugged. "You never know. People have done far worse for money. I don't get the phony ignorance act. How can you not know your wife is having an affair? Or better yet, how can you not know that your spouse is guilty of anything?"

Just then Frank Keller came in the front door carrying some tools under one arm. The other arm was in a cast. He strolled over to them and dropped the tools on the bar. "The storm did a number on those vines."

Deville didn't have to ask what happened to his arm.

Marianne said, "My lovely husband had an accident last night. We had to go to the emergency room. He tried to fix the gutter drain at our home in the middle of the storm. With a ladder and the wind blowing over 40 miles an hour. You can imagine the rest."

Frank went around the bar, grabbed a beer from his secret stash and took a swig. Deville asked, "What time did this accident happen, Frank?"

He looked at Marianne then answered, "Around nine-thirty or so."

"And Marianne took you to the hospital?" He nodded. "Did you pass Allenwood?"

He shook his head. "No need to." He noticed
Marianne coming out from behind the bar and walked
away. Deville stopped him to ask for a glass of water. He
watched the way Frank moved and thought it was a
coincidence that he got injured around the same time
Ryan Ferris was killed and the cottage had their
intruder. He could picture Frank Keller, with his
brooding figure and bald head, coming into a dark room
with the only light behind him. One could mistake him
for a menacing shadow.

Frank Keller could have injured his arm while
vandalizing Deville's vehicle. But why would Frank do
such a thing? He couldn't imagine him killing or
threatening anyone without a good reason. There had to
be a strong enough motive.

Just then another group came in the winery. Frank
Keller observed, "Been busy today with all that fuss
going around. It's been good for business."

As if a veil had been lifted, Deville swallowed and
thought how silly but true his new speculations may be.
He remembered Marianne Keller saying in the
beginning that the wine industry was a cutthroat
business. What better way to kill off your competition
than to actually kill?

Trying to bury Owen Winery was something
Marianne Keller was capable of doing, using her
husband to do her dirty work. But killing Gerard
Bellamont? What motive could there be? Having
publicity such as murder at your vineyard cannot be
good for business.

Deville thought maybe Marianne Keller could have
made up stories about the Ferris scheme or just about
anything to confuse him and get him off track. His mind
felt crowded with all these ideas and he needed to sort
them. He spotted Marianne coming closer and
wondered how she knew about Ryan and Stephanie

Ferris's book deal with Bellamont. He asked her and didn't expect her quick response.

"They didn't speak to me," she answered. "It's all Sydney. People always open up to her. I think she did their horoscopes or something."

Just then, as if the heavens had called her, Sydney Keller appeared from the office. She was looking especially adorable in a flower print dress, showing off her slight curves. Deville also noticed she had a red scarf wrapped around her head and large hoop earrings.

"Louis! I was waiting for you," she said.

Somehow Deville didn't doubt that.

CHAPTER TWENTY-TWO

Sydney Keller ushered him into the office, where she sat him down in an old chair. He felt as if a bib were about to be tied around his neck and he were about to be fed. Well, he thought, she could give me a different kind of nourishment: information. Was there a bib for this, he wondered idly, for all the unimportant information that dribbled out of her mouth? She looked excited, more upbeat than yesterday, sitting across from him and asking for his hand. After a moment he gave in and brought out his right hand. She placed colored stones in it, flipped the hand and told him to drop the stones on a chart, just a few inches below his floating fistful of stones. "What is this for?" he asked, knowing the question was moot. Even if she answered, he still would be in the land of ignorance.

"I'm doing your crystal energy reading," she explained, as a child would a new game. "First ask me— oh, I mean the gods—a certain question. You don't have to say it aloud. Just ask it silently." She looked at him as if she needed to explain further.

"I got it. Then what should I do afterward?"

"Just drop the gemstones, each of which have a special meaning but I'll explain after." She waved him to hurry.

"Go ahead. Ask your question."

He thought for a moment and almost uttered a word. After noticing her wide eyes warning him not to disobey the gods by announcing his question to the public, he stopped himself. She nodded to him that it was okay to let go. The stones came down, spreading out everywhere on the chart like a splatter of pellets from a shotgun blast. She studied the chart and stones with wide eyes, as if she'd found a lost treasure. After a moment, he tried to speak but she hushed him with her finger. Just when he thought another murder would take place that night, from killing her himself, she finally spoke with a cautious voice.

"I see you are troubled." She looked up and noticed his disappointment. "But wait. There's more." She looked down again. "It seems your occupation has you going in many directions. I can see you are confused." She paused. "Have no fear. You see this crystal quartz? It's on the outer circle so it will all be clear soon. Don't worry."

"Thank you because I was worried, you know."

She looked up and noted the sarcasm. "Anyway, see this snowflake obsidian stone? It's near the clear quartz so that tells me something that's hiding will come to light soon."

He noticed a pink one near the other two, almost touching. "What about this stone?"

She cocked her head. "That's a rose quartz. It's the stone of the heart." She pointed to other stones and told him the different meanings. He heard her and nodded several times but he kept coming back to the pink stone. He didn't believe in any of the reading but thought it was odd she didn't explain this stone further. Why was it in such proximity to the clear and dark ones. A stone of the heart, she had said. He couldn't help but think maybe she was embarrassed to explain this further but he needed to understand everything he could. He decided to stay on the subject of affairs of the heart and asked about Ryan and Stephanie Ferris and the book deal.

She raised her arm, which had dangling bracelets, and held her chin, looking like a true fortune teller. "I didn't need for them to tell me about their troubled marriage. The stars already told me." She looked up, as if the stars were winking at her. "Besides, can you believe they came to me for help?"

"For marriage counseling?"

"Dear God, no! I would have told them to get a divorce. They wanted to know about a business deal so I gave them a tarot reading. I told you I did readings didn't I?" Deville said he remembered her mentioning something about that. "I told them about this windfall of sorts. They mentioned the book and I said that's great because I didn't know either of them wrote. They said it wasn't them. It was Bellamont who was writing." She felt her earring, as if to check if it were still there, or in case Deville hadn't noticed them, then continued. "I said I thought writers made lots of money with books. They laughed and said not in this case. It seemed they wrote up a contract with her family's publishing company so they, meaning the Ferris's, would receive a greater portion of the proceeds when the book got published."

"Why wouldn't he publish the book with someone else?"

"They called it a high risk contract I think. This meant no other publisher would publish it or wanted to publish it. Not sure why. I think Gerard Bellamont made a lot of enemies not just here and not just in the wine world. I heard he also reviewed books and art. So I guess he pissed off some publishers as well. Stephanie must have approached him about the book, as it was no surprise he wrote the first one."

Deville almost let it go. "What do you mean the first one?"

"Didn't you know he was writing another one? He started a few weeks ago. Uncle Frank may know more. He heard all about it while he worked on the vines. Bellamont typed away on his laptop while Uncle Frank worked on the vines."

Deville remembered Frank Keller saying something about Gerard Bellamont writing on his laptop outside while Frank was working on the vineyard. He could imagine them both, probably drinking wine or beer in the sun, Gerard procrastinating and Frank taking many unneeded breaks. "Do you know anything about this new book? What or who it's about?"

She shook her head. "I don't even know if it's nonfiction. Could be from his imagination, you know, a novel of some type."

"Did Ryan or Stephanie Ferris know about this second book?"

She shook her head. "I don't think so. I think Mr. Bellamont just told my uncle in confidence."

She reached over to touch his hand. "Why do you ask? How is your investigation going?" He realized she didn't know about the murder of Ryan Ferris. Once he told her, she bolted up, dropping the chart and stones and began to cry. "No! Not another one." She covered her face. "I knew another one was going to happen I felt it. I hoped I was wrong."

He went around the desk and thought about placing his arms around her in an attempt to console her but his hesitation made it awkward. So he stood close to her and could feel the warmth of her body. She didn't seem to mind so he patted her back while she whimpered.

"Why do you flirt so close to danger?" he asked again.

She looked into his eyes. "I'm destined to."

"You don't have to Sydney. No one is forcing you to

be with Paul or Wyatt. You seem so different when you're around them."

She turned her head to stare out of the huge window. "I feel they need me, more than I need companionship, more than I ever needed anything."

Part of Deville suddenly wanted to tell her to stop everything and move in with him. However silly the notion, it was because of her safety, not romance. But he believed she too, was disastrous. No charts or cards were needed to know this. She was like a ship always getting lost in a treacherous sea. He turned to the window to follow her gaze of the vineyard outside, which glimmered from the afternoon sun and gave an excellent view of the grapevines, where just a few nights ago Gerard Bellamont met his death.

Anyone could have seen and watched this death.

Anyone could have seen his passionate kiss with Stephanie Ferris.

Anyone staring out this window, watching the scene under the moonlight. Two figures—either in a passionate embrace—or a murderous rage.

CHAPTER TWENTY-THREE

Frank Keller was arranging grapevines on a trellis wire with his working arm, trying his best not to lose his temper. At least this is what Deville surmised when he met Keller outside after calming down his niece. After a glass of Syrah, assuring her there wouldn't be any more crimes, Sydney Keller seemed more collected. He left her lighting candles and searching for a sage stick then went looking for Frank Keller to ask about this second book.

"I told you he was writing one," Frank Keller claimed.

"I know but I thought you meant the first one," Deville replied.

"Why would he be writing something that was already written? For a detective you don't seem too attentive."

Deville sighed. "I'm going to ignore that statement and ask again. Mr. Keller, did you know what Mr. Bellamont was writing about?"

Frank Keller was on his knees working the trellis wire steadily with his huge sausage fingers. He tried to wipe the sweat from the top of his bald head with his elbow to no avail. "Could you help me, please? I can't let go of this. I am a bit challenged right now. There's a rag in my back pocket."

Deville grabbed it and wiped the bald head. "When are you going to get help, Mr. Keller? You know you can't possibly do this on your own."

"I heard what happened to Ryan Ferris," Keller answered. "My wife told me while you were with Sydney. Ah, there you go!" After he had finished attaching the trellis wire, he stood up, gritting his teeth with pain, but bearing a grin of accomplishment. "You know it was Ryan Ferris who taught me how to attach this trellis wire."

"Before I forget, may I have a sample of your trellis wire?"

He looked at Deville dumbfounded. "Why? Wasn't Gerard killed here with that wire?"

"It could have been from another winery. I'm just making sure." Deville pocketed the sample handed to him and asked, "Ryan Ferris taught you? But he had had little experience himself?"

"But he knew how to study. He took an apprenticeship with other wineries. The Owens flew him to California and I think abroad as well. When he came back, he had a lot of work to do. I met him at Owen Winery and learned from him. He was eager to help me get started. Paul Shepard helped me, too, in the beginning stages. I can't see how we all got tangled into this. They all seemed like good people."

"Sometimes bad things happen to good people," Deville said.

"The winery was my wife's idea. I didn't want to go to California or travel to find out how to make wine. So I read a few books and tried. I was lucky to have Ryan give me lessons. He was very committed, took his job seriously. Never wanted anything in return either." Frank paused and then said, "Ryan was young but he wasn't dumb. He learned everything with ease. You know, Owen Winery's wine is not as bad as some reviewers say."

"So I've heard."

"The Owens took all this time to teach Ryan how to make the wine. Or rather they invested in his education. Not that I know what is the best. You know, one time Gerard Bellamont had us try a French wine, a Beaujolais. I couldn't tell the difference but that's just me."

Keller walked and continued surveying, fixing any loose trellis wire damaged from the storm last night. The rows of grapes looked sad, as if even Frank Keller couldn't help them any longer. It was already November and harvest season was ending. Ice wine was next to be harvested but this wasn't for the dry wine connoisseur. Wine drinkers considered this wine a great match with desserts. He realized if he veered away from the subject, Frank Keller would never bring it up himself.

Deville continued. "Please Mr. Keller, go on about the book Bellamont was writing. You said he was writing another book or started one."

"He was odd, Bellamont, and not just because he was French."

Well that's reassuring, Deville thought.

"Always trying to push himself, anything but lazy. He'd sit here on a folding chair and keep me company. I usually just listen to my music player, something my niece, Sydney, gave me, while I'm working on the grapes. Anyway, Bellamont sat by that hill," he pointed near the cottage where the Bellamont's were staying, "and he took about a week to move closer. Then before I knew it we were drinking beer together."

So it had taken a while for Bellamont to open up to Frank Keller. It didn't surprise Deville. Bellamont seemed to make enemies at every corner. His encounter with Kelly Owen, who stole his father away from his mother, made matters worse. Bellamont had to have been extra choosy before befriending anyone. "Did he say anything about this book? Whether it was fiction or nonfiction?"

"It was about people, a woman in particular. I can't remember the facts but it was about a married woman who was having an affair or a woman who was sick. The woman died tragically but I only remember fragments. He was excited about it. He kept saying if all these celebrities could write books about their lives so could he."

"Can you tell me more about this tragedy he spoke about?"

Keller stopped for a moment and looked deep in thought. "It might have been about love, I think. It was about a very passionate person."

Frank Keller's account of the second book was incredulous. He was a poor witness and Deville thought about what else could trigger the other's memory. More than likely, Keller and Bellamont were both so intoxicated neither of them could make any sense. This second book Bellamont was writing could be nothing but a farce but with the recent events Deville couldn't ignore it. Bellamont's father had died in a plane crash while going back to visit his first wife and child, leaving his current wife, soon to be Kelly Owen, alone in the States. Deville would have to check his notes but he thought Kelly said she and Bellamont Senior had their affair while he was in France, breaking up his marriage to Gerard's mother. "Are you sure the book was about an affair or was it about a tragedy?"

Keller nodded and suddenly looked tired. "I need to rest now. I have to work twice as hard with this arm."

"Why would Bellamont write something like this? It has nothing to do with wine."

"He said he wanted to write a memoir. A tell-all. He said he was getting screwed in the deal from his first book so he was writing this one under another name."

"A pseudonym?"

Keller looked at him curiously. "If that's what it's called, I reckon."

Deville started walking back with him. "So business has improved since the death. You've received some press?"

He was no fool. Keller knew where he was heading. "We wouldn't do anything like kill for more business, if that's what you're thinking. We just opened. I'd like to think the wine itself has been selling because of its quality, not because of the body found in our vineyard."

Deville changed the subject. "How often do you go into the cottage? Do you have your own key?"

"Of course. We own the cottage. They are just renting it."

Deville asked, "Are you aware someone has broken in?"

"No. What happened?"

Deville told him what had gone down the night before.

Keller shook his head. "Why didn't anyone tell us about this? I'll change the locks. I wouldn't want anything to happen to Mrs. Bellamont. Don't need anyone suing us. Her husband died on our grounds. I didn't know she's being harassed." He stormed back inside the winery, leaving Deville in the parking lot.

Frank Keller was an odd man, Deville thought. As he got in the car he thought of the work that had to be done. Now there were two deaths and he needed to work quickly to avoid any more unnatural causes. This second book needed to surface; more than likely it was prominent in this case. This is what the intruder was looking for, Deville surmised. The intruder came in twice to look for files of a second book Gerard was writing. Something about a tragedy that happened in the past.

CHAPTER TWENTY-FOUR

The private high school was in Geneva, a small city at the top of Seneca Lake. Deville had always liked the layout of the town, as if a symmetrical grid was placed on the earth, in the center of the Finger Lakes, above Seneca Lake. Landmarks included the Smith Opera House, a beautiful restored building still being used, and Rose Hill Mansion, a historic building and farm. DeSales High School was a regional Catholic high school on Pulteney Street. It didn't take long to locate Chloe Owen. She followed him down the hall, holding onto her books.

When they were in the car she turned to him and asked, "So what is it now?"

Mrs. Owen was at the station, so Chloe was still in the dark about her father—and more importantly—about Ryan Ferris. He told her to buckle up and while driving he told her in snippets what happened, giving the facts with no other information. She stared out her window, silent. When they arrived at the station, he escorted her inside the building where Mrs. Owen was sitting in a hallway, waiting for news of her husband. She spotted Chloe and stood up.

"Why did you bring her here?" she asked Deville.

Then to her daughter, "Chloe!" When her daughter didn't rush into her outstretched hands, she waited patiently. It was only until Chloe slapped her mother once in the face that the young girl started to cry and show some emotion.

"How dare you!" Chloe said. "First Ryan and then my father! You've ruined both of their lives. You're nothing but trouble, just like your past. Trouble." Tears fell as she let her mother hold her.

Deville motioned for a female officer to separate the two. "We need to ask Chloe a few questions. Place her in the interview room, please." Kelly Owen looked drained from all emotion and energy. She watched her daughter being escorted away and bit her lip.

Deville walked to her and motioned her to sit.

"She's right," Kelly said. "I'm nothing but trouble. Killing Gerard's father then Ryan and now ruining my husband's life. Roger doesn't deserve this."

He brought out a tissue. "Your husband confessed."

"I won't let him take the blame—not anymore." She glanced at the room where her daughter had been taken and turned to Deville. "I did it. I killed them. Both of them. Roger is trying to protect me."

She continued to confess and shed more tears. When it looked like she was finished, he took her to Sergeant Malone's office, where Jessica sat her down. Malone came out of the office and closed the door.

"What's this?" she asked.

"She's confessing to both crimes after seeing her daughter. I will speak to Chloe in the other room. I thought maybe you can get the mother's story and we'll see which one fits."

Malone glanced at Kelly then back at him. "What are you trying to get out of Chloe?"

"The truth."

Chloe Owen looked older than her sixteen years. She sat in the interview room with tired eyes, a withdrawn face and her dull blond hair fell without shine, life or body. Her father was held for murder, her mother just confessed to both crimes and her lover had been one of the victims. How much can one teenager take, Deville wondered, feeling like his own past wasn't so bad. Not knowing what happened in the past may be a blessing for him. He wouldn't wish Chloe Owen's life on his worst enemy. She eyed him with bitterness, as though he were a part of the conspiracy. When he sat, she asked, "What are my rights?"

"You're just here for questioning. You can call for a legal guardian but since your parents confessed to both of the killings, you can contact your family's lawyer. If you don't have…"

She interrupted. "Both of them confessed?"

Deville flipped through some pages of his notebook, which had nothing about the confessions in it, but it acted as a prop to help make her think he was more prepared than he was. "Yes, your mother…"

"Adoptive mother," she interrupted. "She is not my real mother! Why do you insist on ignoring that!"

"Because she and her husband raised you as their own."

"I didn't ask for them to adopt me. I was fine in the orphanage. I don't need to be thankful to them. It's not like I was living on the streets or anything." She moved about in her chair, fidgeting. Anger was flowing through her body. He could imagine she was frustrated, too. "I'm so sick of this. So sick of them. I only felt alive with Ryan. He respected me."

"He made you feel like an adult," he said, watching her.

A thin stare glared back at him. "I was an adult for him. I did everything he asked me to."

"And what did he ask of you?"

"I'm not as innocent as Roger and Kelly think." She referred to her parents like they were strangers, a way of disassociation. "We'd been having an affair for a while. Ryan liked his women young."

"Did it ever occur to you what might happen when you got older? He could have left you for another younger model?"

"He wouldn't have done that. Not Ryan. He loved me. He said so."

"And he said that to Stephanie, too."

She shook her head, "No not her. He never loved her. She lies. She never took him seriously."

Deville kept his gaze on her. "It is you who has been lying, Chloe. And it's time for you to tell the truth. It's time for you to take responsibility, not just for your parents, but for your life. Ryan is dead and you've got to tell me what happened to him."

Her mouth opened but she couldn't form words. Her eyes bulged and tears fell.

Deville didn't want to comfort her. His anger was taking over and he felt the events that happened last night didn't have to happen if she had told him the truth in the beginning. He couldn't stand when people accused the young of being insensitive and careless with their lives but now, staring at Chloe Owen, he understood. Not everyone, he thought. Some teenagers valued their family and still showed respect. Others, like Chloe, and maybe Wyatt to an extent, acted as though the world owed them something. They didn't ask to be born. They didn't sign up for this miserable excuse of a life. He offered a tissue. "Chloe, please, try to calm yourself. It's not too late to make things right."

"It's too late for Ryan!" she cried out.

"When did your parents find out about you two?"

"They suspected months ago and told me to lay off.

Don't stand so close to him, they would say. They didn't want people to talk. They were so worried about their stupid reputation. The funny thing is, they started it. I didn't even notice Ryan until they had him pick me up from school." She paused and took a deep breath, remembering. "He picked me up a few days a week, when he was breaking away from the winery. He always dropped me off at home until I suggested we go out for ice cream. It wasn't right away." She looked at Deville. "It's not like he pounced on me. He wasn't a pervert or anything. I let it happen. I wanted it to happen."

"Why? Were you so unhappy with your family? Was it revenge?"

She rolled her eyes. "That's so childish. No. It was true love. People could see it but were ashamed because they didn't have it themselves. They tried to stop us but our love was stronger."

"Who knew about your affair?"

"I think his wife knew. She was so desperate for attention she started her own affair with that ugly foreigner. They said they were working on a book together but anyone with half a brain could tell what was happening. Ryan said he would tell his wife and my parents. So I guess he told them last night."

"But who did he tell? Your mother or your father?"

She looked away. "So whoever he told, killed him? It was Roger or Kelly?" She thought a moment and then said, "I never would have thought they had the guts to do anything like this."

Deville waited a moment before saying, "They care about you."

"Bull! They're worried about their winery. I told you what they had me do, be some stupid messenger. They never loved me. It's all a front. They needed offspring because everyone else in their class had children and they were too old to produce anything." She straightened her posture. "I'm glad they confessed. Let them both go to prison."

Deville couldn't believe how cold she was. A short lifetime of neglect could do anything to a person, he thought. "Chloe, if both go to prison, you'd have to go back to an orphanage or stay with another family."

"I don't care. I'm turning 17 in a few days so I only have a year before I can be on my own." She watched him write something on his pad. "I'd rather be alone than in a phony family."

Deville let her breathe. He hoped she would calm down. After a moment he asked, "Who killed them, Chloe?" He kept her distant from her parents. "Roger or Kelly? Who strangled Gerard Bellamont and Ryan Ferris?"

She looked at him blankly. "Both of them did it. Both of them need to rot in hell."

The grievous state she was in made being in the same room unbearable. Deville wanted to end the interview but asked her one more question. "Chloe, the second book that Bellamont was writing. The one you were asking Wyatt about. Do you know what happened to it?"

"I don't remember. Meaning, I don't know where it is but I remember he argued with his father about it. He didn't want his father to stir up any more pain. At least that's what Wyatt said."

"So Wyatt knew about this book?"

She nodded. "I think he said he was hiding it from him. Wyatt was funny like that. He was always taking care of them. He hides his mother's medications, puts her to bed when she passes out and makes sure she looks presentable. Wyatt takes care of his father's hate mail, helps by reading his father's works aloud. He didn't like his father's reputation but did everything to get along with him. This second book was an important one to his father. Wyatt said his father was going too far with it. He told me he would stop his father from publishing it."

"I heard he argued with his dad about other things, too."

She shrugged. "His father was disappointed in him. He wanted Wyatt to be involved with more sports, to date and become more rugged." She glanced at him. "I think Wyatt is gay. It's no big thing but I couldn't get close to him."

"What happened to the book Gerard was writing? Where is it?"

"Like I said, Wyatt told me he would stop his father from publishing it. I just assumed he talked to his dad and made him stop writing."

Wyatt could not make his father stop anything, Deville thought. Gerald Bellamont was strong-willed. He was someone who didn't listen to anyone, not even his own son, who could have saved his life.

CHAPTER TWENTY-FIVE

Deville needed a break. He went to grab a piece of fruit and yogurt. He left Chloe in the interview room to deal with her own demons. The station wasn't big enough to handle this many suspects. Having Roger Owen in the holding cell, Kelly Owen in another room and Chloe Owen in the interview room made him feel anxious and nervous. If other sergeants or superiors stopped by from other stations at this stage of their investigation, their team did not look good. Everyone seemed on edge. Even though other officers were helping, Deville never felt so alone.

He thought about Wyatt Bellamont and hoped he knew where his father's second book was. Could Wyatt have hidden it to save the family more grief and despair? Wyatt proved to be more than just a kid who wanted to skip town. He remembered how much the teenager wanted to leave and felt guilty for not knowing how much the young man was going through. Wyatt may know what happened to the missing book.

He remembered Scudder leaving a manuscript on his desk and asked him if he took it. Scudder didn't have it nor did anyone else in the station. The manuscript, which could be the second book, was missing.

Investigator Christine Wolanski said there was somebody asking for him. He followed her and discovered Stephanie Ferris at his desk. She had her hair pulled back in a ponytail and was wearing a simple black dress. She had showered since discovering her husband's body this morning, looking more refreshed. As he sat, he gave her a slight nod and couldn't believe the circumstances. The family of Owen Winery were all here and now Stephanie Ferris, its manager. He felt as if he'd had enough and wanted to lock them all up. Put them all in a holding cell and watch what happens, he thought. He almost predicted why she was here but asked, "Mrs. Ferris, what can I do for you?"

"I just wanted to check up on what's happened to Ryan. Do you have any leads?"

"It just happened a few hours ago. I can call you when something comes up."

"Something?" She looked around. "Is everyone working on this or just you? Two murders don't happen every day here. Can you get more people on this?" She shook her head, opened her purse and grabbed her cigarettes. She looked at Deville, sighed when he shook his head, and threw them back in her purse. "Who is your supervisor?"

"I will gladly let you speak to my supervisor after you answer a couple questions."

"More questions? Should I have recorded my statement myself? Didn't you do that?"

"Mrs. Ferris, these are different questions." She looked at him with disappointment and waited. "The first book Gerard Bellamont was writing about Finger Lakes wineries, the one that is being published by your family's company, is that still being published?"

"Of course."

"And the contract you created, with you and Ryan Ferris as sole receivers of the royalties, is that still binding?" The question got her attention. She sat on the edge of her seat now and gave a short nod. "Now that your husband and the author is dead, do you get all the royalties?"

She swallowed and looked for words. "I don't know. I may but I'm not thinking about that right now!"

"Mrs. Ferris, you do know. Your family's in the publishing business. In fact, you know too well what will happen. You've known all along. The affair with Gerard Bellamont, Chloe, your husband's love interest, the book, the contract, it all involves you." He paused. "Both murders involve you. I should arrest you right now. You had the motive and the opportunity."

"I don't have the strength!" she said in a loud shrill voice. A few officers turned to see what was happening. "I couldn't kill them. He was a big guy."

"The wire took little strength. A woman could kill both men. All it takes is to stay focused. You just wrap the cord around the neck—and pull." He made a gesture of pulling. "Holding it steady with just a little strength makes it easier than you think."

"No. I didn't. I couldn't. Why would I kill him?"

"You had your husband kill Gerard. Ryan thought he would get the book royalties when you knew all along you were planning to kill him. You could sweet-talk him into doing anything. He listened to you. He may have been having an affair but he still listened to you." Deville leaned forward. "How long have you been planning this? Did he approve of your affair with Bellamont? I find it hard to believe he didn't know about it. Was it some twisted agreement? You sleep with Bellamont, he sleeps with Chloe? Was this the master plan?"

She didn't look like she enjoyed being questioned that way. "Are you done?" she asked, pursing her lips and shaking her head. "That's no way to treat a lady."

"No. I'm not done. I'm just getting started. For killing

your husband, the wounds were slightly different. The assailant struggled but not too much. If Ryan were drunk enough, he wouldn't struggle too much either, plus it wouldn't take much strength. It would only take a few moments. Wouldn't it?"

She crossed her legs and continued to glare at him. "Why don't you lock me up right now? Oh, that's right. You need something don't you? You need proof. That's so hard to come by."

Deville felt like slapping her. He couldn't believe what this case was doing to him. He would never do that, especially to a woman, but Stephanie Ferris needed a slap on the face, even if it was figuratively. "Mrs. Ferris, tell me what happened to the second book Gerard Bellamont was writing."

She seemed surprised. "What second book?"

He cocked his head. "Oh, come now. We stupid police could not have overlooked such a thing." He leaned even closer and hoped he was out of earshot of the other officers. "Listen, either tell me what happened or I will create an offense I don't need proof for and stick you in a cell with a bunch of other women who will show you a thing or two about how to treat a lady." He straightened his posture and watched her squirm. "Cooperate with me or you'll never see a dime when that book is published."

She opened her purse again and this time lit a cigarette. "What the hell do you want to know?"

"The second book."

"After our first agreement he wrote another book. He realized what was happening and tried to renegotiate the contract. I made sure it was ironclad, at least for the first printing. I don't know much about this other book he was writing. Ryan and I tried to find out but our methods failed. Gerard wouldn't tell me. He wanted to end the relationship but I pressured him. I told him I cared for him, not the book. I wanted to know what else was he writing about but I wanted to make sure it wasn't about me."

"Or Ryan?" Deville added.

She nodded and tapped her ashes into his coffee mug. "Ryan was to find out from the Owens what was happening with the winery itself. He was stupid. He actually thought he loved that little slut." She paused and then added, "If you haven't noticed, I don't believe in love."

Deville had noticed. "So do you know where this second manuscript is?"

"Beats me. I tried to get it out of him but he wouldn't tell me. And no, neither of us killed him. Ryan and I thought about it but we didn't. We don't have the guts. It was purely about the money."

"And now that your husband is dead?"

"I don't know what will happen. His wife, I suppose, will get the share that Bellamont would get."

"What makes you think this book will sell well?"

She looked at him in disbelief. "Come now, you can't be that naïve? Wine sells and this part of the world is still undiscovered. I don't feel guilty about the contract we did. It was my idea to write the book. He already had a name for himself and a notorious one. Gerard was happy just being a critic. I was offering him so much more."

"What do you know about his past with the Owens?" Deville wasn't sure if Stephanie knew of Gerard Bellamont's father's marriage to Kelly Owen. Kelly was the catalyst for almost everything that happened, perhaps inadvertently. Gerard Bellamont moved to the Finger Lakes, even temporarily, because of this. Deville was sure.

Gerard Bellamont came seeking revenge against the woman who had caused his family to fall apart. Stephanie Ferris had given Bellamont a reason to stay longer, more time to cause more havoc and make Kelly Owen regret she had ever gotten involved with his father. He imagined Bellamont was so distracted he wasn't aware of the manipulative contract that Ryan and Stephanie Ferris had written. This new book, however, would change things. Bellamont would look after himself after being wronged with the first deal. The subject of the second book must have been crucial to him and his son, Wyatt, for it could well be the reason he was killed.

"I didn't know Gerard had a past with the Owens. No wonder he was so intent on ruining the winery! It was at the point of being silly, how much he hated it."

"How did you meet Bellamont? He didn't just walk in Owen Winery. It wasn't customary to visit the wineries he was trying to ruin?"

"I went to see him when I found out where he was living. Sydney Keller from Allenwood told me they were boarding this critic. Once she told me who it was I almost didn't believe it. You see he had already started with the bad reviews for Owen Winery. Sydney didn't pay attention to his reviews but I did. I went to see what was wrong. Why he had it in for us." She sighed, stubbing out her cigarette. "He didn't tell me why he hated the wine, just that he hated it. I knew my husband was devoted to making wine so I took it as an insult. When we met I knew he was trying to get in my pants."

"So you used him to write a book."

"The opportunity was there. I'm sorry it all ended up this way."

Deville wasn't sure if she was sincere. "Jan Bellamont, was she there on your first visit to the cottage?"

"No. She was doing some charity work, at an arts council. I get all those philanthropic activities confused." Stephanie didn't look like the type to give back to the community. "She doesn't even know we saw each other behind her back. We'd meet at hotels and sometimes at our winery itself. Gerard got a thrill meeting there, said it made sense."

Of course it would. It was adultery that ended his father's life and robbed him of his childhood. By meeting at Owen Winery, Bellamont was bringing it all back home. He wondered if Bellamont was ignorant to what was happening all around him. His wife's addiction to prescription drugs, his son's hidden feelings. How can a man be so intent on focusing on the past yet ignore his own family's dysfunctions? One would think having a troubled childhood would ensure a plan not to repeat the abuse, even if it were adultery.

Deville watched as Stephanie spotted Chloe Owen being escorted out of the interview room with another officer and a couple, who were her closest family. He remained silent and noticed Stephanie's sad glance. "There she is," she said. "Young, pretty. My husband definitely had a type."

"Mrs. Ferris who do you think killed your husband?"

She looked back to him and shrugged. "Roger Owen. Who else? He was upset when I told him."

"Told him?"

"About my husband and his daughter."

"When was this?"

"The night Gerard Bellamont died. I let him know because Ryan said he wanted to be with Chloe and I couldn't let that happen." She searched for a tissue. "I guess he's dead because of me."

Deville thought for a moment. If Roger Owen knew for some time about Ryan Ferris and his daughter, why did he say he just found out the night he killed Ryan? This supposedly was the trigger for the murder but if Roger had already known then killing Ryan was planned and Deville wasn't sure if Owen could have committed the crime.

Stephanie Ferris asked if she was free to go. Deville

told her not to go far. The case was turning up new leads and it would be wise to stay near a phone. When she left, Deville thought he had reached her. Stephanie Ferris was a manipulative, money-hungry woman. She used her sexuality and cunningness to get what she wanted and she probably had to fight for everything she had. He'd seen her type before but didn't know how much empathy one could feel. He knew, however, that killing Bellamont and her husband was something she could have done but more likely didn't. Evidence was not there to support this but Deville still had his suspicions.

Investigator Wolanski appeared, handing a file to Deville. "Shit. Doesn't she know there's no smoking inside buildings?"

"Yes. She was trying to prove a point." He opened the folder.

"She looked like she was ready to start some trouble. Not exactly a mourning widow, I daresay." She sat on the edge of his desk, something she did on all the desks. "The file shows what I found out about the Kellers. Frank Keller has a record of assault. His wife was sued for a real estate deal. It seems she sold a property to someone who was under the pretenses that the property would be torn down for a shopping complex. The new owner found out there was never such a deal and overpaid."

"Frank Keller has a past?" Deville asked. He looked through the file and there was his mug shot, looking dim-witted as ever. "Any more info about what happened? It says here it was at a casino. An Indian reservation."

"The casino was trying to throw him out. Apparently he lost big money. The real estate deal was a separate incident with the wife. It seems Keller likes to gamble."

"And lose," Deville said, closing the file. He was not happy with the news. Frank Keller admitted there was a problem with his gambling but never mentioned the assault. Keller had the strength and now a record of assault. Was owing money to Bellamont enough of a motive to kill him? Deville didn't think so. This still gave no motive for Frank Keller to kill Ryan Ferris.

"Would you like me to dig deeper into this?" Wolanski asked.

He almost didn't hear her. "No. I think that will be all."

"Geez, do we have enough people confessing to these murders or what?" she asked, still sitting on the edge of his desk. "That young girl, Chloe, her aunt and uncle came in to pick her up. Poor girl, both of her parents are confessing. What if they both are guilty? What will happen to her? Perhaps foster care. I can't imagine anyone going to foster care."

Deville didn't utter a word and wondered if Wolanski knew about his own years in foster care. He tried to change the subject. "This property, the one that caused all these problems with Marianne Keller, which one is it?"

She stood up, opened the folder he had just closed and pointed.

He sighed. He'd missed the information right in front of him.

"It's in Geneva, some arts council. It appears they're not going anywhere. And the new owner is pissed. Thought they would get a chunk of change if the shopping center was coming but since it's not…"

Deville couldn't hear Investigator Wolanski anymore since his mind was racing. Where else did he hear about the arts council? He remembered Jan Bellamont being involved somehow. The cookies. She had baked cookies for the arts council. She said she had donated some time there.

He got up and thanked Wolanski, "See if Mrs. Owen needs anything and I'll be back."

"Where are you going?"
As he was walking away he said, "To see some art."

CHAPTER TWENTY-SIX

He needed to speak to Wyatt Bellamont but the arts council was on his way to the cottage. The building in Geneva was a large brick and stone at the corner of a busy road. The huge windows displayed local art pieces and there were some posters of a musical show coming soon. He parked a block away and walked. The streets were busy with townspeople who were enjoying the mild day. Inside the building was dark and he noticed people rehearsing for an upcoming show. Music flowed throughout the building and Deville had to go past the stage area to get to the gallery. Inside there were several people setting up. He noticed sculptures, paintings, drawings, photographs and unusual pieces.

As he strolled through the gallery, he wondered how many pieces were from local artists. He glanced at his watch and almost bumped into someone.

"Louis, it's you," Sydney Keller said, holding a box of bottles with somewhat of a struggle.

"What are you doing here?" Deville asked.

She handed the box to him. "An art show starts in ten minutes and I'm providing the wine. Can you please carry it over to that table?"

Deville did so and helped her unpack. "Is this

customary?"

"To get the word out, yes. It's good PR." She sighed and Deville could tell she was still feeling troubled from earlier today. The news about Ryan Ferris was on her mind. "I don't feel like doing any of this. I may just leave a little early. If it weren't for Jan, who invited me, I would have canceled."

Jan Bellamont appeared and greeted Sydney. She noticed Deville and walked over to him. "Oh, my God. I heard what happened at Owen Winery. That poor young man!" She grabbed Deville's shoulders. "Thank God you were with us last night. That monster could have killed us."

"Mrs. Bellamont, I remember you said you donated your time here. Do you have a moment?"

"Just a minute. The show is about to start. Why don't you walk with me?"

They walked in a brisk stride. Jan Bellamont made sure everything was perfect. She brushed cobwebs with her hands, straightened anything framed and on the wall and ordered people around. She looked at Deville and noticed his pondering gaze. "This is what I used to do before Gerard. Event planning. Art openings, private parties. I was quite good."

Indeed she was. Deville was impressed when four people came to her at once and her instructions came out fluently and without effort. When she finished with her orders, she took a breath. "Dear me, I haven't worked this hard since a fashion show in California. Gerard used to say I worked too hard. He didn't want me to work this hard and he didn't want me to do without. He didn't want me…" she broke off.

"To have a life?"

She turned to look at him. "I know what you think. Why did I stay married to him?" She shrugged and walked over to a colorful painting. "One gets comfortable and forgets how life used to be." She lowered her head, fixed the card on the colorful painting, which showed tulips, and then stepped back. "Paul Shepard donated this. It's lovely."

Deville recognized the artist. A vivid red background with white tulips.

Jan Bellamont asked, "It's a holiday preview show. Are you staying? You can bid on something. I'm sure your wife or girlfriend would love this."

"Not on my salary but thanks. Mrs. Bellamont where is your son?"

"I was going to ask you. He's not answering his cell phone. As soon as this starts I'm going back to the cottage." Another person came to her and she almost yelled. "We said tea, not iced tea. Back where I'm from, tea means hot tea. It's November, for crying out loud, do you think people want iced tea?" She shook her head and covered her face. Deville heard her whimpering. "I'm sorry. I just need a moment. I'm worried about Wyatt. He usually answers his phone."

Deville found a tissue and gave it to her. "Mrs. Bellamont can you tell me about your husband's second book?"

She grabbed the tissue that Deville handed her. "I don't know. Some book. I don't think he's even started. My son Wyatt knows more. He helps him. Wyatt helps me. too."

"Do you know what the book is about? It's important."

"To the case? Will it help you find the killer? I don't know what to say. How hard can it be to find whoever killed my husband? Was it robbery, as the papers are saying? I don't think so. Why would they come after me? I can't see how this other endeavor will help you solve the case."

"Anything you know, whether you think it's important

or not, you need to tell me."

She looked at him as though she were losing her patience. "Tell me, investigator, did you fall asleep last night?"

He said nothing.

"The intruder came into my room and could have gone into Wyatt's. I know you were watching because you came as soon as I screamed but didn't you notice anyone?"

Deville's mouth opened but it took a moment before he could talk. "I'm so sorry."

"How does it feel to be questioned? Not knowing all the answers makes you feel less of a person, doesn't it? That's how I feel. Like I should know something about his murder or about what caused this but I don't." She closed her eyes. "I don't need your apology. I am just scared. That's why I can't stay at the cottage all day. I need to keep busy." She patted his shoulder. "Maybe you can tell me who my husband was having an affair with? Do you know? Because I am that wife who doesn't know. All I know is he was spraying himself like a man whore and now every woman I see, I sniff." She looked past him to where Sydney Keller was getting ready for wine tasting. "I am more interested in who was sleeping with him than who killed him." She patted his cheek and walked away.

Deville watched her greet people at the door. She was truly elegant and after all she'd been through, she continued to show dedication to her commitments. Deville believed Jan Bellamont kept her mind off her husband's death by keeping busy. He also believed she was scared to stay in the cottage by herself. She wanted her son to be there while she was, Deville thought. It was only a matter of time before she moved back to California and left the Finger Lakes for good. He needed to solve the case soon so Jan and Wyatt Bellamont could move back to the West Coast before something awful happened to them.

He noticed Sydney Keller pouring wine for people. Her face looked pale and her movements mechanical, like she was someone in a factory or at a job where time just dragged. She was not her usual self.

He watched Jan Bellamont leave and wondered if he should escort her. He decided he would go to her after speaking to Sydney. "Sydney, can I ask you a few more questions?"

She shook her head. "I'm too tired." She touched his arm. "But you can stay with me." A glimmer of a smile appeared and then a little color in her cheeks.

There it was, he thought. An invitation for him to stay with her. Though it was short, somewhat curt and not terribly romantic, Deville accepted it for what it was. Sydney Keller was interested in him, making him feel young again but also nervous and uncomfortable. Was this how infatuation felt? He tried to recall and told himself this was silly. He was reading too much into this. What would he do next? Carry her books home from school?

"Are you seeing anyone, Louis?" she asked while looking anywhere but at him.

Maybe he wasn't reading too much into it He couldn't believe his hands were in his pockets. He didn't remember placing them there. "Not anyone exclusively." He made a face. It sounded ridiculous even to him.

She laughed. "You're quite a fox then, just as I suspected." She poured more wine. "Well, I'm not seeing anyone. But I'm not sure if I'm ready." More people came to her table and she continued pouring Allenwood wines, explaining each varietal as though she had rehearsed it. At one point there were about 20 people at her small table. She became flustered, forgetting words and spilling wine.

Deville wished he could help but knew he couldn't. When one person got belligerent, Deville flashed his badge. At once everyone was polite and soon enough they were alone again. "I can't help you pour, sorry."

Sydney smiled. "You've helped enough. I can't believe how people get when they want more wine. Let them go to a bar. This is only a tasting."

"Did you know your aunt sold this building?" he asked, getting back to work.

She didn't seem to mind. "Yes. She was hysterical about it. The person who bought it thought it would be torn down for a shopping plaza. Aunt Marianne said it was what she heard but it wasn't so. She sold the building under false pretenses but she didn't know. It's just a mess."

"So what's happening?"

"Aunt Marianne has to pay some legal fees and the difference of what the property is really worth, about thirty grand. It's a lot for them. I don't know where they will get it."

The Kellers needed cash. Between Frank's assault charge and Marianne's litigation, Allenwood Winery needed to produce cash, quickly. He couldn't get Frank Keller out of his mind, saying how business was picking up for the winery ever since the murder. Stranger things have happened and Deville couldn't bear telling Sydney how he felt. Seeing Frank Keller in an arm sling stirred up speculation. Learning the Kellers' desperate situation made matters worse.

Just then his phone rang. It was Jan Bellamont.

"It's Wyatt," she said. "He never turned up. I think he's missing."

CHAPTER TWENTY-SEVEN

Deville drove to Allenwood Vineyard in just a few minutes. He pulled into the driveway, almost crashing into other cars that were blocking the path to the cottage. When he reached it he parked, got out and ran. When he arrived, he found Jan Bellamont searching the cottage frantically. She was looking under couch cushions and he could see she had even tipped over houseplants. She was looking for the drugs her son had hidden from her, Deville thought. When she noticed Deville, she said, "He's gone. I don't know where he is!"

"Don't worry. He'll turn up but I don't think he's under couch cushions."

She didn't want to hear it. "We have to find him right now. He's left me. They've both left me, first Gerard and now my Wyatt!" She turned to Deville, "Look for him. Don't just stand there. Look for him now!"

They both turned when they heard a noise.

Frank Keller appeared at the front door.

"What happened?" Keller asked. "I saw your car pull into the driveway like a bat out of hell."

Deville reached for his phone. "Wyatt is missing and I need your help, please."

Deville searched Wyatt's room while he heard the

other two on the first floor. Frank Keller kept Jan Bellamont company in the kitchen. He offered to take her to his winery but she didn't want to leave in case her son called. Listening to Deville's suggestion, Keller placed a pot of water to boil, called his wife Marianne and they both sat with her. Jan Bellamont shook with nervous energy and looked more disoriented than usual. Deville couldn't guess which prescription drugs may be circulating in her bloodstream at the moment but he surmised it was more than her usual dose. He continued searching for any clues of Wyatt's disappearance and evidence of a second book.

While he searched Wyatt's room, he also called the station and asked for them to search Bellamont's laptop further. He told them to search high and low, knowing documents could hide in folders and could be locked by a password too. He hoped there still would be something on the computer itself but if he kept a copy on a flash drive or other storage device there was no telling where it could be. So while he searched the cottage his eyes were also searching for Bellamont's second manuscript. From what he learned, Wyatt would have hidden it somewhere if he hadn't thrown it away.

Wyatt's room was neat, as usual, but there was something different and missing, besides the obvious inhabitant. The room, bright with afternoon sunlight, gave a view of Allenwood's grape vines and the spot Gerard Bellamont was killed. Deville paused a moment to stare out the window. Could Wyatt have seen his father's death through this window? It was possible but because of the time of death it was dark and the figures wouldn't be discernible. Besides, Wyatt would have been too busy with Chloe Owen. Two teenagers, around the same age, a perfect opportunity for both of them to explore each other, but something had happened. Could this have been when Chloe discovered Wyatt was gay?

Did Wyatt even know he was? At his age, a person knows if he is gay but being brought up by Gerard Bellamont he might still be in denial, trying to become the man his father wanted him to be.

He did one final search around the room and realized the kid's knapsack was missing. He remembered Wyatt Bellamont talked about moving back to California so he had to act in haste.

A squad car pulled up outside. He rushed down the stairs to meet Reginald Scudder and Jerome Miller.

"Wyatt Bellamont's bike is not here," Deville said, "nor his knapsack. He couldn't have gone far but he may have hitched a ride." He told Scudder to search for any transportation leaving the state, trains, buses. Wyatt would take any means to go back to California.

He turned to Jerome Miller and asked him to stay to search the cottage, beginning with Gerard Bellamont's room. "Look for a flash drive of some sort, a storage device for…"

Miller said he knew what it was. His huge frame walked away and climbed the steps to the second floor. Deville couldn't remember ever seeing Miller move so fast. Another car pulled up, a car he recognized. He ran outside to meet Sergeant Malone.

"Your cars are on my grass!" Frank Keller shouted from the doorway of the cottage. "Can you please be careful! Don't drive into the vineyard itself. Use the driveway for Christ's sake!"

Marianne Keller came from behind, grabbed her husband and encouraged him to leave them alone. Keller looked at Deville, gave a worried frown then followed his wife back into the cottage.

"Louis," Jessica said, "the case is over. Why are you doing this?"

"It's not over. Wyatt is gone."

"I know. I heard the call. We'll search for him but

having another officer search the cottage? For what?"

Deville told her without delay about the second book. She shook her head. "We have a confession, Louis, and someone else who is confessing. One or both of them killed, I'm sure of it. They each have motive and opportunity. Don't do this. Don't let this case drag on!" She grabbed his shoulders, "If you don't, I will order you to stop! I will not let you spend more of your time, or any officer's time, on this. I can't let this go on, especially with a confession."

"The Owens may not have killed him."

"Who? Bellamont or Ferris?"

Deville took her hand off his shoulder and paced. Here they were on a hill overlooking a vineyard in the fall. Somehow this spectacular view went unnoticed by both of them. Deville inhaled a deep breath and took a moment to take it in. "It's indeed beautiful, isn't it? I can't believe this is happening. In a place like this."

Jessica Malone came to him to admire it. "We often forget how nice it can be when we're faced with this sort of crime." She looked at him. "You didn't know what you were getting into when you transferred here did you?"

He didn't reply. "There's something I'm missing and I think Wyatt can help."

"Let me drive you to your car then," she said, "and we can figure out how to find Wyatt." He inhaled one last breath of fresh air and let her do just that. While driving past the vines she asked, "Are you okay?"

He bit his lip. "I'm having flashbacks. I'm remembering more things about my past."

"About your father?"

He nodded. "These images are disturbing. I'm running through the tall vines, I feel my father is near, and then..." he stopped.

She pulled up next to his car, "What happens then,

Louis?"

He looked at her. "I don't know. That's when I feel a sense of dread. There's something there. I'm about to find him—my father."

She brought out her hand once again to hold his. "Why don't you take off? The case is over. We can talk about it."

"Talk about it! My God aren't you tired of it?" He paused. "That's right, of course. You thrive on it!" She pulled back her hand. Her face turned pale. He continued, "There you go again. The deeper I get into my past, the more passionate you get. The only time our relationship worked well for you was at my darkest point. You have no use for me when my past is not in the picture. Am I that boring to you?" He sighed. "That's it. It's over between us. You can't just want to start something because you get excited whenever my memory kicks in."

"That's not how it is."

"It is, Jess. You get a thrill from my anguish."

She slapped him. Hard. "How dare you!" She turned away. "Get out. Get out of my car. That's it. You're off this case. I request that you transfer. Maybe then you'll see how excited I get. You bastard. I can't believe I ever loved you. Get the hell out!"

Deville opened the door, feeling like a heel. So there it was. She finally admitted she had loved him. He still believed she did, which created a problem. He needed to leave her, leave the station and expeditiously leave his past. While he buckled himself in his car, he saw her peel away and tried to feel something. Sadness, or anger? He looked in the mirror where his face seemed larger than life but lacked emotion. His brown eyes stared back at him as he dared his reflection to show some emotion. He almost begged for tears. When none came, he screamed at his own reflection.

CHAPTER TWENTY-EIGHT

Humans could only be stretched to a limit and Deville felt he had reached his. After a few moments of deep breathing, he decided he needed to collect his thoughts. Just then, he noticed people leaving Allenwood Winery. If Sydney Keller were there, she might know where Wyatt is. Then a thought occurred to him. He would try the next closest person to Wyatt. He drove out of the driveway, went up the road and turned into Catalina Winery, looking for Paul Shepard. If there was anyone who knew where Wyatt was, it would be Paul.

Shepard had his back to him when Deville stepped up. Shepard turned around, as though he were expecting him. He looked troubled and forlorn, even a bit sad. When he found out about Wyatt's disappearance he poured himself a glass of wine.

"Mr. Shepard do you know where Wyatt is?"

Shepard took off his apron. "I've got to go look for him."

"Mr. Shepard…"

He raised his hand. "I have to help you. Wyatt is not himself. He's troubled. Lately he's more troubled than usual." He shook his head. "I saw this kid, this young man who reminded me of myself when I was younger. I gave him some attention and listened to him. Made him feel like he's worth something. Then what happens? The kid doesn't leave me alone. People talk." He paused and then added, "You think I'm unaware of what they are saying? I know how bad it looks for a man like me to have Wyatt around all the time." He sighed. "Wyatt just needed a friend. Sydney and I just wanted to help."

Deville didn't know what to believe. All he heard was an imaginary clock ticking, taking precious time away from Wyatt. "You and Sydney know him the best. Should we be worried about him or will he turn up somewhere? Right now I don't care about your relationship with him; whether it's emotional, supportive or something else. I just want to make sure the boy is safe."

Shepard gave him a serious look. "I would be worried. I am worried."

"So where could he be?"

Shepard shook his head. "I don't know. I need to think."

"We don't have time, Shepard. Where did he like to go?" He slammed his fist into the bar. "Think, dammit!"

Shepard jumped, startled. He thought for a moment and then looked hopeful. "Waterfalls. He enjoyed waterfalls. We took him to see waterfalls a few days ago. He loved it there. Said something about being buried there. I told him not to say such things. It was so out of place. And then he looked at me and asked if I could write a lament for him." He looked at Deville and swallowed. "Is it normal for a teenage boy to say such things?"

"Wyatt is not a normal teenage boy. I don't know anyone who's normal."

Moments later he drove, wishing Wyatt was alive and well and could help him unravel the mysterious deaths that had been plaguing the Finger Lakes.

He thought again about the haunting memory of who

his father was. He had never been this close to discovering what happened in his past and this case meant more to him than life itself. It was the reason his memory was working and it may be the key to the truth.

As he passed more wineries, he felt a tug of sadness. How could a tragedy happen in the midst of all this beauty? Indeed, these grapes were the key to this misery, from his past to the present case. So little is the fruit that bears the pain of a lifetime.

Wyatt wasn't on foot and he could find a ride with anyone. Deville requested help from other stations from here to the Rochester Airport and visited the area's waterfalls. Finding Wyatt Bellamont was not an easy task.

Deville phoned Jan Bellamont. From what she recalled, which wasn't much, they deduced Wyatt might have gone to Watkins Glen, which wasn't too far. Jan remembered she was walking (staggering, Deville thought) to the bathroom and saw her son pacing around in his room earlier this morning. Did you see his knapsack? She didn't remember. She wasn't feeling well she admitted. But she remembered Wyatt talking about moving back to California weeks ago, before his father's death, but she didn't pay attention. She asked him why he would go there. He had no friends.

Deville thought this explained Wyatt's reluctance to run away to California. What was waiting for him there? Fictitious friends and a better life? Jan Bellamont didn't know what was going on in her son's life, perhaps because he was busy trying to fix his parents. Hiding pills from his mother, helping his father, the young boy had no time for friends. Too much responsibility and no one there to help him become a man.

Watkins Glen State Park was about ten miles away, south on Route 14. He rushed and drove well over the speed limit, passing cars swiftly. He also passed more wineries on either side of the road, wondering how so many wineries survived fighting for the same dollar. Each must be unique in their own way. One winery, he noted, specialized in red wines, while others mentioned their ribbons and awards by billboards and some poked fun at the award-winning wineries, claiming they were not pompous. One even mentioned they featured a "redneck" wine. Deville continued driving, watching the sun setting, hoping he would reach his destination in time before dark.

Watkins Glen, in Schuyler County, was famous for hosting the NASCAR Winston Cup and other racing events. It stood at the bottom of Seneca Lake, where an impressive pier housed massive ships and quaint boats. There was also a recently built six-story hotel overlooking the lake and the town. He passed Main Street and turned right. After going uphill, he noticed the entrance to the park. Watkins Glen State Park held 19 waterfalls, the highest ranging up to 60 feet. Deville loved the park, admiring the cascades, plunges and chutes where water fell without effort, creating a marvelous spectacle. He asked the attendant if he saw a teenager with a bike. The attendant said he hadn't. After finding out he was the police, he shared that there were a few places where bicyclists parked to enter the park for free. He learned the locations of these places and began his search with the directions given to him.

He found one place where there were two bicycles. One looked familiar to him. He began his hike at a moderate pace. There were several trails, each bearing slippery walkways, dirt and stone steps and wooden balconies and bridges where onlookers could view the beauty. Walking the gorge trails was risky in November but Deville thought that Wyatt wouldn't mind taking the risk. The park was regulated but because of its size a person could disappear for just a few hours or even a day.

Coming to the State Park to escape from your problems was a different way to use this place, Deville thought. Instead of camping with a family or spending a romantic afternoon with your lover trailing the cliffs, Wyatt was using it as a haven. One place where he felt safe. Serenity can come in many places, even in a steep craggy ravine.

Wyatt Bellamont was not answering his cell phone. So his only company was his mind and memory. Deville could justify that these were enough sometimes. Having a stained past, whether you're 16 or 40, meant living with your ghosts. Sometimes they kept you company even when uninvited. He called out to Wyatt. After yelling his name several times and hearing his own echo, he continued down the slopes of the gorge, walking gingerly. He came across an archway of stone, which led to a dark tunnel. He moved toward it, slipping a few times on the wet path of stone and held on to the sides as though he were entering a mystical cave. Fear came across him in a precise moment, paralyzing him for a few minutes. He stood there, in almost complete darkness, noticing reflections of a wave further up, dancing on the walls of the tunnel. Then he heard a few splashes of water and found the courage to start again, picking up his speed. There was light ahead. Before he knew it, he was out the other side, in front of a pool of water. Just beyond, a waterfall continued filling the pool, creating splashes of light and color, and amidst all of this, the body of a young man floated near the pounding water.

Deville didn't hesitate a moment and he couldn't remember much of what happened next. After taking off his coat, he dove into the water. The pond, shockingly cold, made his muscles numb, and if it weren't for the act of trying to save a life, he thought he may have drowned himself. As he desperately swam, his feet flailed in the water behind him. He was relieved when his foot touched the bottom. Thank God, he thought, as he realized the water to be shallower than it appeared. This new knowledge gave him a boost of energy and he reached Wyatt a few seconds later. After pulling the shirtless body to the side and out of the water, he checked for breath. Wyatt was still breathing but he was out cold. Deville had made it just in time. However, the body felt cold and numb and he shivered himself. His phone was not working due to getting wet so he took his dry coat, wrapped Wyatt in it, and carried him back through the cave, following his path back to the car.

He drove to the nearest hospital in Watkins Glen, where they admitted Wyatt Bellamont immediately. A few nurses and doctors checked on Deville himself and would not let him leave until he took off his wet clothes and agree to a checkup. While in a hospital bed, waiting to be released, Deville made phone calls to the station with the hospital phone. He asked a few questions and suddenly felt dizzy. Jessica Malone's voice loomed at the other end of the line, asking where he was. He found it difficult to breathe and couldn't speak any further. Before he knew it, he drifted off to sleep, where his body could feel warmth again and where his head would stop pounding.

While he slept, he could feel the rough terrain of the ground, where the earth felt damp against his naked feet. He was running but he did not know from what. Grapevines and trellis wire were on either side of him, like a labyrinth of verdant twigs and fruit. He felt his pulse rush, his breath short from a terror swelling in his heart. Again, he was in shorts, breathing in the crisp air of France. The sun shone down; a perfect day in hell.

He recognized his uncle's voice shouting his name. Was he running from his uncle or running to him? The voice continued but now it seemed closer. From the tone, he could tell he would be in trouble.

"Louis, can you hear me?"

Deville opened his eyes and saw a blurry figure in front of him. Malone leaned over, placing a hand on his forehead. She looked tired and haggard herself. He looked around and discovered he was in a hospital room.

"It's great to see you're okay. You had quite a shock from rescuing Wyatt."

"Where is he? How is he?"

"He's a few doors down from you." She paused and took a heavy breath. "He's in a coma from pneumonia and shock. A few minutes later and he would have died." She sat on the side of the bed. Deville noticed what appeared to be another gray streak in her hair. She was dressed in a skirt and dark sweater, with little makeup. She brought up a cup of hot cocoa and urged him to drink. He did so but felt a shiver. He pulled up the covers and realized he was in a hospital garment.

The door to his room was open and he could see nurses walking past. "When I discovered where you were I rushed over." She paused and looked uncomfortable. "I'm so sorry about today, yelling at you." She reached out her hand to caress his cheek.

She must be in hog heaven now, he thought. Taking care of him was in her element. He didn't want to seem ungrateful or rude but he didn't know what to feel right now. After he had decided today that he would transfer and get away from Jessica, she had come to visit him. He pulled back her touch. She lowered her hand and head, as if she'd been rejected. "I'm just trying to help," she said.

She stood and he watched her move around the

hospital room, like she felt at home. She switched on a lamp and went to the window to open a curtain showing a new moon. "Roger Owen will go to trial and going to be sentenced. I am officially closing the case."

"Has he said anything else?"

She shook her head. "No. I took a recorded confession from him so we have something."

Deville moved, trying to get warm. He could still feel the cold in his bones. He tried to keep his mind occupied and thought about the case. Roger Owen had confessed but Deville couldn't ignore his other leads and unanswered questions. "What about my trellis wire samples? Did you hand those to someone?"

"I told you the case is…"

"Dammit, Jessica! We need proof, regardless of who did it."

She nodded silently. After a moment, she moved around the room. "Okay, I can take them and see if it's a match with the wound."

"What about Bellamont's laptop or the cottage? Was there a second book found?"

"No. Jerome Miller looked through the cottage and our computer expert went through the laptop again and found no second book."

He sighed, looking at the clock. It was ten forty pm. and he felt useless.

She moved away from the window and grabbed her purse. "I sent Mrs. Owen home to be with her daughter. When she confessed, it was surprising."

He shrugged and said, "She loves her husband. It's a toss-up. Two confessions, one from each of them. A couple who both have motives is misleading to the case. She's confessing the same reason he is."

"Because she thinks he did it? So he confessed because he thinks she did it? How terribly romantic."

Deville said, "They're protecting each other or

someone else."

"The only other person is Chloe. There's no way she could have killed those two men. You've seen her."

"That child is manipulative. I don't think she killed anyone herself but she may have been involved or be the reason behind the killings." He explained about the affair of Chloe Owen and Ryan Ferris. "A lover's quarrel could have been a motive to kill Ryan Ferris, but Gerard Bellamont had a different motive."

"I would certainly hope. I can't see Bellamont and Chloe Owen together. The thought of her and Ryan is upsetting enough." She put on her coat. "But if Chloe Owen is the reason, who did the killing? Her mother? Her father?"

"Maybe neither." He thought about Wyatt Bellamont, lying in the water, his head floating, eyes closed facing the heavens as if he were a human sacrifice. Finding Wyatt in this state meant the young man was trying to kill himself. One reason for suicide was remorse. He couldn't imagine Wyatt killing his father but Ryan Ferris, possibly. Though Jessica Malone was closing the case, Deville considered Wyatt still very much a suspect. The troubled soul was just a few doors down from him and he thought he would try to get up to visit Wyatt. After trying a few times he couldn't believe how weak he was. He leaned back, listening to the message his body was giving him.

The two teenagers were on his mind now, Wyatt and Chloe. He wondered how much more trouble they would be in after this. Killing people who got in your way was nothing new, Deville thought. Chloe Owen could have been the mastermind and the reason for these crimes. He could still remember the time he saw her, standing above the staircase, with a worried look in her face. Was it fear or was she concerned he was on to her? Using Wyatt as a pawn for her evil work was something he wouldn't put past her. But why would Wyatt submit? She knew he was confused and attracted to men but did Wyatt know she knew?

Jessica Malone was heading out. "Get plenty of rest and don't come in tomorrow. I'll let you call in sick." She gave a small smile and grabbed the door handle to leave. "Closed or open?"

"Closed. And thank you," he said with a strained voice.

It was warranted and he didn't want to be rude.

"You're welcome," she said, with glassy eyes. "It's what any friend would do."

CHAPTER TWENTY-NINE

His heartbeat was the only thing he felt. A glimmer of light appeared in the darkness and he could see the clear sky again. A moment later, the tall grass, and subsequently, the vineyard. His movements were quick. He was running as fast as he ever had, wishing he could just fly over the vineyard and away from his pursuer. Still, his heartbeat prevailed and Deville counted eighteen in six seconds, meaning that his heartbeat was reaching 180 beats per minute. Dangerously close for heart failure if he were old, he thought, but not while he was young.

And indeed he was young, at least in the dream world. Everything else came back at once. The smell of grapes from the vines and the ground when his bare feet stomped on them while he was running. It was not only his heartbeat he could feel but other senses were developing. He could hear a hush and a murmur of voices. One stronger voice called his name.

Papa, he called out.

The voice that responded wasn't his father's. He thought it was because he was searching for his father. It was a frantic search because he was running. Running away from someone. Not from his home but from someone who was after him.

He cut across the vineyard and his tiny stiff body got caught in trellis wire. The blood and grape juice splattered on his legs. He went through, row after row, for what seemed like hours, trying to make the distance greater between him and his pursuer. He cursed his feet for not moving faster and cursed the rest of his body for not being flexible.

His head felt the pressure of his heartbeat and the effects of how much wine he'd drunk last night. He could still feel the wine in him and when his mother took it away he became violent and hit her. He felt sorry for doing this but he knew he wasn't his usual self.

Watching his uncle hit his mother, right after dancing with her in the kitchen made his stomach turn. They would always dance after eating a huge dinner, and usually a row followed. On those particular nights, when the two were nearly passed out from drinking, Louis hid under the furniture. Whenever his father's name was mentioned, the hitting began.

He hated his uncle. He hated everything about him. His looks, the smell of him after he made love to his mother, the feel of his palm when he slapped the hell out of Deville. The fear in him when his mother told his uncle she was leaving him. And taking her son with her. She would look at Deville and know it was enough—the wine, the treachery. It was all enough for him to leave. Leave it all behind and seek safety.

He wished his uncle would just die.

That was the last thing he remembered before running. The fear of his uncle. A fear that made him forget all the times...

He spotted something ahead of him, a figure. A scarecrow. He rushed toward it, getting tangled in more wires and vines. He felt blood dripping in his ear from a wire cut but he kept moving. If you stop moving, you die, he told himself, not sure where he'd heard it before. Probably from some American movie, he surmised. They were always so bloody violent.

The scarecrow was in front of him now, gawking back at him. But it wasn't a scarecrow. He remembered now they didn't own a scarecrow. The lifeless figure in front of him, covered with dried blood and insects, was almost unrecognizable. If it weren't for the torn, ragged clothes he remembered, he wouldn't have recognized that it was his father. The figure looked like a maniacal clown. However, the makeup was human flesh, exposed.

That's when the death of Deville began, at least the death of a part of him, and that's when he couldn't remember anything else.

Just then he opened his eyes and tried to move. He opened his mouth and tried to scream from the terror of his dream but there was no one around to hear. No one except for the shadow in the doorway.

A figure, dark and mysterious, loomed by the doorway of his hospital room.

Deville, half awake, could see the brightness behind the figure.

He realized he wasn't in a dream anymore.

He almost made out who it was—but before he could —he reached for a button that called for help. A moment later the door closed then re-opened to show the nurse on duty.

"Someone was here!" he exclaimed.

"Calm down, Mr. Deville. You had a nightmare."

"No, it was real. Someone was here," he pointed. "By the doorway. A shape."

She pushed him back and pulled the covers to tuck him in his bed. "There's no shape, sir. It's just the medication."

"What medication? I don't take medication!"

She grabbed a vial at his bedside, "And what do you

call this? I don't think the doctor authorized this. You're going to be in a lot of trouble, Mr...."

He grabbed the vial. It was something from Jan Bellamont. He tried to read what it was but couldn't. His blurred vision prevented anything from focusing. A moment later, the nurse yelled for a doctor and soon everyone around him was a dark figure, exploring his body. A light flashed in his eyes and a moment later, they were injecting him with something. He heard someone mentioning how high his heartbeat was climbing and that his heart may fail. It was beating so fast it wanted to burst out of his chest.

The dark shadows around his hospital bed soon faded away and right before they did, he heard another nurse from the doorway say they'd just lost the other one. The young kid who came in the same time as this one.

CHAPTER THIRTY

They had injected him with Anistreplase, which was given to prevent a heart attack. If it weren't for their fast thinking, Deville would have developed cardiac arrhythmia and could have died. Just like Wyatt Bellamont did, a few doors down from him. Deville never said goodbye to the young man and he was angry for not preventing his death.

An image of Wyatt Bellamont taking care of his parents tugged at his emotions. So much responsibility for a teenager, especially when he had his own demons to work through. No wonder he sought refuge with other grownups and felt at home with them. He was leading an adult life himself.

The mysterious figure who came in had given him and Wyatt a therapeutic dose of Chlorpromazine, a prescribed drug commonly used for anxiety. The bottle of pills lay by his bedside. Although his dose, along with Wyatt's, were administered by a shot. Who would have taken the time to create a lethal dose then inject it? Whoever it was must have known he was asleep; so tired he couldn't stop anyone from injecting him. The vial was left as a cruel joke. He knew there would be no prints on it.

When the nurses came in, they opened the curtains and asked him how he was doing. He could move around and had enough strength to lift his head.

"You gave us a scare last night," one of them said.

The other one remained silent. Both were being fussy, making sure he was comfortable. He wondered if they thought he would sue the hospital. Not paying attention to anyone who came into a room should be a crime but he knew it was difficult to keep track of all the patients and their visitors, even after visiting hours were over.

Two officers from the local police department walked in and said they needed to speak with him. He agreed and asked them to retrieve his clothes. They obliged and while he was dressing, they asked questions. Deville asked if there had been videotapes and they said no. It was not a big hospital and security was not high on their priority. Deville couldn't complain since they may have saved his life.

"There are a few more questions," the officers said.

"Then you follow me."

They helped him stand and waited while he dressed. Deville walked with a cautious pace, grabbing the walls for support. He answered their questions while he searched for Wyatt's hospital room. When he found it, they stopped asking their questions. The body was covered in a sheet and an officer guarded the door. Too late, he said to himself, wishing he had authorized an officer to guard Wyatt. He didn't have to die.

Deville looked around but didn't see Jan Bellamont anywhere. He walked inside the room but was stopped by the guarding officer. When the others waved him through, Deville went straight to the closet. "So the book must have been found," he said aloud.

"What book, sir?"

His body felt weak and his hair was a mess but he continued looking through the clothes that Wyatt had worn. "The book. The second book his father was writing. Was anything found on him?" They shrugged and shook their heads.

After going through all the clothes in the room, he turned around. "All right, I still have a little more work. First, I need a strong cup of coffee." One officer left the room. Deville turned to the other, who had been silent all this time. "Next, I'll need a ride to the station. Since you haven't said a word, I guess you're the driver, correct?

CHAPTER THIRTY-ONE

He knew his sergeant had asked him to stay away from work but it wasn't the first time he disobeyed her orders. Plus if he didn't arrive she would probably be more worried about him. Romantic relationship or not, Jessica Malone had proven to be a valuable friend and he didn't want his friends to worry about him. Though he disappointed himself for being such a weakling from the consequences of diving into icy waters, he was glad he had tried to save Wyatt Bellamont's life. At least once. The second time he wasn't as successful. In his drugged state he was lucky to be alive himself.

As he was driven to the station, he thought about his dreams the previous night, before the killer had visited him. For once he was thankful for the dreams and memories. He knew memories were always a good thing for his psychosis but the delivery method had been less than desirable. Running through a vineyard for your life was not like remembering someone's grandpa on a rocking chair, smoking a pipe.

His visions were sheer terror to him, a horrific movie he could not pause. At least his latest vision was this way. Last night was the worst flashback so far. He could still see the body of his father in the vineyard, set up in a similar fashion as Gerard Bellamont had been. He now knew why these images were coming back to him. This case was making him remember. Seeing the first victim triggered these memories. He'd heard images and smells could do this and wondered if a combination of these things caused the memories to surface. Walking around in vineyards, being around the grapes or even the wine itself, could have provoked them. Whatever it was, it was getting more difficult to manage, and he wondered if he'd reached the end.

He now knew how his father had died: by the hands of his father's brother, his own uncle. The danger was all too real. A part of him wished the whole past would unravel at once, so he could take action and be done with it. This prolonged agony was doing a number on his nerves and emotions. It could even hinder his performance on the job.

But he wasn't sure if these images were real memories. His father's death was too similar to Gerard Bellamont's. He wondered if his investigation influenced these dreams. Did his father really die like this or was the case getting to him? Should he remain silent about what he saw or how he felt? Disclosure came at a price. He kept quiet. He didn't need more visits to psychiatric hospitals, more sessions with psychiatrists or more mind-altering drugs, especially after last night.

If he didn't stay quiet, a new army of specialists would emerge to guess what made his mind tick. He dreaded the process of discovering his demons and let nature run its course, knowing whatever happened, would happen soon. He would have plenty of time to research his past at some point.

The station was crowded, although it seemed there were no more officers than usual. He tried to move without causing any attention. There were a few stares and Deville greeted everyone the same way. He wondered if he looked any different to them. Was there a near-death-experience people showed on their faces? Or perhaps it was visible in their aura and a handful of gifted people could see it? Whatever it was, this would have to cover the stench of not showering for a day.

He found on his desk folders from the other investigative officers who were helping him. A note on one said, "You're welcome" and on the other, "Thanks for wasting my time. The case is closed."

He looked at the first report from the lab, which held the information about the trellis wire he had collected. All three were comparable but it was unlikely any were used for the murders. The tests weren't conclusive. They needed permission to continue and Deville wasn't sure if they should since the case was closed. He read the report again carefully to make sure. It was unlikely any of the trellis wires were used, he repeated to himself.

He looked at photos inside the folder—which had been rushed—two close ups of each victim's neck. Bellamont's thin red line microscopically close. Ryan Ferris' neck, all cleaned from the blood that was surrounding the wound, showed the same characteristics as the first. It could mean the killer was the same person. Except the second victim had a more jagged, coarser line, which could mean Ryan Ferris could have fought.

The second folder listed the contents of the laptop plus held photos of the first victim's room. Bellamont's room looked like it had been searched for something, with clothes disarrayed, bed unmade and dust everywhere. Where in this mess was a flash drive of Bellamont's second book? He had searched and not found anything. It didn't help that Bellamont was untidy, just as his wife was. He wondered why Wyatt had kept a neat and clean room. He thought about searching Wyatt's room again but Malone called him into her room.

Jessica Malone stood by the open doorway to her

office, with her hands crossed. She started shutting the door, then stopped, leaving it open. He felt relieved she kept the door open. She was taking this friendship more seriously, he thought. Maybe he would stay here after all.

"I knew it was impossible to keep you away. I'm not even going to ask how you are, although you're paler than usual."

"Thank you."

"I heard you had an intruder last night."

He nodded. "The same one Jan Bellamont saw. The same person who vandalized my car."

She cocked her head, "This person tried to kill you."

"That person succeeded with Wyatt Bellamont."

She looked good. She was dressed in a tight but respectable sweater, long dark slacks and her hair pulled back in an easy no-frills fashion. "I'm sorry about him."

"So what happens to our suspect in custody?"

She went around her desk to sit in her chair. "I imagine you heard the press conference, stating we caught the killer." He nodded, remembering an announcement he'd just heard on the officer's car radio. "I know you may not agree but we have a smoking gun."

"Jess, Roger may not be our killer. He told me he discovered the relationship of Ryan Ferris and Chloe the night he killed Ferris but he knew before." He told Malone about the conversation he had with Stephanie Ferris. "Spiteful wife came clean to Mr. Owen. If he wanted to kill Ferris, why wait days later?"

Malone explained. "We charged Mr. Owen because he has motive and opportunity, plus there's the confession."

"Why not charge Mrs. Owen too? Mrs. Owen has everything you mentioned as well, including the confession."

She pursed her lips, "I knew you would say that."

"She was gone for a while," he said. "When I visited

their home on the night of Ryan Ferris's murder." He remembered going to visit Chloe and then walking downstairs to see Mrs. Owen's boots. "She had opportunity. Plus, while her husband was incarcerated, she could have come to the hospital last night to finish Wyatt off and try her best to scare me."

"Finish Wyatt off? Do you think someone tried to drown him?

"I don't know right now. It's possible. He was distressed about his father, about other things, too. It looks more like a suicide attempt but someone could have driven him to it."

"And Kelly Owen is your suspect for this?" When he said nothing she continued. "What happened last night could be a separate thing. Maybe Wyatt tried to kill himself. Maybe it's unrelated."

"And the attempt on my life?"

"Could Wyatt inject himself after injecting you?"

Deville couldn't believe what he'd just heard. "Jess, he was in a coma. You said so yourself."

She closed her eyes and took a deep breath. "We are going in circles. I cannot hold this case in limbo."

"So do others know about the attempt on my life last night?"

"It's not public knowledge," she said.

"The drugs were prescribed to Jan Bellamont. Where was she?"

"When I left you she was at her son's bedside." A moment later she uttered what they were both thinking. "Do you think she would kill her son and then try to kill you?"

He remembered her last night, how much in charge she was. Jan's life before Gerard Bellamont seemed so alluring, so different from when he first met her as a grieving widow. The drugs were hers. She had access to them. Leaving the vials there with her name seemed so incriminating but also misleading. Would Jan Bellamont kill her own son? Deville didn't want to think she would but he felt a moment of dread, and thought it could happen. Jan didn't know they had someone in custody. She still thought the public feared a murderer on the loose so the police would not suspect her.

He could still feel his body throbbing. The nurses said traces of the drug may still linger in him and its side effects. He needed no one at the station discovering what happened but it would be a matter of time before the word got out.

There were more important things he had to worry about though. If there was a killer still out there, something had to be done soon. The public thinking a killer was in custody was a good thing. However, confessing to their supervisors about their doubts of arresting the wrong person was not. "How long are you going to wait before you tell the lieutenant about me and this new lead?"

"He's still in California with his family. I talked to him yesterday. He's happy we finally have our man. I don't know, Louis. Should I tell him we are not sure?"

He shook his head. "Why disappoint him? Let's wait."

"For what? For you to gather more evidence? How much more time do we need?"

They both sat silent, neither wanting to look at each other. Deville stood and asked, "Any word on the pizza delivery person?"

The question seemed to have come from left field. "I don't understand what you're talking about."

"The pizza left in the room where Ryan Ferris was found. It was a delivery. I asked Scudder…"

"The case is closed. I told everyone to stop. We have other cases, Louis!"

"You're wrong, Jess!" He turned to go and she called out to him.

"Louis, I can't stop you from investigating. I'll keep Owen here a little longer. Have you thought about what you said yesterday about leaving? Were you serious?"

"Yes." He stared into the hallway, not looking at her, his hand on the archway. "I'm still thinking about it. I'm thankful to you but things have to be handled differently if I stay. I want to be treated like everyone else. I want to pretend we don't have a past. That is if you don't transfer me. It's your call."

After a pause he heard her say, "I'd be lying if I said it wouldn't be difficult. I care for you, just like I care for all the officers."

"Then let me be," he interrupted. "The first sign of treating me different, I'll leave. It's not a threat. I'm just letting you know."

"That is fair" he heard her say as he left her office, feeling lighter than when he'd entered. He strolled to his desk, where he found Scudder.

The young man seemed nervous. "Sergeant told me the case is closed."

Deville wobbled over and sat down.

"What happened to you, sir?" Scudder asked.

"Life," he replied. He noticed Scudder holding a pad. "What did you find out, Scudder?"

Scudder swallowed and continued. "I asked if they had delivered to Owen Winery the night in question. One place did but the driver was off today. I asked for the name, phone and address, which I got without a problem. I called and left a message when no one answered, letting the driver know that it was important to call me back." He paused. "Sir, I know she said the case is closed but I also know you. You asked me to follow up, and I did. I'll wait for him to call me and let you know right away."

He nodded. "Thank you. I appreciate it."

The young officer left leaving Deville alone to look at

his notes again. He went into the interview room, where it was quiet. There he replayed his videos and studied his notes, going over different scenarios. He watched the video of the crime scene of Ryan Ferris, saw the pizza, the bloody mess, the wine bottles and a single wine glass. No prints on the glass nor on the wine bottles. However, something stood out to him. The wine bottles. There were several of them laid out. Ryan Ferris seemed to reach out to one in particular. He couldn't see clearly which bottle but thought it might be something. Once they enhance the video, they might tell which wine bottle.

Just then the door opened to reveal Investigator Jerome Miller.

He stood up, hoping he didn't look like he felt. "Miller, what can I do for you?"

Miller's heavy frame stood by the doorway. "Case is closed. You had me wasting my time."

Deville sighed. "I know but I didn't realize it. You may work on your other cases."

"I heard what happened to you," Miller said. He walked over to him. "Been here long enough, you know the officers well enough. They tell me everythin'. I heard you saved the boy's life." He raised his hand to keep Deville from talking. "And I know what happened to him and to you. You know, I'm always thinkin' about how dangerous it is, out there, in a major city, with guns. But no one could have seen this comin'. Someone shooting you up to kill you?" He dropped another folder on the table. "I could have stopped callin' but I thought you might want to see this."

Deville opened the folder and saw images of Jan Bellamont.

Miller nodded to him and said farewell. "Stay safe, Frenchman."

The folder Miller left was all about Jan Bellamont and

her life before Gerard's career had taken off. Free spirited, successful, eager—a woman with so much promise. There were several photos of her from different newspapers. Art openings, private parties, book launches. One photo showed her and Gerard looking like a bright, fresh couple. Another photo, which he stared at with interest, showed Jan with another woman. It was an art opening, and paintings could be seen in the background. The other woman, standing next to Jan, seemed meek and worried, while Jan flashed a smile with a drink in her hand. Deville read the caption which read Jan Bellamont had hosted another successful art opening, this time with the rising artist, Danielle Shepard.

He remembered seeing the painting last night from Danielle Shepard, Paul's late wife and he also remembered Jan staring at it. Thoughts were flooding his head and he could feel his body shake from a chill crawling up his spine. The thought of Jan Bellamont chasing women around to sniff them. Jan, making sure no other woman went near her husband and possibly taking great lengths to keep her marriage alive.

The door opened again to reveal a grave-faced Jessica Malone.

He stood up and dared to ask, "What is it?"

"It's Sydney Keller. She's unconscious. And you'll never guess who found her."

"Jan Bellamont?" he asked, already knowing the answer would be yes.

CHAPTER THIRTY-TWO

Jan Bellamont had called the police station. Sydney Keller's apartment was in Geneva, just a few miles from the Owen residence. It was a small apartment—neat, tidy but it lacked any color whatsoever. The dark drapes wouldn't let sunlight in and the drab, beige walls were bare of any pictures, frames, or posters. It had all the fixings of a temporary residence, as though the renter used the pad as a start-up or somewhere just to lay their head for a while. He followed other officers into the bedroom, where Sydney Keller lay, surrounded by a slew of medical EMTs. From what Deville saw, her body appeared to be in the middle of a struggle, as though she were tossing and turning, but there was no blood. She looked as though she were sleeping, except for the dried up vomit. Luckily, she was still breathing but the uneasy breaths and slow rhythm concerned everyone.

An accidental overdose from a sedative, they were guessing. He watched as they carried Sydney's small body on a gurney into the ambulance and almost ran in with her. A part of him wanted to hold her hand, tell her she will be okay and be the first person she sees when she awakes.

But there were other duties. When the EMTs left a

few officers remained, treating the apartment as a crime scene, just in case Sydney lost her battle. There was no forced entry. While the officers took pictures of the bottles and pills by the bedside, Deville reached for his video device and remembered he'd left it at the station. Just as well, he reflected. Can't take a video with shaking hands. He moved about, still not steady on his feet, trying not to get in the way. He found the bathroom, off to the side of the bedroom, went inside and closed the door. There alone, he tried to collect himself. He wondered if he was falling apart.

Sydney Keller was on her way to the hospital and most likely will die. And he felt responsible. In his mind, she was already dead. The young, vibrant and mystical woman would forever remain a memory. He took a deep breath and went to the sink to splash cold water on his face. His temper rose while he tried to compose himself. This killing spree needed to end before anyone else died, or before he lost his mind. He heard a knock on the door and wondered how it would look if he fell to pieces, in front of everyone. He would give them a reason to talk. The sicko finally went insane, he imagined they would say, right there in front of a drugged passed out woman. He completely lost it.

He came out of the bathroom and asked to see the person who found the body. In a small kitchen, a wide-eyed and sleepless Jan Bellamont sat. She wore no makeup. Her face showed strains of age. She wore what appeared to be rabbit fur attached to the top of her coat and around her neck. Deville grabbed a glass, poured water from the sink into it, and handed it to her. She drank the entire contents and continued swallowing. This time for air.

He wanted to slap her. Shake her. Ask how she was involved with Sydney's current condition. He stayed silent and waited to hear what she had to say.

She shook a little when she spoke and Deville wondered if he needed to call an ambulance for her. "I gave her the drugs," Jan Bellamont said. "I gave her an old bottle of something I didn't take anymore. She said her pills weren't doing the job, only getting her dizzy but not helping her sleep. I told her I had my own little pharmacy."

"What were you doing here? Why not stay with your son's body?"

"He's asleep now. He doesn't need me now." She hugged herself, trying to keep warm even though the kitchen wasn't cold. "I can't bear to say he's dead. I have no one now. No more family."

Isn't that what you wanted? Deville thought to himself. You're free to do what you want. Live your own life; no one there to tell you otherwise.

"I needed to see Sydney," Jan continued. "To find out why." She looked at him, and when she saw his perplexed face she said, "I needed to know why she had an affair with my husband. Gerard wasn't a great husband but he was mine. And now he's dead and my son's dead, too. All because of her!"

He grabbed a chair and pulled it up. "Mrs. Bellamont, how did you get in here?"

"The landlady. I told her it was an emergency. She remembered me from the night before. Wyatt and I stayed here the night of the intruder. Sydney thought I didn't know about her and my husband. Maybe she felt guilty but I knew. How stupid do people think I am?" She grabbed his hand. "I saw the manuscript on your desk at the station. I took it. I read Gerard's second book."

Deville instantly remembered when she arrived at the station, she had dropped her pills on purpose so she could grab the manuscript that had been laying on his desk. He cursed himself for not catching it.

"The book was a tell-all. He mentioned a girl here in the Finger Lakes, a girl he was infatuated with. I suspected Sydney but I wasn't sure."

After a pause Deville asked, "So you gave Sydney pills, knowing the pills would kill her?"

She lowered her head, "God forgive me. I knew she wouldn't be able to handle it but I never thought she would have to go the hospital. I just thought she would get sick." She looked back at him with frightful eyes, "If she took the normal dose this wouldn't have happened. I swear. She wanted to kill herself. It's the only explanation." She covered her face with her hands and began crying.

"When did you give her these pills?"

"The night my husband died. I had the pills in my purse. I thought to myself this bitch had some nerve, asking me for something after what she's been putting me through. But I'd forgotten about all that. I forgot about giving her the pills. You saw me looking for them. I didn't know where they were."

Deville wondered if she meant to kill Sydney Keller by giving her an extra strong dose of sleeping pills, then why would she come to see her? Unless she wanted to make sure Sydney was dead. Deville remembered the crystal stone reading Sydney Keller had given. She had said the case would be cleared and the answer related to the heart. Love and relationships were the motive all along for the crimes, not profit. So why was Jan Bellamont here and not at her son's body?

"Do you think she had an affair with your husband, Gerard?"

Her voice sounded dry and weak. "I knew he was having an affair but I didn't know who. He would come home late to the cottage, smelling like perfume, or smoke and neither of us smoked. I confronted him. He told me to shut up and asked why I even cared." She wiped her tears with her hands. Deville handed a paper towel to her. "He called me a drug addict and said that I was of no use to him anymore. He said he had a queer for a son and an addict for a wife."

"Do you think Wyatt was gay?"

She shrugged. "I suspected for a long time but he's never mentioned it and I never asked. He knew I'd love him anyway." She blew her nose. "But Gerard, he was such a pompous asshole, thought of himself so manly, which made me laugh. He was short, always dressed to the hilt and he never liked getting dirty. Hardly what I call a man, but there it is." She blew her nose.

Jessica Malone came in and led Jan away. She asked to be taken back to the hospital to see her son. Before she left the room, she turned around. "Investigator, I rushed here to ask her why she ruined my life. That's all. I didn't kill her. Maybe she won't die. It was an accident. I didn't want to leave Wyatt but while he sat there motionless, I kept thinking about Sydney."

"What made you think it was Sydney your husband was having an affair with?"

"Who else would it be?" She looked at him in astonishment and grabbed his elbows. "What do you know? Was there someone else? I just thought it was Sydney. She would be the one, wouldn't she? She's younger and she not married. Why? What do you know?"

Deville said, "The late Danielle Shepard. Was she having an affair with your husband too? Is this what you thought? Was this what your husband was writing about?"

The question apparently surprised her. She frowned, looking disappointed. "You and that book! What does his book have to do with anything?"

"It may be important. Tell me please, about Mrs.

Shepard."

"It happened a long time ago. She died tragically. Gerard had a history with women and tragedy. Started with his mother dying."

Deville said, "Gerard's mother died right after his father died in that plane crash. His father was having an affair with Kelly Owen and then his father married Kelly. Did you know?"

"Of course I knew!" Jan Bellamont said. "Why do you think he wrote about Owen Winery so harshly? He blamed Kelly Owen for his father's death and soon after his mother died, we moved to the States."

She came forward suddenly—a couple officers stopped her. She tried to get loose. "Let go of me!" she screamed.

"Tell me what else happened then, Mrs. Bellamont."

Her eyes widened and she seemed a different person. She was remembering something troublesome. "He was so bitter after it happened. It was when he became harsh, not just as a critic but in general. He had no sympathy for anyone. Authors, artists, anyone." Her grasp tightened, "It all started when the woman drove off a cliff, Paul's wife. She killed herself because of his review of her opening. Ever since then, Gerard wasn't right. It's what he was writing about in his new book." Her eyes rolled back and a moment later she fainted, her body falling into Jessica Malone's arms.

Malone asked for more help. She looked up at Deville.

"I guess this clears the Owens," she said in an almost disappointed way.

CHAPTER THIRTY-THREE

Back at the station, Deville sat in the office of Jessica Malone, feeling tired, used and upset. Sydney Keller's life was hanging by a thread. If she died it would be another death in this bizarre case, which has taken over Deville's life. Though he wasn't sure if it would be a homicide, Sydney's death would be real and the questions still left his mind racing. His mind and his body had reached their limit. The drugs he had in his bloodstream should now be completely out of his system. He wondered if this was what was keeping him from going insane.

Malone could see his distress but she had her own troubles to worry about. Roger Owen was now asking to be released. Jan Bellamont was hysterical, not admitting to any crime. Malone received a phone call from her superior, who was on his way back. She was looking worried and Deville noticed she had already started biting her nails. When she spoke, it was with caution. The usual authoritative assured voice was now replaced with uncertainty, the sounds of a panic-stricken sergeant.

"I saw you go into the bathroom at Sydney Keller's apartment," she said. "I knocked on the door. Are you okay?"

He nodded, feeling a weight in his head that could smash a melon. He knew he needed rest and he couldn't wait to go home to his sanctuary.

"I knew I should have pulled you off of this case," she continued. "You had too much going on and these memories are not helping. They're hurting you."

He didn't want to talk about his memories, if there were memories. They were still a concern but it wasn't what was affecting him now. Sydney Keller's overdose made him feel something he hadn't in a long time. Feeling responsible for someone's life meant he cared. Deville wasn't sure if he cared for Sydney any more than he would a friend. He admired her youthfulness and humor and found her thoroughly entertaining. How could someone find her a threat? And why would Jan Bellamont kill her?

"Did you hear me? Jan Bellamont is not admitting to anything. We need to get more proof." She picked up her phone. "I'll get Christine Wolanksi on this. Is that okay with you? I think you've had enough."

Deville sat hunched in the chair. "I'm not dead yet."

"True but 'zombie' would describe you right now."

She was trying to make things a little lighter but was failing. "You need to go home. Now."

Investigator Wolanski came in and greeted them. Malone asked her to find more evidence to help convict Jan Bellamont for killing three or possibly four people. It sounded so absurd when she said it that Deville almost laughed. "It's not official," Malone continued, in a soft voice so they wouldn't be heard, "but Mr. Owen may not have done it, even though he confessed. I don't want you to broadcast this, Wolanski. It's just between us."

Wolanksi nodded. "Ain't that a crock?" she said. She noticed Deville. "What can I do for you, Louis?"

Deville stood. "Nothing. I'm going home, to rest."

She grabbed a file handed to her and took Deville by

the arm. "Come on, sweetheart," she said. "It looks like you could use some help. I've seen war veterans look better than you." They strolled out of the office together. She whispered in his ear. "Everyone's talking about you."

"What's new?" he asked.

"They're saying you were right, all along. That you French guys have something other guys don't have."

"Manners?"

"No, something in here." She let go of him and pointed to her head. "The brain cells. Maybe they're bigger in France." She watched him sit at his desk. "I think you know a lot more than you tell us. I think you could teach us a thing or two."

"Believe me, what I know, you want nothing of it."

She smiled and grabbed a pencil out of her hair. "Like my new do? It works as a compartment too. I have my pens here. I'm always losing them." Her hands went up to her hair. "I like having more than one use for things. My latest phone is also a music player and a computer, you know."

"Wolanski, your point, if you have one?"

She gave him an intense look. "My point is sometimes it's okay to have only one feature. My coffee cup, for instance. I use it to drink coffee but sometimes I store paper clips in it. The brakes in my car, they're good for one thing, to stop my car." She paused handing him another report. "And you, you try to do everything. Solve this case, save that young kid's life. All while trying to figure out what happened to you when you were a child."

He looked at her blankly.

"Don't think we're all stupid. We are investigators. We know you come from a troubled past." She leaned forward and whispered again. "It's okay to be good at just one thing. You can't be everything to everyone."

She walked away, looking more than ever like a hair stylist, ready for her next client to waltz through.

Deville couldn't help but feel just a little better. Even though Wolanski knew little about him, it appeared she felt he deserved to be cut some slack and some empathy for trying to do so much. He looked around the station and wondered if the other officers were glad to have him back. Safe and out of harm's way. No matter what differences they had, no one wanted to see another officer down.

He looked through the report and signed off the case, closing the file.

The second book of Gerard Bellamont would never be found. He wondered if it was lurking in the bottom of Seneca Lake. Jan Bellamont could not recover the manuscript and it was missing again. Just a few days ago she had snatched it from him and this had caused Sydney Keller's condition. He also never found Wyatt Bellamont's knapsack, which he deduced carried the second book and possibly more of his mother's prescribed pills.

The thought of Jan Bellamont killing so many people, including her own son, mystified him. Some people would do anything to start a new life, he decided. Killing Sydney Keller for thinking she had an affair with her husband was nothing new for Jan Bellamont. She had done it years ago with Paul Shepard's wife. Danielle Shepard had run off a cliff in her car and Deville guessed Jan had been responsible for her death as well. When moving to the Finger Lakes, Gerard Bellamont continued his wandering eye but with Stephanie Ferris, not Sydney, as Jan had predicted.

Ryan Ferris had died for other reasons. Maybe blackmail after witnessing what had happened? He already believed there was more to Ryan Ferris than what everyone thought. Ryan and his wife's consorting with Bellamont proved this already.

As he drove back to his home, he wondered how this case had gone so wrong? How did he not see the clues that were in front of him? Jan Bellamont's paranoia was evident from the beginning. She cried in hysterics when her son went missing the night of the first murder. She made a point of telling everyone she hated her husband's cologne and after his death, she didn't try to hide her dissatisfaction with her life.

Deville could remember her baking cookies, looking out of her kitchen window and longing for the past she once had.

And at the stakeout while Deville fell asleep in his car, she would open the front door to the cottage herself, claiming that a mysterious figure was lurking over her in her room. It had been all a ruse. She had instructed Wyatt to damage his car to clear suspicion.

He yawned and suddenly swerved, almost driving into oncoming traffic. He balanced the wheel, knocking a few things over inside the car. He tried to stay focused on the road and grabbed the fallen items. A cup, papers, pens, and a tool. He lifted all of these items and placed them all the in the back seat, except the last one. The tool proved to be a wire cutter. The young crime scene officer named Scudder, who was related to Investigator Scudder had given this to him. He smiled idly, remembering the youngster's enthusiasm.

What was it that Scudder had said? "A tool that served two purposes" or something like that. Just like Investigator Wolanski said: something that had dual purposes. Use it once, and use it again for something else.

He pulled over and stopped the car.

Use it once for something and use it again for something else, he thought again to himself.

The device in his hand had cut trellis wire but was also

used to cut cable wire. And the trellis wire from his collections proved to be the wrong wire used to strangle the first two victims.

It was the wrong wire. No wonder they didn't match.

He called the station before making a U-turn to pursue his final hunch.

CHAPTER THIRTY-FOUR

The road back to Canandaigua seemed to be the longest drive he'd ever taken since living here. It was just a few hours after the discovery of Sydney Keller's condition and the sun shone especially bright. The road seemed to open up for him, inviting him to take the lead. As he drove, he thought about the past few days, which would forever stay with him. He did not want to encounter another week like this ever again. The mental anguish of his past, coinciding with the recent case, and the events leading to the conclusion, created a mini mental breakdown. The term "need a vacation" seemed fruitless but ever so rightly deserved. He didn't know where he would go, but that it would be alone and away from the Finger Lakes. What he'd called home the past few decades seemed a cruel and vicious place to him now, even though the natural beauty surrounding him said otherwise. Even in a place that seems like paradise, bad things happen. He pondered this as he turned on to the same pier he'd been on just a few days ago.

He knew Paul Shepard would be here, at the pier. He turned off the ignition, he spotted the boat, Danielle, floating soundlessly alongside others. Most of the boats were now being parked inside the historical boathouses for the season but true diehards, like Shepard, waited until the first snowfall. He unbuckled his seatbelt, looked at his notes and hoped he was right this time. The pizza delivery person had turned up and proved to be more valuable than he'd thought.

Investigator Reginald Scudder called, after speaking to the young pizza boy who had delivered the last supper for Ryan Ferris. After finding out the investigator wasn't interested in recreational drugs, just some information on a certain night and a certain delivery, the pizza boy was a little more helpful. A large mushroom and pepperoni was delivered to Owen Winery the night Ryan Ferris died. The pizza boy remembered a guy, whom he described as Ryan Ferris, answering the door to the establishment, and after the man had paid, the delivery boy asked about possibly exchanging the pizza for some wine. Ferris, being veritable, declined the proposition, exclaiming that the driver was too young.

Yes, he'd heard about the murder and he hoped he wasn't indicated in the crime but didn't they catch someone already? Someone who had confessed even? The pizza boy also said the man who paid for the pizza was not alone. When Scudder asked who else was there, the boy could not help. He didn't see the other person, but he saw a second car in the lot.

A car, which, incidentally, had paintings in the back. The driver said he remembered saying to himself they must have been setting up for some fancy party, because of the art in the backseat. Scudder thanked the boy thoroughly, and when the boy asked if he would get in any further trouble for not reporting what he saw after finding out about the murder, Scudder told him not to worry.

Deville told Scudder not to worry as well. He also told him he needed back up.

Shepard came out after Deville called for him. He was

dressed in jeans and a sweatshirt, and held a fishing pole in his hand. "There you are," Shepard said, in a matter-of-fact voice. "I thought you'd be here earlier."

"So you're expecting me?" Deville asked.

Shepard showed Deville some bags on the boat's deck. "I've been busy packing. No use for all this stuff where I'm going is there?" Shepard made a weak attempt at a charming smile but his dark eyes and furrowed brows showed his resignation. It reminded Deville of those ugly sad clown paintings. Shepard was no clown though. He had methodically orchestrated three or possibly four murders, and had taken advantage of several people.

Wyatt Bellamont's knapsack lay next to Shepard's things on the deck The knapsack held Jan Bellamont's prescription drugs and Gerard Bellamont's second book. Deville was sure of it.

Paul Shepard disgusted him. Sydney Keller and Wyatt Bellamont were his pawns and he'd used them all along, discarding them after he no longer needed their help. Deville wouldn't be upset to see Shepard die and it was a fitting punishment. All it took was just to shoot him now and claim self-defense. There were no witnesses around and he could plainly deliver justice himself.

"So, when did you decide on me?" Shepard asked. He mimicked a drum roll, "This is your moment of glory isn't it? Too bad there's no one else here to witness it."

Deville said, "Backup is coming. Don't you worry."

Shepard suddenly disappeared into the cabinet and Deville quickly took the mini Glock out from his ankle strap.

Deville took a deep breath and hoped he wouldn't have to use it. A moment later Shepard came back with two wine glasses and a bottle of his wine. "Easy there, investigator, I was just getting something to help us celebrate. Well, I guess you wouldn't call it a celebration, would you?" The bottle had already been opened. He poured two glasses and offered one to Deville, who declined. "It seems fitting we drink Catalina Vineyard's wine, don't you agree?"

Deville didn't reply. Instead, he took a moment to think of what to say next. "I don't think we should celebrate," he said.

Shepard smiled. "This is your moment of truth, isn't it? When you lay all your cards on the table? Impress me with all your speculations?"

Deville sighed. He couldn't believe Shepard's arrogance. Deville said, "Your wife ran her car off the road, on the Catalina coast, after hearing Gerard Bellamont's reviews. He remembered your wife's paintings, the night of the party."

Shepard drank from his glass and showed Deville the bottle, "This one is the sunflower one. You saw it, remember? It's my favorite watercolor. She was brilliant." His voice dropped and Deville could see his manner change. "But Bellamont was a cruel man. I doubt he knew what he'd done. It was years ago, and I'd almost forgotten myself. Not what happened but about him. You see she was always..." He waved his hand, "emotional. Most artists are. She was feeling depressed, took pills, had some wine to drink and off she went." He swerved his hand downward. "Drove down to her death. It was the worst day of my life."

Deville waited for Shepard to continue but he didn't. Deville said, "Bellamont said something at the party that brought it all up again, didn't he?"

Shepard took another sip of wine. "Bellamont said, 'I didn't like it the first time I saw it.'"

Deville said, "He meant your wife's paintings. Bellamont was staring at your wine bottle but he meant your wife's paintings."

Shepard nodded and finished his glass, "The bastard remembered and mentioned a book he was writing, about the power of critics. That's what he called it. The power they have. They can make anyone famous. They can also run them out of their house and force them to live on the street. And they can also kill."

"Where is the book?"

Shepard smiled, "Good ole Wyatt had it. We searched for it at his cabin and couldn't find it. But it turned up. He said his mom found it." He checked the cabin door to make sure it was locked. It was as if he was leaving and not coming back.

Deville heard the cruisers approaching. He kept the gun aimed at Shepard.

"So did you get the clues I left you?" Shepard asked. He saw the look on Deville's face. "Come now. Killing with the wire I use to hang the paintings, and admitting I always have paintings in my car might have been too much but it didn't seem that you were catching on. And what about Ryan's hands, reaching out for a bottle of Catalina Vineyard's latest Cabernet?" Shepard reached grasping into the air. "He was pointing to my wine bottle, giving you a clue!" He shook his head. "You police may be just as stupid as I'd thought."

Deville felt nauseated and remained silent.

Shepard laughed, "You know you and I would have been great chums in different circumstances. Both of us cultured, creatures of habit and a flair for the dramatic."

"Don't compare me to you," Deville said.

"But why not? We are both daring souls, aren't we? That night at the cottage, you were there! I thought that was it. I thought the game was over. You had me."

"It was never a game," Deville said.

"Maybe not for you and maybe not in the beginning, but come now. Smashing your windshield, stealing Jan Bellamont's prescriptions, and making her crazy. You've got to admit, that was pure entertainment."

"And what about Wyatt Bellamont? Was killing him

pure entertainment?"

Shepard shrugged. "Wyatt got nervous when I threatened him for the book. The poor kid, he was smitten with me, you know?" Shepard moved and almost fell over. "When did you suspect me?" Shepard asked.

Deville said, "When no one bought your story about Bellamont refusing to sell you Californian grapes. That's when I knew you were lying about something. But why kill Ryan Ferris and Sydney Keller?"

"Ryan saw me kill Bellamont at Allenwood's. They have a huge window in their office." Shepard staggered and lost his balance. He sat, holding the edge of the boat, looking as though he were ready to faint.

Deville cursed himself for not seeing it happen. Shepard had drugged himself. Shepard continued, "That big old window looked out across the vines. Ryan saw me with Bellamont. He had a great view of me squeezing the life out of the little foreigner. After the deed was done, I spotted Ryan watching. He was calling Chloe and needed privacy. Can you believe it, he had his way with that young girl?"

"And you and Wyatt?"

"He wanted to run away with me. To sail all over the world. He actually thought I might be gay! Do I look gay?"

Deville ignored the question. "And you did nothing to stop him. You led him on."

"Only to help me finish what I started." Shepard spotted the other officers approaching. "I never did anything. I never touched the boy. He knew I killed his father. I honestly thought he was—well, a good kid. Once I told him I wasn't interested in him, he tried to kill himself. I just helped him along at the hospital." He keeled over and thrust his head over the side of the boat and gagged.

Deville put away the gun and leaped on the boat to help Shepard, holding his head.

"Throw it up, Shepard, stay alive damn you! Don't do this. It's over. It's all over. You don't need to do this."

The body was getting weaker by the moment. Other officers were there, some with guns out. They were watching and waiting for orders. Deville noticed Investigator Reginald Scudder among them.

Shepard's eyes bulged and he began sweating. Soon after he vomited. He looked up to Deville in desperation, as if he was a priest.

He is looking for forgiveness, Deville thought, as Shepard's hands held onto Deville.

Shepard's steady gaze deteriorated. His eyes became glassy and he appeared to be losing focus. "Sydney thought we could have a life together," Shepard said, shaking now. "I told her we couldn't but she didn't understand. I told her what I'd done and she didn't care. Said she was destined to a life of turmoil. The stars said she would have to sacrifice herself."

He looked up and Deville could see the fear in Shepard's face.

"And last night, she said she wanted nothing to do with me. I think she took a liking to you. She mentioned she would tell you everything."

Shepard started vomiting again, only this time there was blood.

"Can I get some paramedics?" Deville yelled out to the other officers. "Put your guns away. Don't just stand there, hurry!"

"I'm coming, Danielle," Shepard said, uttering his last words.

EPILOGUE

Sydney Keller was tired of gelatin. The hospital's idea of nourishment was laughable. Although she didn't think her stomach could handle anything more solid at the moment than the green jiggly substance. She had been in the hospital for almost a week. The drug nitrazepam, a powerful benzodiazepine known for its hypnotic effects, was finally out of her system. The breathing tubes were gone, the IV made her skin itch but she was out of the coma and alive. She was thankful the ordeal was over.

Jan Bellamont had accused her of having an affair with her husband. The shock of it all was unbearable. Being accused of killing her husband would have been easier to take than having an affair with him. However, she couldn't stay angry at Jan Bellamont. The woman had lost her husband and son and she wasn't in her right state of mind.

That could also explain her own behavior with Paul Shepard. The charming man who swept her off her feet, the man who had lied to her, the destructive man who had brought so much death. After the devastation of Wyatt Bellamont's death, she didn't think things could get worse. She had wanted to come clean and tell

Investigator Deville everything. Paul Shepard begged her to not say a word and came to console her. The next thing she remembered was Shepard injecting her with one of the prescription drugs from Jan Bellamont. It all felt like a dream to her.

The sadness of death was all around and her carelessness almost led her into the spirit world prematurely. She had never seen so much death and mayhem. From discovering Gerard Bellamont's body in the vineyard, to holding his son's hand before he slipped away, not to mention her own near death her first few weeks in the Finger Lakes were not at all what she envisioned. Those cards were right all along, but she had no idea how to stop any of it. What was more upsetting was that it was just the beginning. She wished she had seen the true devil before the madness began.

She could still smell Shepard's cologne and remember the thrill she got when she saw him smile. Now remembering his beguiling smile made her stomach turn. She heard on the news he had killed himself. Why didn't he just kill himself in the beginning, she thought? Why bring so much tragedy and then off yourself? Then she remembered his determination. Paul Shepard was on a mission. To avenge his wife's death. Nothing stood in the way of that; no other thought, deed, or person. Not even Sydney.

The nurse came in to announce a visitor. She was curious about who had filled the room with flowers, juices, and snacks. The door opened and Investigator Deville appeared, bearing a small bunch of irises.

"Are you up for visitors?" he asked.

She nodded and wished she had a mirror. "Come in. The flowers are so beautiful."

He handed her the flowers and while she admired the bouquet he stood by the bed, with his hands in his pockets. He looked like a confused man who had a lot on his mind.

"Sit Louis," she said. "I think it's time we talked." He followed her order and she continued. "I know you've been through a lot. We both have but I don't think we should rush into things."

"Well, actually…"

"I understand that perhaps you have already fallen for me and who could blame you? I have that effect on men. I hope you don't think I led you on?"

"As a matter of fact…"

She raised her hand to let him know she heard enough. "Don't defend our passion. We both know it is strong. You can't put out this fire."

Deville said nothing and just stared.

"Good, don't argue. I don't think we should just jump into things. I need to be alone right now. Especially after —" a thought of Paul Shepard came to her mind.

"I understand Sydney," Deville said. "I value your friendship more than anything else."

"Don't read too much into this. Caring for me can be hazardous to your health. Just look what happened to Paul Shepard and Wyatt."

"It's not your fault, it never has been."

She grabbed his hand. "Louis, you just have to love me from afar."

"Sydney, I never said I loved you."

She took a deep breath. *Had she been wrong about him?*

Deville took his hand away. "I didn't say it because you were unavailable." Color returned to her face. He gave a heavy sigh and said, "The stars and destiny are your soulmate, I would only get in the way."

She sat up and gave him a small embrace. "Oh Louis, you are not as dense as I thought! I'm so glad you understand. I didn't know how to break it to you. Your heart has been wounded so many times and I didn't want to distress you." She wasn't sure if he was telling the truth or whether she was hearing him correctly but it didn't matter. She was relishing the moment. "You need to be strong and continue saving lives." She gave him a hopeful look. "I can help you. When you have a tough case. Kind of a sexy sidekick?"

He thought for a moment and said, "Perhaps. That is, if I can bear the torture of being in the same room with you without ravaging you." He pulled something out of his pocket and handed it to her. It was the amulet that she'd given to Wyatt.

She held it with both hands and sighed. "I made this to protect him from harm. Didn't help much did it?"

"Sometimes we do all we can and it's not enough." He placed a hand over hers. "Maybe you did everything you were supposed to do?"

She looked up into his eyes and studied his awkward but handsome face. "Destiny?" she asked.

A slight smile appeared. Something she predicated happened rarely from him. "Yes, destiny," he agreed.

Hearing that from this intriguing man made her smile too—and feel better about herself.

THE END

SACRED VINES

A preview of the next Finger Lakes Wine mystery.

PROLOGUE

The night sky was almost flawless. It appeared to be showing off, displaying its stars like a proud peacock's feathers for every night viewer to enjoy. Dudley Steiff considered himself lucky to be in the hills of Lakeview, off the shores of Conesus Lake, overlooking the magnificent splendor, waiting. Few people can expose themselves to an event such as this. Playing Warcraft or conquering other worlds digitally in his video games is one thing. To actually witness something spectacular, live and in the flesh, can't be measured.

He crossed his arms and felt a chill. Waiting was something he abhorred. He had the patience of child, or so he was told. This was a similarity he agreed with. All the other mannerisms associated with a child's behavior —his communicative skills, his shyness—were said to be attributed to Asperger's. People rolled all the symptoms together and made their own decisions. They told him he was childish, wrote him off or simply gave up trying to understand him.

Dudley wondered how people could understand him when they couldn't understand themselves. There were layers of sensory activity in an average person that others couldn't comprehend. With someone diagnosed with

Autism, there was much more. There was too much going on, like a rush hour traffic jam on the highway.

He felt his senses were stronger, perhaps like a superhero, at pivotal moments such as this. His sense of smell was one. He could smell gas and the burning of metal and rubber.

That's when he witnessed a burst from the corner of his eye. He saw the blaze, a flightless meteor, rolling down with a flashing speed from the community of homes, the winery and the monastery. The fiery spectacle continued down its destined path toward the lake, creating tracks on the damp canvass of green. It destroyed everything it touched; bushes, small trees, budding flowers the late spring had brought.

Rubbing his eyes, he couldn't believe the contrast of darkness and how bright the fire had become. *Katie,* he heard himself say to the blowing wind, as it muffled the screams coming from the moving car. The hysteria of the scene caused a panic attack. Lately he'd managed them well but there was no time for medicine. He could hear himself yelling for help as he ran closer, realizing the screaming from the car stopped. The car hit the shores and continued its journey into the lake, where just a few weeks ago young Andrew met his death.

CHAPTER ONE

Investigator Louis Deville watched the car being pulled in slow motion from the shallow part of the lake with a wench. The wreckage of the vehicle, still possessing the stench of a burned metal marshmallow, caused a mild sensation with news reporters and spectators who gathered around this part of the lake.

The April rain continued, melting what was left of the snow. It had been almost a week of fog and after a hard winter of snow and record-breaking freezing temperatures, the Finger Lakes residents seemed grateful but restless. They took any opportunity to get them out and about. Whether it was trying a new bottled wine or watching a burned car being pulled out of the lake, it kept them from boredom.

He pulled his coat tighter as the crowd started dissipating into the fog. No questions as to what has happened to the car or the victim inside. It seemed the crowd had enough of the suspense, or lack of, and decided to go home.

"Don't know why we were called," Investigator Reginald Scudder said, standing beside Deville. He was at least eight inches shorter than Deville. Strands of red hair escaped from under his cap.

"There is a body in that pile of metal," Deville

remarked, hoping to shed some light. He tried to appear astute, hoping he had more info to give the young man but there was little to divulge. The police had called for help and had asked for Deville specifically.

The young investigator's gleam and steady gaze suggested he was excited about the possibility of a new case. His tone, however, implied that this type of thing occurred regularly. He had arrived at the scene showered and fresh, as if he were on a date. "Do you think the car is from the village up there?" he asked, motioning the top of the hill, where light from the windows glowed like small torches from a distance.

Deville didn't reply. He turned back to the vehicle, which was now out of the lake. It was a sedan, an older model and dull looking, as if the fire relieved it of its misery. Neither said another word. Deville took photos and a short video. Scudder got called to help the crime scene officers so he walked away, carefully, his boots squishing in puddles. The task force was light with only a few officers examining the scene. Taking evidence during the rain is challenging. They were at risk of little to no footprints and latent prints possibly being washed away. The temperature fluctuations also could disrupt decomposition.

Deville wondered who had been in the vehicle and what happened. The hills surrounding the lake had little civilization or wildlife. He spotted only a few homes, a monastery and a winery. The scene was familiar to him. There was a haunting deja vu about this place. Lately there have been many memories coming to surface and this could be a false memory triggered by another occurrence. Some of the lake towns looked alike. The fog blanketed the hills and the shore like a shroud, creating an atmosphere similar to places he's visited in the past. Or towns he's read about in books.

Conesus Lake was one of the minor Finger Lakes in

western New York. The lake stretched eight miles long and about thirty-eight feet deep. This point of the lake wasn't open to the public so a car wouldn't just drive itself down the hill without knowing the consequences.

Deville didn't remember seeing any roads where a driver could veer off because of lack of visibility due to fog. He decided it was a deliberate attempt. Driving your car into the lake meant you wanted to end your life. So who wanted to do such a thing and, as Scudder had wondered, *why did they call them?*

About an hour later Deville and Scudder sat in an office in the nearest police station in Geneseo, about ten miles west of the lake. The station was smaller than their own but it was well-built with bricks. Deville heard it used to be the town library that closed due to remodeled —and larger—one in the university. It was near the campus and Deville expected that most of the town's crimes generated from there. While he was relieved to take shelter from the gloomy weather, the mood inside the office wasn't much better. The sergeant, who met him earlier at the scene, sat in his chair studying Deville and Scudder as if they were uninvited guests. The sergeant looked tired and overworked. He seemed like he was displeased at what the world had become. His glum face showed many disapproving lines and this case didn't seem to help his demeanor. "Would you like some coffee?" Sergeant Adder asked.

Deville shook his head. "No, thank you."

"Perhaps some tea," Scudder announced. "Investigator Deville likes tea. He was brought up by a British family, you know."

Sergeant Adder forced a smile. "I almost forgot. The Fitzhughes. Walt Fitzhugh was a dedicated officer. I knew your father. We're about the same age. He brought so much tact to the office. His work ethic was so impressive. I hoped it would rub off on you, although you aren't really his son, are you?"

The offering of tea was clearly forgotten with the question of Deville's bloodline. "No, sir. I'm not. Although I remember his determination to his work." *And I remember his discipline. And how many nights I didn't see him,* he almost added. His foster parents raised him in a cold emotionless house; stiff and stringent. He was always reminded that he didn't belong and felt unwelcomed. Although their kindness in raising him was apparent, Deville didn't think they knew how to show love or affection. The moments he shared alone with Walt Fitzhugh that he could recall were slim and those resembling anything close to a father and son relationship were scarce. His real father was a mystery and he dare not try to bring up those memories again. Growing up in France was like a nightmare from another life.

"But he's French," Scudder added.

"I've heard," Adder said harshly. He went through some files on his desk. "Don't you French have a knack for sniffing things out? Or is that bloodhounds?" Adder stood and limped to his poncho, which was hanging, dripping wet. Deville noticed an old framed picture of Jesus behind Adder's desk. He tried to recall if anyone at his station had any inclination or clues to their faith and he couldn't remember. "We heard all about you from your last case," Adder continued. "You've been through as much crap as anyone with years on the force because of that case. Heard you have a flair for wine."

Deville swallowed. "I am familiar with wine but it has no bearing on the past case."

"Well, it does. He was a wine critic wasn't he? And from France?" Adder found what he was looking for—a small, clear plastic bag. "The Finger Lakes are known for wine. I heard the press say God laid *His* hand on this spot because of the beauty and wine. I'm as religious as they come and I don't believe that. But what do I know? I've worked here for over two decades and never seen a burned vehicle with a body inside."

He handed Deville a folder and Scudder the plastic bag.

Deville opened the folder to see recent photos of the body found inside the vehicle. "In the bag is a ring found on the body," Adder continued. "We can't tell who it is but the car is registered to a Corrine Blanchard, a nurse at the Geneseo hospital."

"Have you notified next of kin?" Deville asked. He studied the pictures that showed a corpse with some skin not fully burned off. In one picture he could see a gaping mouth forming what looked like a scream. Each photo was more disturbing than the next.

"Not yet. Her family is from Maryland and she has no living relatives nearby. We are waiting for dental records to confirm." Adder sighed. "Troubles me to think that accidents like this happen."

Deville looked up. "Accident?"

"What else could it be?" Adder leaned forward and the bags under his eyes seemed to grow. "Do you think it's a homicide?"

"Judging from where the road is, I don't think someone accidentally drove into water without intending to end their life."

"Suicide, huh? I suppose that's an idea but what about the fire?"

"If it wasn't a suicide then maybe an accident after all. Fires happen all the time; faulty wiring, especially in an older car." Deville read the report in front of him. The vehicle was a twenty-year-old Chevy Impala. "Was she from the village?"

"There is no village, just a cluster of homes. Bungalows they call them."

"She could have been on her way to work and was already driving when the car burst into flames." Deville had heard of things happening like this before but he never did any research. The thought of this being a homicide troubled him. Not because of the act itself, which was a terrible ordeal, but at the task at hand. Working on a case in Lakeview with Adder and his officers seemed such an arduous task. He would be away from the other officers and his own sergeant, Jessica Malone.

Adder adjusted his tie. "This case is delicate. I wish it was an accident. I don't want a homicide."

Deville could imagine Adder adding, *not on my watch.*

"This town has had its share of accidents. Just a few weeks ago a child drowned in the lake, not far from where the car was found. He was six years old."

"Good God!" Scudder said.

Adder shook his head. "The family doesn't need any more attention, especially this kind." Adder suddenly started coughing. He hunched over and covered his mouth with one hand while the other held on to the desk for support.

"Are you okay, sergeant?" Deville asked. He turned to Scudder. "Grab some water." In an instant Scudder was gone and back again with a cup of water.

Adder drank it and his coughing subsided. "Thank you. My days of running this office are coming to a close. I don't want to see any more evil and sadness in this town." He glanced at the picture and for a moment it looked like he was about to pray. He turned his attention back to them. "Sorry about that coughing. This weather doesn't help with all my ailments. Now where was I?"

"The boy who drowned," Deville replied.

Adder thought reflectively. "Yes, the Hollingsworth boy. They own the winery up on the hill. Willows Pond. They make the wines for the monastery, which is on the same grounds as the winery. Joann and Richard Hollingsworth bought the winery a few years ago from the Willow family. They moved here from the East coast. They do everything. They make the wine, bottle it, grow the grapes on the monastery. It's small but still in business."

"The business of saving souls?" Deville questioned.

Adder cocked his head. "You don't seem like the religious type, investigator. Am I wrong?"

Deville said nothing. The thought of empty churches, unanswered prayers and priests taking advantage of the innocent crossed his mind. It was easy to forget all the good a church can do because of this.

Adder continued. "Years ago, the nuns ran an orphanage at Saint Felicia's Monastery. I am a guardian to a boy who grew up in that orphanage so this place means something to me. The orphanage closed and is now the winery. Nuns used to harvest the grapes themselves without machinery but now there's only a few of them and the winery is run by the Hollingsworth family."

"Is this pertinent to the case?" Deville asked.

"They are what attracts people to the area. The monastery, the winery and their story. It's all tourism, investigator. They are what is keeping this town on the map. The college and hospital are in another town but this burned car is in Lakeview, where there is little else."

News of a murder at the town's one attraction would cause distress for the community. That's why Deville was called. At least that was the reason he thought. He didn't think there would be much concern because it wasn't ruled a homicide. However, there was no way to hide the facts of the case, even if it was a grim accident.

"We called you, investigator," Adder continued, "because of your experience. We don't want it to be a homicide. Damn we don't want it to be a suicide either. I heard good things about you and your relationship with wineries so it made sense to contact you."

So he was enlisted because of his experience with wine and/or wineries. Deville bit his lip. He didn't know whether to laugh or leave. How much did the sergeant know about his past? Was he called because he didn't drink wine or rather couldn't? Surely they had capable officers here who could work on this? Being known as the expert who investigated crimes in wine country wasn't something he wanted to be known for. He was the last person they needed and if they dug deep enough they'd know why. He glanced at the picture of Jesus again and wondered if this a twisted joke from the heavens. If this was karma because of his lack of belief then perhaps it was destiny to be stuck here, traipsing through the vineyards while piecing together his tarnished past. A thousand prayers, not even the monastery, could help his situation.

A noise could be heard in the station. They turned to see the vision of a woman speaking to someone impatiently. A moment later an officer led her into the office. All three men stood to greet her. She was medium height, thin and fragile, with a pale narrow face and silky brown hair. She looked young but her deep blue eyes told them she was older than she appeared. Her softness flowed into the room with her presence and even her distraught state couldn't hide it. She looked at the men with worried concern.

"Who found my car?" she asked in a calm breath.

"Your car?" Adder inquired.

She nodded. "I heard what happened. Is it true? Was there someone in it?" She took a deep breath. "Please tell me no."

It was Deville who asked, "Who are you?" He motioned her to sit.

She refused to, acting as though she'd wasted enough

time. "Corrine. My name is Corrine Blanchard. My car was found in the lake."

Adder fell into his seat, both hands on his desk. "But you're dead!"

She walked closer, saw the grimacing photos of the victim and shuddered. *"I'm* not dead *but I know who is."*

AUTHOR NOTES

Thanks for reading, I hope we can keep in touch. If you enjoyed the book, please leave an honest review on Amazon, Goodreads, or other sites you see the novel. Visit my website to keep updated on other books and promotions.

Keep in touch:
Website: http://donstevensauthor.com
Facebook: http://facebook.com/donstevensauthor
Twitter: http://twitter.com/donstevens

CPSIA information can be obtained at www.ICGtesting.com
Printed in the USA
LVOW10s1810120716

496029LV00014B/281/P